"Hey, why are you crying ... ing out to wipe away the track of Gabby's tears with his thumb.

"Oh, I don't know, maybe because I just made a fool out of myself," she answered, hating that tears welled up in her eyes again. All her insecurities came washing back in tidal waves that she felt herself drowning in.

"Aw damn, don't cry, Gabby," Maxwell told her huskily, as he sat up on the couch and pulled her upper body into a comforting embrace. "It was just an accident. No big deal. And don't worry, the ones who laughed were the first ones I let Addie give the boot."

Gabrielle actually smiled at his serious tone. "Even Penelope?"

"*Especially* Penelope."

Gabrielle was surrounded by Maxwell's scent, his face caressed her nape as he pressed her against his chest. It was all just too much and she tried to pull away. "I'm fine, Maxwell, but thanks for checking on me."

"You stopped crying?" he asked, looking down at her as he tilted her chin up to inspect her face.

Their mouths were just inches apart, and when his eyes dropped to her lips, Gabrielle's heart actually surged. That was definitely another of those cues. Maxwell wanted to kiss her!

Oh, what the hell. I'm going for it.

"Kiss me, Maxwell," she begged sweetly as she felt his heart pound hard against her hand.

"Gabby—" he began.

She lifted her head and captured his mouth with hers, using her tongue to trace his bottom lip before she sucked it deeply. "Kiss me," she begged again throatily, not wanting her boldness to be for naught.

Seconds later he took the lead, capturing her tongue with his own.

BOOK YOUR PLACE ON OUR WEBSITE AND MAKE THE ARABESQUE ROMANCE CONNECTION!

We've created a customized website just for our very special Arabesque readers, where you can get the inside scoop on everything that's going on with Arabesque romance novels.

When you come online, you'll have the exciting opportunity to:

- View covers of upcoming books

- Learn about our future publishing schedule (listed by publication month and author)

- Find out when your favorite authors will be visiting a city near you

- Search for and order backlist books

- Check out author bios and background information

- Send e-mail to your favorite authors

- Join us in weekly chats with authors, readers and other guests

- Get writing guidelines

- AND MUCH MORE!

Visit our website at
http://www.arabesquebooks.com

NIOBIA BRYANT

Can't Get Next to You

ARABESQUE
BET BOOKS

BET Publications, LLC
http://www.bet.com
http://www.arabesquebooks.com

ARABESQUE BOOKS are published by

BET Publications, LLC
c/o BET BOOKS
One BET Plaza
1900 W Place NE
Washington, DC 20018-1211

All Kensington Titles, Imprints, and Distributed Lines are available at special quantity discounts for bulk purchases for sales promotions, premiums, fund-raising, and educational or institutional use. Special book excerpts or customized printings can also be created to fit specific needs. For details, write or phone the office of the Kensington special sales manager: Kensington Publishing Corp., 850 Third Avenue, New York, NY 10022, attn: Special Sales Department, Phone: 1-800-221-2647.

First Printing: March 2005

10 9 8 7 6 5 4 3 2 1

Printed in the United States of America

You were a lover of sweet hot
Lipton tea and buttered toast.
You were always faintly scented with a mix of Noxema
and Avon's Timeless talcum powder.
You were an odd mix of love and
brutal honesty . . . when needed.
You were the epitome of "keeping it real" before
hip-hop even thought about it.
You were a vessel of wisdom and advice.
You were funny with your unique
one-liners and wisecracks.
You were a mother, grandmother,
sister, aunt, and friend.
You were one of a kind.

You are truly missed.

In Loving Memory of My Grandmother,
Bertha Mae Bryant

ACKNOWLEDGMENTS

Thank you, dear Lord, for giving me life.

Thank you, Mama, for everything you've done for me, including passing on your intelligence, your humor, and your looks (smile). I am so blessed that the Lord saw fit to send me to you.

Tony, thank you for your love. Who'd have thought fifteen years ago that we'd be together today? And remember, Karl Malone has nothing on you (smile).

Thank you to my big brother, Caleb. I know we argue, but I love you. We all we got.

Thank you to all my aunties and uncles: Ernest (Dick), Jim, Randy, Pete, Toe, Agnes, Mary, Doris, Margaret, Lloyd, Alberta, Rodgers, and Marsha. A special shout out of love to my great-aunt, Margaret.

To my editor, Demetria Lucas: girl, big thanks for your guidance and your patience.

For those who have gone on before me but still guide me from heaven, I thank you all: my father, Ernest; my paternal grandmother, Bertha; my maternal grandparents, Clarence and Sally; my aunt, Marion; and my godmother, Claudie.

Chapter One

"Party over here . . . Party over there!"

Growling in frustration, Gabrielle "Gabby" Dutton buried her head deeper beneath the pillows, trying desperately to drown out the sounds floating into her bedroom. "One of these days I'm gonna hurt you, Maxwell," she mumbled murderously under her breath.

Gabrielle rolled her slender body over in the bed, causing some of the pillows to fly up in the air briefly before floating down to the hardwood floor like oversized snowflakes.

The two-bedroom guest house she resided in on her boss's estate was more than 400 feet from his sprawling main house. Still, the distinct sounds of his party goers floated back to her little domicile, disturbing her sleep.

The multimedia artist loved a loud, boisterous party and threw at least one every other month. Even though the planning was left up to her, and Maxwell always encouraged her to attend, Gabrielle never did. She was usually tucked away in her cottage with a good mystery novel when his guests began to arrive. She planned it and then coordinated the cleanup afterward, but she knew absolutely nothing about what went on in between.

Working as Maxwell Bennett's personal assistant for the past six years certainly had its ups and downs. The erratic working hours, odd requests, and flamboyant lifestyle were definitely outweighed by the live-in quarters, set salary, and plenty of free time.

During her senior year at the University of Richmond in Virginia, Gabrielle had attended an Art Expo at the Greater Richmond Convention Center. The five-day event was one of the country's leading art and framing-industry trade shows. A lover of contemporary art, Gabrielle had been able to enjoy the work of many artists she was already familiar with and was introduced to a few she did not know, like Maxwell Bennett. She could still vividly remember the way they first met.

Gabrielle immediately thought that the artist was just as beautiful as his colorful and thought-provoking artwork. She had to force herself not to stare at the tall man with the most amazing deep-set mocha eyes. His smile made her toes tingle.

She had to force her attention away from the artist and back to his art. She was studying a piece entitled *Eyes to the Ceiling All Night Long* when the hairs on her nape stood on end. She glanced over her shoulder, and there he stood behind her.

"What do you think of it?" he asked, his voice sounding to her like syrup poured over warm biscuits.

"I think that it's beautiful," she told him, her voice shaking with nervousness.

He walked up closer to stand beside her, tilting

his head up to study the painting. "It's beautiful? Okay. Thank you, but what do you think of it?" he asked again, seeking more.

Gabrielle turned her bespectacled eyes from his profile to look up at the painting hanging suspended by wires in the air. "When I look at the man lying in bed, unable to sleep, I immediately think that he's in love, but for whatever reason, he can't have the woman he loves. He's thinking of her, wishing she was there with him."

Maxwell clapped as he turned to face her again. "Very good, Miss . . . "

She flushed under his praise. "Gabrielle. Gabrielle Dutton," she told him, accepting the hand he now offered her.

"I'm Maxwell Bennett."

"Yes, I know."

"You live in Richmond?" he asked, crossing his arms over his strapping chest.

"I'm originally from Georgia, but I attend University of Richmond. I graduate this May," she told him, surprised at the excitement she felt at sharing her future with this total stranger.

"In May?" he balked. "This May?"

Gabrielle nodded.

"You barely look old enough to be a freshman," Maxwell told her in disbelief.

Gabrielle bristled just a bit but tried not to show her annoyance. "Well, I'm not," she told him lightly.

"You have family in Virginia?" he asked, obviously curious.

"No, my only family in the world is my older sister, Ape."

"Ape?"

Gabrielle smiled as she pushed her glasses up on her face. "It's short for April."

"I hope she doesn't live up to her nickname," he teased.

Gabrielle laughed, ending on a snort that was very unladylike. "No. No, she doesn't," she told him, as she dropped her head and flushed with embarrassment.

"Good," he said, his eyes crinkling at the corners as he smiled broadly down at her. "Well, Gabrielle Dutton from Georgia. You mind if I ask what your plans are after graduating?"

Gabrielle's face became a mask of confusion as she looked up into eyes she could get lost in. "I plan on remaining in Virginia or the Washington, D.C. area."

Maxwell nodded. "Plan on working?"

"Oh," Gabrielle sighed with understanding. "I'll probably get an entry-level position in the government that will let me pay the bills and have great benefits while I advance."

Maxwell stared down at her, his eyes reflective as he did.

Gabrielle felt uneasy under his stare. "Mr. Bennett?" she asked.

"I'm looking for a personal assistant," he began suddenly. "The position pays thirty thousand dollars a year with benefits and a cottage on my estate—rent free."

Gabrielle looked up at him as if he had two heads and one eye.

"Ms. Dutton?" he asked. Now it was his turn to draw her attention.

"Gabrielle."

"Huh?" he asked.

"Call me Gabrielle," she told him, completely stunned by his offer and totally confused. *What if he's a psycho?* she thought. "You're offering that to me? Why? You don't even know me," Gabrielle said.

"Why not?" he returned quickly. "Listen, this is my card, think about it and let me know."

Gabrielle accepted the card with shaky fingers. "I'll think about it."

He nodded with an indulging smile. "I look forward to hearing from you, Gabby," he told her, before moving over to a young couple who had stopped to view his art work.

"Gabrielle," she corrected him softly as she walked away, the card still in her hand. She looked back at him over her shoulder and smiled briefly when he looked up to smile back.

That had been six years ago.

Curious as to the actual factual goings-on at the party, Gabrielle kicked the covers from her body and climbed out of her queen-size bed. The hem of her cotton nightgown fell down to her slender ankles. After grabbing her spectacles from the bedside table, she moved easily in the moonlit darkness to the living room and out the front door.

She winced as the music became considerably louder. Quickly she made her way up the stone-paved walkway leading to Maxwell's mansion on the hill. Thankfully, the grounds were well lit so Gabrielle found her way easily to the back of the sprawling house.

The sounds of music, laughter, and chatter echoed through the night as Gabrielle dashed behind a bush at the sight of two uniformed security guards patrolling the grounds. Holding herself still as a statue, she questioned her impetuous decision to leave her house in her nightgown just to sneak a peek at what went on at one of Maxwell's parties. Taking a deep, steadying breath, she leaned forward slightly to peer through a break in the leaves at the two men.

Relief filled her as they moved toward the front of the brick mansion. Glad though she was that they had not discovered her, Gabrielle made a mental note to hire a new security company. If *she* could slip under their radar, anybody could. "Bad idea, Gabrielle," she reprimanded herself aloud, as she stepped from behind the bushes, releasing the twigs that were snagged to her nightgown. "Very bad idea."

The sounds of glass crashing startled her. Her curiosity once again piqued, she pushed her glasses up on her nose and moved to the nearest window, being sure to stay lower than the ledge. As she slowly raised her head, Gabrielle hoped no one inside happened to be peering out.

Seventy or so people were in the den. Some lounged on the sidelines sipping Maxwell's popular Cosmopolitans, but most were dancing in the center of the floor. Her eyes immediately fell upon a scantily dressed woman gyrating to the music as her breasts struggled to not pop free of their confines. The woman's motions were so lewd that Gabrielle could easily picture her working the pole in a cheap strip club.

Gabrielle's eyes widened and her mouth circled in shock when the woman proceeded to tear off her tank, her long hair barely covering her breasts. "Oh my God," she exclaimed in a whisper, slapping her hand over her mouth. Thoroughly disgusted, Gabrielle jerked away from the scene, having had her fill. She had gathered that Maxwell's parties were a little wild, but she had never imagined that they went *that* far.

She raced toward her cottage, squealing as the lawn sprinklers came on and showered her from head to toe. The late August night air was surprisingly cool as it swept over her, making the cotton plastered to her skin all the more uncomfortable. Gabrielle was glad to spot the tip of her roof.

"Gabby?"

Her steps sped up as she heard her name being called. It could only be Maxwell, because only he dared to call her by that inane nickname.

"Gabby, will you stop running. Don't you hear me calling you?"

"Oh, great mother of all things embarrassing," Gabrielle mumbled under her breath as she stopped to turn to him, shivering and wet like a drowned rat.

Maxwell jogged up to her. "Is everything all right? You're not usually up and about this time of the night."

Gabrielle tilted her head up, using her fingers to wipe the water from the lenses of her glasses as she struggled to regain what little composure she could. "I'm just fine, Maxwell."

"Really, Gabby, if you want to enjoy a late night swim, wouldn't wearing a bathing suit be the best thing?" he drawled, pushing his hands into the pockets of his slacks as he smiled down at her as if

she were an amusing child. His eyes darted down
briefly before they quickly diverted. "Ahem, Gabby,
you're uh . . . "

Gabrielle looked down at herself and nearly
shriveled to the size of an ant as she realized that
her less than ample chest was shown clearly
through the wet material. She immediately crossed
her arms over it, ready to flee, but knew she *had* to
offer up some sort of explanation of her late-night
wanderings. "I heard glass break and, I, uh, came
out to see what was happening and got caught by
the sprinklers."

"In your nightgown?" he asked, obviously amused.

"Good night, Maxwell," she told him curtly, before turning to move down the lit path to her
house. She scurried inside, leaning her upper body
over in the darkness to peer out the window at his
retreat. Her heart hammered in her chest.

Maxwell loved life and having fun, wanting to
enjoy every bit of it to the fullest. His long, almost
feminine lashes surrounded eyes that were always
filled with laughter. His full, sensual mouth constantly seemed to be formed into a smile. It was
nothing for him to leave at a moment's notice to a
faraway place for a vacation. He was a carefree soul,
an artist with no limitations, inhibitions, or worries.

What little organization and order he had in his
life was supplied by Gabrielle. She made sure his bills
were paid, ran his household, had his clothes dry-
cleaned, made sure he kept his appointments—she
did it all. She liked to call her job: "the wife without
bedroom privileges."

Not that she would mind. Truth be told, Gabrielle
had loved Maxwell since her first few months on the

job. He was handsome with his goatee. High cheek-bones and a strong jaw were completely offset by his supple lips. And his body was lean and toned. Just downright sexy.

Even though Gabrielle was wet and shivering, the tender spot between her legs was warm and throbbing as she watched him until he disappeared completely from her sight.

Gabrielle began to pull her nightgown over her head as she made her way to the bathroom. She turned on the shower, set her spectacles on the sink and then pulled back the white shower curtain to step under the spray. She welcomed the warmth of the steam and the feel of the hot water pulsating against her skin, but it was the very thought of Maxwell, naked and wet in the shower with her, that knocked the chill from her bones.

In the six years she had worked for him, erotic dreams of wild, passionate sex with her boss were the only bit of sexual activity in her secluded life. "And to think, most lonely women just buy a vibrator," Gabrielle mused.

Rinsing the last of the soap from her body, Gabrielle leaned down to turn off the water before stepping out of the shower. She immediately reached for her spectacles, wiping away the condensation on them before she slipped them on. Quickly, she dried off with a plush towel and then wrapped it securely around her slender frame.

Heading straight for her dresser in her bedroom, Gabrielle immediately felt tiny goose bumps race across her exposed limbs. She opened the top drawer containing her lingerie. That is *if* thirty pairs of white cotton underwear, brassieres, and nightgowns could be considered lingerie. She opened the next drawer and pulled out yet another full-length nightgown with long sleeves and a high, ruffled neck.

She dressed in the darkness and removed her glasses before climbing beneath the covers of her bed. As soon as her head hit one of her many pillows, she felt her eyes become heavy with sleep. Just moments later, she smiled as she welcomed Maxwell into her dreams.

"Good morning, Gabrielle."

Gabrielle smiled at Addie, Maxwell's lovable housekeeper/cook, as she walked into the large, airy kitchen. "Morning, Addie. Something smells good," she sighed, inhaling deeply of the aroma as she strolled over to the stove.

Addie smiled with pride. "Just banana nut pancakes with turkey sausage," she told the younger woman, handing her a warm plate of food. "Your favorite."

"My favorite," Gabrielle affirmed, before taking her seat at the island in the center of the kitchen.

Addie moved to lean her hip against the island near Gabrielle. "After that mess I saw in party central, I thought you deserved a special treat."

Gabrielle paused over a forkful of pancakes as she cut her eyes up at Addie through her glasses. "That bad?"

"Chile, please." Addie waved her hands in the air as she turned to walk over to the sink.

"Any sight of our fearless leader?" Gabrielle asked.

Addie slid a pan into the sink of hot, sudsy water.

"They way it looks in there, I doubt if we see him before noon."

"That's what he thinks," Gabrielle muttered, thinking of the day of appointments she had scheduled for him.

"What I wouldn't give to be a fly on the wall at one of his shindigs," Addie told her with a mischievous smile. "What do you suppose goes on so?"

Gabrielle's face flushed with warmth as she recalled her little escapade last night. A clear vision of Stripperella came to mind. "Nothing I want any parts of, that's for sure," she snapped, then softened her words with a smile at Addie's odd look.

"I don't know why you won't curl your hair, put a pretty outfit on, and go. You're too young to live with your head in a book all the time. Live life and stop reading about it before your hair is as gray as mine, Gabrielle."

Gabrielle self-consciously touched her hair and looked down at the plaid short-sleeve shirt and cotton stretch pants she was wearing. An image of the scandalous outfit that Stripperella wore appeared in her coffee. With a spoon, she viciously stirred the image away with a frown.

"Oops! I'm sorry, where's the front door?"

Both Gabrielle and Addie looked over their shoulders to the doorway where Stripperella stood, still dressed in the skimpy outfit she had on last night. Gabby didn't try to hide the distaste on her face, and Addie flat out snapped, "Girl you *need* to go to church."

"Huh?" the woman asked in a childlike manner, every bit of her make-up gone and her hair a mess.

Gabrielle felt her heart drop to the floor, just low

enough for Maxwell to walk all over it. It was quite evident that this woman had just awakened from a night of lascivious sex with *her* Maxwell. "The exit's this way," she said, rising to escort her out. *The sooner the better*, she thought.

Gabrielle said nothing to the woman, who introduced herself as Mercedes, as she strode quickly down the hall toward the front door.

"Are you Max's little sister or something?"

Again Gabrielle ignored her, pulling the front door open wide with a false smile.

"Woo, what a night!"

"I'm sure it was," Gabrielle said snidely before slamming the door with pleasure in the woman's face.

Maxwell felt as if elephants were stomping on his forehead as he rolled over slowly onto his back in his king-size bed. Groaning, he blocked the light from his eyes with his forearm and wished like hell that his infamous Cosmopolitans weren't so damn good. "Gabby!" he roared at the top of his lungs, wincing as darts of pain swarmed his clean-shaven head.

"Why are you yelling, Maxwell?" she asked quietly, stepping closer to the bed.

Startled by her sudden appearance, he moved his arm and cocked one eye open to peer up at her. "I want—"

"Your special, I know," she finished for him, setting the awful hangover drink on his nightstand. "Plan on getting up today, lover boy?"

Maxwell struggled to a sitting position, the leopard-skin coverlet falling to his waist to expose a smooth, hairless chest. He reached for the reddish brown brew. "What would I do without my little Gabby?" he asked, gulping down the liquid in one quick swallow.

Gabrielle winced at the thought of the drink's ingredients. She wouldn't dare consume it, but it always seemed to work for Maxwell's I-partied-last-night-and-drank-too-much hangover.

"Ready for today's schedule?" she asked him, using an index finger to push her wire-rimmed spectacles up on her nose.

Maxwell grimaced and then waved his hands as if he were signaling an SOS. "The only thing I'm ready for is a hot shower," he grumbled, deep into his customarily grouchy morning demeanor.

Deciding to ignore his protests, Gabrielle opened her portfolio and looked down at his schedule for the day. "I have to arrange for the cleaning crew for your latest event, so before you shower—"

The bathroom door shut firmly.

Gabrielle looked over the rim of her glasses to find Maxwell's unkempt bed to be empty. Soon the sound of the shower could be heard. "Okay, *after* your shower," she mumbled, still annoyed by his female companionship last night.

Here he was an intelligent, enlightened brother who preferred women who didn't know the difference between a paint-by-number art kit and an original piece of art. Like Mercedes, for instance. *What kind of name was that anyway?* "Maybe if I change my name to a vehicle, he'll notice me," she mumbled sarcastically. "Something like Lexus, or Volvo. No, I know. PT Cruiser sounds good."

It would take more than a name change for

Gabrielle to become one of Maxwell's trophies. Unlike the women he usually favored, Gabrielle was intelligent, conservative in dress, and shaped more like a prepubescent girl than a voluptuous woman. "I guess that's why I'm the assistant and not the girlfriend."

Quite confident that if she didn't wait for Maxwell, he would climb back into bed, Gabrielle strolled around his master suite. She deliberately avoided looking at his bed, hating the images of Maxwell making love to another woman on those very sheets.

Her eyes darted up to the oil painting above the bed. The mocha-skinned couple was nude and face-less, their bodies locked in a rather erotic pose as the woman straddled the man's hips. His strong hands intimately cupped her buttocks as she rode him.

Gabrielle bit down on the tip of her pen as the face of the man clearly transformed into that of Maxwell and the face of the woman became that of her own. She released a shaky breath that seemed to breathe life into the picture, making it animated. Her vivid imagination beat out reality as she watched herself ride Maxwell's shaft in vibrant color.

Gabrielle nearly bit the pen's top in half.

"Gabby . . . Gabby?"

Surprised by the sudden sound of his voice, Gabrielle literally jumped. "Uh, yeah. I mean, yes, Maxwell?" she stumbled, fanning herself with her portfolio as she turned to face him leaning his upper body out of the bathroom.

Maxwell instantly noticed the nervousness in his assistant's face, the way her cheeks were flushed and her eyes glazed. He made an odd face. "What's up with you, Gabby? You okay?"

Gabrielle cleared her throat. "Did you need something?" she asked, ignoring his question.

"I had an unexpected houseguest last night. Could you make sure that she's gone?"

Gabrielle's face became aghast. "In my six years working for you I have at times gone above and beyond what I believe to be my job description. I've gotten out of bed at midnight to go get your favorite ice cream. I've nursed you and wiped up puke when you've had the flu. I've even dragged you to bed after you got wasted at the bachelor party you threw for your friend." She took a deep breath before continuing her tirade. "These things I did with a smile. A forced smile—but a smile nonetheless. Now I must draw the line at taking part in disposing of one of your little bedmates in the morning after you're done with doling out your wares."

Maxwell's handsome face shaped into surprise.

"What next, Maxwell? Will you ask me to parade the women in for you? Where will we draw the line of inappropriateness?" she finished with an angry stomp of her foot.

"All done?" he asked calmly.

She nodded.

"My houseguest—"

"Mercedes," she drawled, already guessing correctly that he had forgotten her name.

"Uh, yes, Mercedes, hung around after the party to get a chance at my—how to you say—*wares*. She was a little drunk and since I wasn't interested in adding her to my list of *little bedmates*, I let her sober up in one of the guest rooms last night."

Gabrielle diverted her eyes from his, feeling embarrassed by her outburst. "Oh."

"Uh-huh. Just pick it up."

Gabrielle frowned. "Pick what up?"

"Your face," he teased with a huge grin that was adorable.

Forgetting all about reviewing his schedule for the day, Gabrielle turned and walked out of his bedroom, his laughter following her as she did.

"When are you going to realize that you are not Maxwell's keeper? You are supposed to have a life of your own, Gabrielle."

Gabrielle bit at one thumb's fingernail, a nervous habit she had had since childhood, as she listened to her older sister, April, berate her for the thousandth time. She had heard it all before until she could recite April's speech right along with her. "This is my job, Ape," she told her, rising to carry the cordless phone with her as she walked around her tiny office in Maxwell's loft.

"Yes, but what about your life?" was her sister's soft reply.

"Don't be so melodramatic, Ape," she spoke around her thumb.

"When's the last time you took a vacation? Went on a date? Did anything for yourself without Maxwell in mind?"

The honest answer was never, but Gabrielle would not say it. "I am quite happy with my life the way it is, Ape," she insisted sternly, wincing as she bit too deeply into her nail bed.

"You need a man," April told her sassily.

"Why? So that I can call my sister every two weeks with another sad story of broken hearts, bad sex, and betrayed trust? I don't think so."

Gabrielle wasn't at all surprised to hear the line disconnect.

She sighed as she hung up the phone. The last thing she wanted was to hurt April's feelings, but she also wanted to be left alone about the way she chose to live her life. Truthfully, she didn't have the heart to date someone else, because as far as she was concerned, her heart belonged to Maxwell.

Gabrielle turned from the large bay window of the renovated loft that Maxwell used as his studio. The sunset became her backdrop with beautiful shades of lavender and burnt orange blazing across the darkening sky. Directly in front of her was a painting of a similar sunset that Maxwell had painted. His talent could not be denied. His work was more beautiful than the real sunset, and as always, she found comfort in his art.

Moving past her cluttered desk and all the work she had to get to, Gabrielle walked the full length of the loft, which was filled with Maxwell's art. Paintings leaned against the wall and were positioned on various easels. They could be counted in the hundreds. That was the reason she had fallen for the man. Not just his bronzed good looks and charming demeanor, but his depth. In his work his moods were clearly evident, but the major theme in most was the anger and seemingly hopeless nature of many urban communities: The girls jumping rope among crack vials in the street. The low-income housing where people were grouped together like caged animals.

The deteriorating schools. The wise and aged people who had seen better days long before.

It was all there in every hue, every stroke, every canvas.

Gabrielle stopped in front of a black-and-white oil painting of a young woman sitting on a stoop, surrounded by seven children. Her children. In her eyes, Maxwell had so clearly depicted her plight. A person knew without asking that she was single, poor, and struggling. In the children's eyes, there was hope and the innocence of youth.

Gabrielle felt herself sadden. This was the Maxwell many never knew—the young boy with six brothers and sisters who grew up into the man who painted his past. He refused to sell the picture. He wouldn't even show it.

This was why she excused his excess. She understood his reasons. His mother was gone, and he regretted that he never had had the chance to give her everything she desired in life but could never afford. And Gabrielle mailed the many checks Maxwell sent to some of his brothers and sisters as he tried desperately to give them all a precious piece of the life he enjoyed.

She loved Maxwell, that she knew. Would he ever return her love? She had no idea. But she also knew she wanted him in her life. Not just the flamboyant and carefree artist everyone loved but the quiet and reflective soul who wore his emotions on his sleeve. The man whose eyes lit up at the sight of his nieces. The man who cocked his head to the side and pouted playfully when he was pleading with her for a favor. The man who continued to pay Addie for cleaning even though he had a professional cleaning crew come in every other week.

The man was multifaceted, and unlike so many other people, Gabrielle knew him, really *knew* him, and she loved him to death.

Chapter Two

The late summer air was heated and humid as Gabrielle left her cottage and headed up the paved walk to the big house. She fanned herself and quickened her pace. She craved a glass of Addie's sweet tea and the breakfast she knew was already prepared.

"Excuse me, little girl. Where can I find Maxwell Bennett?"

Gabrielle was just about to enter the front door. She immediately bristled at being referred to as a little girl and because the woman's tone was abrupt and rude. Turning, her hand still on the doorknob, she squinted her eyes through her glasses as she looked at the woman climbing out of a platinum Jaguar XKR coupe.

She instantly reminded Gabrielle of those girls back in high school who used to make her life hell. Everything about the woman spoke of wealth and arrogance: her costly car, the designer clothing, her perfectly coiffed bob, her flawless make-up, and the tilt of her chin. Gabrielle disliked her instantly.

"I'm Gabrielle Dutton, Maxwell's assistant. Can I help you?" she asked firmly as the woman stepped onto the porch.

The woman arched a brow. "Yes, lead me to Maxwell Bennett," she answered coldly.

"And you are?"

"Impatient, sweltering in this heat, and ready to see Maxwell Bennett."

Gabrielle's spine stiffened. "And I'm busy and waiting for you to identify yourself."

"Listen—"

Suddenly the doorknob slipped from Gabrielle's tightly knuckled grasp as the door was opened from inside.

"Where in the hell is Gabby this morning?" Maxwell was saying aloud to himself, just before his presence filled the doorway.

The woman took another step onto the porch, and Gabrielle turned to face Maxwell, blocking the woman's path. "Hey you," Gabrielle greeted him.

"Hey." Maxwell's eyes briefly lit on Gabrielle before moving to the woman behind her. "Penelope, is our appointment today?" he asked, sounding surprised.

Penelope? That's almost as bad as Mercedes, Gabrielle thought spitefully.

The woman smiled at him as she continued up the stairs. "It most certainly is. I didn't know I was that forgettable," she teased, cutting a "so there" look at Gabrielle as she stepped past her to kiss Maxwell's cheek warmly.

"I guess I did forget," he told her apologetically, stepping back into the house to allow her entrance.

"Well, the first thing I am going to do as your new consultant is buy you a Palm Pilot."

Gabrielle's mouth dropped open. *Consultant? Did she just say she's Maxwell's consultant?* She stepped into the foyer behind them, trying not to show her surprise.

Maxwell stood in between the two women. "Gabby, this is Penelope Tillman. Penelope, this is Gabrielle Dutton, my personal assistant. We all call her Gabby."

Penelope removed her shades and extended her hand. "Gabby, huh? How . . . adorable."

Gabrielle accepted her hand briefly. "Actually, I prefer Gabrielle."

"Yes, of course."

Maxwell was oblivious to the tension between the women as they stared each other down. "Gabby, I completely forgot to tell you about Penelope. She came by my exhibit at the museum last month."

Gabrielle forced a smile. "Oh, and you just hired her as your consultant. Sounds . . . productive. What role will Ms. Tillman play?"

Penelope smoothed her hands over her tailored linen slacks. "I will take over marketing and career development for Maxwell. That means construct-ing press releases, getting him into more feature articles in newspapers and periodicals, as well as handling his art exhibit bookings, with new gal-leries if necessary."

The way Penelope's frame filled out the sleeve-less silk sweater and slacks she wore, Gabrielle felt like shriveling to the size of a pea and rolling out of the woman's condescending eyesight. "Well, I did the best that I could," Gabrielle said weakly, feeling so awfully self-conscious next to the woman. She was so beautiful, voluptuous, and confident. Every-thing Gabrielle wasn't.

Maxwell hugged her to his side playfully. "You did

a great job, Gabby, but I know you're so busy with everything else that I thought it was a good idea to hire Penelope."

Gabrielle forced a smile. "Of course. Welcome, Ms. Tillman," she said, wanting so desperately to be out of the woman's presence. "Will you both excuse me, I have to . . . to . . . check on a project Addie was working on for me."

A bold-faced lie.

Gabrielle quickly walked down the stairs leading to the sunken kitchen. She was actually pleased to find that it was empty. She was so furious at Maxwell. Hiring Penelope Tillman was just another of his antics, even topping the time he had hired a homeless man sleeping outside the gallery to be his chauffeur. Very chivalrous indeed—except the man didn't know how to drive and did not have a license. Needless to say, Gabrielle wouldn't dare let him near any of the vehicles. Still, his job as Maxwell's new gardener—with no gardening experience—allowed the man to get his own apartment.

Instinctively, she new that learning to work with Ms. Tillman would be a far more harrowing experience than even that. Gabrielle paced the length of the kitchen.

"What did he do now, Gabrielle?"

Gabrielle turned to find Addie standing in the doorway, looking at her with a sympathetic smile. "He hired a manager or consultant or whatever she is. I have never heard of this woman. I have no idea if she's qualified. I don't know diddly about any of it, except she's here."

"Where is she?" Addie asked, walking to the stove to turn the burner down under a boiling pot.

"I'm Penelope Tillman, and I'm right behind you."

Gabrielle and Addie both turned in surprise.

"Max is off to his loft, and he sent me to you to get updated on what's what," Penelope said, her stiletto heels clicking against the tile floor like the constant cocking of a gun barrel. "But first let me update you on some things, little Gabby."

At her tone both Gabrielle and Addie immediately bridled.

"I have worked in the art industry for well over a decade. I currently have ten artists on my roster with seven of them generating well over a total of one million dollars in sales last year. I have connections from the East to the West Coast. I can and will take Max to an even more successful career as an artist because I'm smart, I'm experienced, and I'm not one to take lightly. Oh, and I guess my master's in fine arts doesn't hurt either."

Well, la-di-da.

"Now . . . any more questions?" Penelope asked, coming to stand nearly nose to nose with Gabrielle.

Addie frowned, placing her hand on her hip. "Oh, *I* got a question for you. Just who in the world do you think you are?"

"Certainly not a maid."

Addie dropped the hand towel she had been holding to the floor and bustled over to the woman with her finger pointed. "Now you messin' with the right one."

Gabrielle's eyes widened and she rushed to step into Addie's warlike path. "I'll handle Ms. Tillman, Addie. Is breakfast ready, because I'm so hungry this morning."

At Gabrielle's pleading look, Addie shot Penelope a hostile glare before she turned to walk over to the stove. Her mumblings of less than pleasant commentary on the newcomer could clearly be heard.

Gabrielle forced a smile before she faced the woman. "We've all gotten off to a rough start, Ms. Tillman," she began, using her index finger to push her glasses up on her nose. "Since Maxwell has brought you on the team—"

"To *lead* the team," Penelope asserted, as she tapped her fingernails against the marble top of the kitchen island.

This really is an aggravating woman, Gabrielle thought, instantly scrapping any idea of trying to be cordial.

"If you have a pen and pad I have some things I'm going to need you to get for me," Penelope said.

Gabrielle's face became incredulous. "Excuse me?"

"You're the little assistant, aren't you? Well, I need you to—let's see, what's the word—*assist.*"

The sound of a metal pot noisily hitting the countertop echoed in the large kitchen.

"First of all, Ms. Tillman, I'm about to have breakfast. Secondly, and most—oh, let's see, what's the word—*importantly,* I'm Maxwell's assistant, not yours. Let's get that clear."

Penelope smiled like a viper. "Well, the little kitty has claws, does she?" she said with satisfaction.

"Come and eat your breakfast, Gabrielle," Addie said abruptly, obviously still upset.

Gabrielle's stomach grumbled loudly at the sight of the grits, salmon patties, and scrambled eggs.

"Care to join us, Ms. Tillman?" she offered, not sounding at all like she meant it.

Penelope frowned in distaste. "Those grits are swimming in butter. On behalf of my arteries, thanks but no thanks."

"Suit yourself."

Addie sat down at the island as well as Gabrielle, and they both began to enjoy their breakfast. They exchanged a look as Penelope began to wander slowly around the kitchen.

"This really is a wonderful house. With a little womanly touch it could be quite a showcase," she said slowly with pleasure as she opened an ornately carved wooden door that led to the wine cellar.

Gabrielle had a clear vision of herself kicking Penelope and her insufferable attitude with a enormous size-twenty shoe down into the cellar. *Why did Maxwell bring this woman into our lives?* her eyes asked as she looked meaningfully at Addie.

Because he needs my size seven and a half up his behind, that's why, Addie's eyes seemed to say in return.

The two women broke out in laughter.

Penelope turned quickly to stare at them with a wary expression.

Maxwell could honestly believe that he had been born with a paintbrush in one hand and a chisel in the other. As long as he could remember, his life had revolved around art. From crayons and Play-doh as a child to paint and sculpting clay as an adult. From graffiti art in the eighties to the modern urban landscape he honored with oils and acrylics today, art had always been his salvation.

His parents, Al-Tarik and Melissa Bennett, had met during their sophomore year in high school. He liked her green eyes, and she adored his toothy smile. Ten years and seven children later they were still together—until the night he was murdered during a random drive-by shooting on his way to the corner grocery store to buy Pampers. An innocent victim who unwittingly left his young wife and small children alone.

Maxwell was the last of the seven children. The baby. His mama's baby boy. She raised him and all of his older siblings alone, never even remarrying or moving another man in to watch over her dead husband's children. And although they were poor by most standards, neither he nor his siblings had ever been hungry or homeless. Even if they had fried bologna and rice for dinner, their bellies had been full. Even if they were all crammed in a three-bedroom apartment, they had never felt the bite of winter or the heat of summer.

He had been glad for his hand-me-down clothes and toys. And he had cherished the meager art supplies his mother scrimped to buy for her baby boy. She had been his biggest supporter, emotionally and financially. His art work was always displayed on any available spot in their apartment, transforming the dull walls with vibrant colors and images. She would hold him close in her arms and tell him to never give up his art. "God blesses everyone with a special talent, son," she would always say. "Never give up your gift."

Once he asked her what gift God gave her, and she looked down into his eyes and said: "Being a mother. My children are my blessings." And she meant that.

Although they had all split over the years, moving to different cities and states for jobs and spouses, each of them was doing relatively well. No convictions, no addictions, no excuses.

Maxwell blinked away tears that threatened to fall from his eyes as he stood in the center of his loft and looked at his mother's face in the painting with seven children. He felt no shame for the grief he had felt ever since she became ill and died from colon cancer during his senior year at Arts High School. He hated that he could never give her all the things she'd wanted in life but had sacrificed so that all seven of them could go to college and have a better life than she had. After her death, her will stipulated that any remaining insurance money was to be used toward sending Maxwell to college, where he eventually earned his bachelor of fine arts.

Just one year after graduating, a member of a nine-panel art-buying committee for a leading computer corporation's art collection saw his exhibit at the outdoor Canal Art Work exhibit. She recommended his work to the committee to be included in their collection of young, contemporary living artists. The panel soon agreed, and Maxwell's career had soared ever since.

His work now sold for six figures or more. The apartment he grew up in would fit in the kitchen of the house where he lived now. His backyard was bigger than the small park where he used to play. Public transportation had given way to the expensive cars he owned. The gritty urban landscape he still painted had given way to the suburbs of Richmond where he now lived.

Maxwell knew that his mother was smiling proudly down upon him from heaven. That fact made him happy and sad all at once.

There was a soft knock at the door, and he knew it was Gabby. Using his sleeve, he wiped his eyes and moved away from the picture of his mother and her seven blessings. "Come in, Gabby," he hollered, as he took his seat at her desk. Maxwell couldn't fight his tears, so he dropped his head in his hands and let them fall.

She walked in with a smile, and he felt comforted by her presence.

"How'd you know it was me?" she asked, looking down at the folders she held as she put them in alphabetical order. "Ms. Tillman is quite a woman, isn't she? Subtlety is not her strong point. She actually told me that I was a twelve-year-old boy trapped in a woman's body."

Gabrielle walked over to the pair of cherry-wood file cabinets in one corner and squatted down to place some of the files in the bottom drawer. "I hope I'm not too forward in saying that I was glad to see her tail lights. What do you really think of her?"

Gabrielle rose and wiped her hands together as she finally turned to face Maxwell. Her face immediately became concerned at his drooped shoulders and the way he held his head in his hands. "What's wrong, Maxwell?"

He used his strong, agile fingers to wipe the tears from his angular face. "Just wishing my mother was here," he told her wearily as he looked up at her with a weak smile.

The dampness of his tears still clung heavily to his long lashes, and Gabrielle thought he had never looked more beautiful. She forced herself to look away from those eyes. "You really should spend more time with your sisters and brothers. Maybe a big gathering or something. Then you won't feel so alone in the world."

Maxwell reached up and tweaked her nose playfully. "I'm not alone. I got you, Gabby."

Forever and a day if you want me, she wanted to say, but she knew that he meant as his friend, or more like the little sister that he treated her as. "How about a big reunion?" she asked instead, hiding her emotions easily as she had so many times in the past six years. "I would love to finally meet all of your family, Maxwell. Come one, let's do it."

He rose and nudged her shoulder with his own. "Let's get past this exhibit first."

"Well, you hired Penelope the Pit Bull. Put her to work. That will free some time up for me, and I'll get the ball rolling on the reunion. This is one party you will throw that I'll actually grace with my presence," she told him eagerly, bouncing into her chair and causing her ponytail to whip around her head like a propeller.

"You don't mind?" he asked, looking down at her.

"Not at all," she answered him softly.

Their eyes met.

Gabrielle felt her heart swell with love for him.

Maxwell felt blessed for her friendship. When he had seen the awkward young woman with the big glasses and ill-fitting clothes at the Art Expo, Maxwell had felt a little sorry for her and completely protective of her. He struck up a conversation, and she spoke to him in a rushed, breathless way that let him know that she was eager for a friend and nervous from the attention all at once. When she told him that she was originally from Georgia but was staying in Virginia, or even moving to D.C. after graduating that summer, Maxwell had awful images of her alone and naive in a big city. Although the last thing he needed was an assistant, he had offered her the position on the spot.

That was six years ago, and now Maxwell didn't know what he would do without the little imp. He knew that he became so engrossed in his art that things like paying bills, attending meetings, and actually selling his work fell to the wayside. For six years, Gabrielle had made herself an important element in his life. She was his safety net. He could lose his mind painting because he knew Gabrielle had his back. He honestly didn't know anyone he trusted more in his crazy and hectic life.

"Maybe if we get some family up and through here you won't feel the need to surround yourself with people who are just looking for free liquor and food for the night."

"Ha ha, you're so funny," Maxwell drawled dryly.

"And right," she insisted as she steepled her fingers.

"You're gonna make some man a great wife one day," he told her.

Someone like you? Gabrielle pushed her hopes away. "Will you let me have my wedding here?" she asked, forcing lightness into her voice.

"You would get married here?" he asked in disbelief.

"Yes. I would love a beautiful garden wedding out

by the pool. It would be a small wedding, with lots and lots of lit candles. The people I'd invite are there to be happy for me because they love me and not to just gawk. I'd have lots of gardenias, including one in my hair. And everyone, even the guests and my future husband, would wear white. The reception would be kind of casual just as the sun sets, with a buffet of good old-fashioned southern food and lots of soul music. And our first dance would be to 'Always and Forever.'"

"For a kid, you got it planned out really well," he told her, coming to sit down on the edge of her cluttered desk.

"I'm twenty-eight years old and that's far from being a kid," she told him with a meaning that she knew he was clueless to.

Maxwell reached over and mussed up her hair. "I don't care how old you are. You will always be a kid to me, Gabby."

Gabrielle hid her sadness and disappointment with a forced smile. "Just because I'm not as old as time doesn't mean I'm a kid, grandpa. How old are you, anyway? Forty?"

"Forty!" he balked in astonishment as he lunged for her.

Gabrielle scurried from around her chair with a squeal. "Careful, grandpa," she teased at him from across her desk.

He dashed around the desk after her, and Gabrielle squealed again as she ran toward the other end of the loft.

Maxwell caught up to her easily, grabbing her around her slender waist with one solid arm. He wrapped his other arm around her from behind and began to squeeze her lightly. "Say sorry," he growled low in her ear.

He had absolutely no idea that Gabrielle was actually reveling in the feel of being so close to him. His arms brushed against the base of her breasts. His hard chest pressed into her back. His groin molded onto her hip. Her nipples hardened into tight buds, and she felt warmth spread and throb between her legs. "Why are old people so sensitive?" she teased, half-heartedly trying to get out of his hold.

Maxwell tightened his grip further. "Okay, come on and say it like a good little girl. Say you're sorry, Gabby."

Gabrielle shivered slightly as his breath tickled her ear. She felt near to passing out for want of him. She realized then that if she didn't give in and he continued to press his body against hers, that she would beg him to strip her naked and make love to her atop one of his paintings on the floor.

"Excuse me. I didn't mean to . . . interrupt?"

Coolness filled Gabrielle as Maxwell released her and turned to face Penelope. "Hey, Penelope. You weren't interrupting anything."

Gabrielle quickly regained her composure with effort. "Nothing at all."

Penelope walked the length of the loft toward them. "I forgot to get you to sign these contracts," she said, handing a large manila envelope to Maxwell.

Maxwell immediately passed the envelope to Gabrielle. She already knew she should fax the contracts to Max's attorney to be looked over before he signed.

Penelope took in the move with calculated eyes. "It's just a standard contract outlining my fees, duties, and such."

Maxwell looked at her with distant eyes and Gabrielle realized his mind was already focusing elsewhere. "Okay," was all that he said to her.

"I was on my way to dinner and thought I'd invite you. Have you eaten?" Penelope asked with an alluring smile as she lightly touched Maxwell's chest with her scarlet fingertips.

Gabrielle swallowed back her irritation.

"Actually I got this painting that's been nagging me in my dreams for weeks that I want to start on. I'll pass, but thanks," he told her kindly.

Gabrielle just loved Maxwell's dedication to his craft. She nearly jumped for joy.

"I'll leave you to your work, then. See you tomorrow," Penelope said, turning to leave.

"Maxwell leaves for L.A. tomorrow, Ms. Tillman," Gabrielle told her with satisfaction.

Penelope stopped and turned on her heel. She pierced Gabrielle with her eyes. "Yes, I know. I'll be traveling to Los Angeles with him, dear."

Gabrielle hid her surprise.

Maxwell looked down at her. "Oh, yeah, Gabby, Penelope's going with me to Los Angeles," he told her teasingly with warm, laughing eyes.

It was at times like these that Gabrielle could strangle her handsome boss.

"Gabrielle . . . Gabrielle. Wake up, baby. Wake up."

Gabrielle blinked rapidly as she awakened. Her

heart raced as she reached over and picked up her glasses to put on. She turned over in bed and looked up at Maxwell's face framed beautifully by moonlight. "Is something wrong, Maxwell? What time is it? And why on earth are we whispering?" she asked, sitting up in bed.

Maxwell sat down on the bed, facing her. His expression was intense in the moonlight as he reached for her shaking hands. "Gabrielle, I—"

Her eyes took in the silk housecoat he wore. "What is it, Maxwell?" she asked, her voice frantic.

"I need to talk to you before I go to Los Angeles in the morning, Gabrielle. I just can't keep this inside any longer, baby."

Gabrielle froze in shock and her mouth dropped opened comically. *Did Maxwell just call me baby? Is he really massaging circles on my hand with his thumb? What on earth is going on?*

With wide and frantic eyes she watched his hand like it was a snake as it rose to lightly grasp her chin. He closed his eyes as he leaned his head toward her. "I love you, Gabrielle. I always have and I can't keep it from you any longer," his words whispered over her quivering lips.

"Maxwell, are you drunk?" she asked.

"Yes," he answered. "Drunk with love for you." His mouth pressed down on hers as his hand moved to her nape and pulled her face closer to his. The kiss deepened as his tongue tangoed with hers. They both moaned in pleasure.

Gabrielle felt the stiffness in her body fade as she reached up to remove her glasses and fling them across the room as Maxwell's tongue seemed to make love to her mouth in the most erotic fashion.

"Oh, Maxwell. Yes, Maxwell," she moaned against his lips, as she let her hands rise to grasp his face tenderly.

She didn't resist as he gently pushed her back down among the many pillows on her bed and covered her upper body with his. His lips kissed a trail from her mouth to her neck as she moved her hands down his chest to remove his robe. She gasped as her hands felt nothing but the heat of his skin under her eager fingertips.

Maxwell lifted his hips to fling the covers away from her body. She lay there, his willing captive, as he slipped his hands under the full length of her nightgown to raise his fingertips up her thighs to play in the slick wetness between her legs. She gasped harshly and arched her hips off the bed as he slipped first one and then another finger deep into her core while using a thumb to tease the swollen bud.

Gabrielle cried out, flinging her own arms above her head to clutch wildly at the pillows as he pleasured her. She felt no shame as he watched her with close intensity. She had waited for this for what seemed like forever, and she was not going to ruin this night with silly frigidity.

With his other hand, he continued to pull her nightgown up and over her head. "You're beautiful, Gabrielle. Just like I knew you would be," he whispered huskily as he lowered his head to capture one of her pert breasts in the warmth of his eager mouth. His tongue circled her nipple before he suckled nearly the whole mound into his mouth.

Gabrielle cried out in abandon as she felt her climax nearing. Tears of love and pleasure filled her eyes and raced down her cheek as she came. "Maxwell . . . Maxwell . . ."

"Yes, Gabby? Gabby, don't you hear me talking to you?"

Gabrielle blinked rapidly as the last beautiful vision of Maxwell making love to her faded into the distance out of the loft window. She turned and looked up at him, her cheeks as warm with embarrassment as the sun blazing in the morning sky. She felt her heart racing and core pulsating like it had all been real. *And* she had called out his name!

"Gabby?"

"All set to go?" she asked, rising to walk around the desk and stand beside him.

"What on earth were you just thinking about?" Maxwell asked, his face incredulous.

Gabrielle had another vision of Maxwell naked and proud standing above her nude body on the bed and shook her head to send it away. "Nothing," she lied.

Together they walked out of the den to the foyer where the driver was picking up Maxwell's luggage to load into the trunk of his taxi. Penelope climbed the front steps and walked into the foyer as well. She looked pretty in an ivory silk blouse and slacks. "Good morning, Max," she said with a warm smile.

Gabrielle longed for a cup of coffee to accidentally spill on her outfit. Instead she ignored the woman. "You have your tickets, Maxwell?" she asked, turning to face her boss.

"I knew I forgot something," he told her, turning to head up the stairs at a jog.

The women watched him before turning to face each other.

"You know, Gabby—"

"Gabrielle," she insisted shortly.

"Yes, whatever," Penelope said dismissively, actually waving her hand in the air as if she were shooing away a fly. "I noticed that you have a little crush on Maxwell."

Gabrielle was startled, but she didn't know if it was because the woman was astute or because she had actually let her guard slip. But she didn't show it. "You're not very observant are you, Penny?"

"It's Penelope, dear."

"Whatever," Gabrielle said dismissively, imitating the waving motion Penelope made with her hand.

"Anyway, you may as well use these few days to begin healing your little broken heart because I plan to use this time Maxwell and I will have alone to form a bond that will lead to the start of a wonderful relationship between us."

Gabrielle laughed. "You're not his type, trust me."

Penelope gave her a once-over that was meant to belittle. "Oh, and you are?" she asked with pity.

Gabrielle swallowed back embarrassment. "Maxwell and I are friends, nothing more, so if you want to use your class in Tricking 101 to get him, then feel free to do so. But trust me, Maxwell ain't falling for it."

"We'll see," Penelope said just before he came back down the stairs.

"Got it," he told Gabrielle, showing her the ticket before he slid it into the back pocket of his jeans.

"All ready, Max?" Penelope asked with a seductive smile.

"Bye, Gabby," he said before turning to leave the house.

Penelope wove one arm through his as they went down the steps. She threw one last meaningful glance over her shoulder at Gabrielle.

Chapter Three

"What in the world are you doing in there?"

Gabrielle looked up at Addie from her spot on the floor of the pantry. She smiled weakly. "I noticed this morning that it wasn't organized so I decided to . . . organize it for you."

Addie gazed at Gabrielle like she had two heads. "There ain't a thing wrong with my pantry. Come out of there. You been acting fool all day. Now what's going on?"

Gabrielle rose to her feet and left the pantry, pretending to wipe dust from her bulky green pants and sweatshirt. "I was a little bored without Maxwell shouting my name all day to do something. I was just trying to help. Sorry," she lied.

She had plenty to do, her desk was filled with bills that had to be paid, but she couldn't focus on work. She needed something physical to keep her mind off the fact that Penelope might be successful in her attempt to seduce Maxwell. A woman like Penelope was so different from the usual trollops Maxwell dated. She was intelligent, beautiful, classy, and above all—confident. This woman was the first real threat to Gabrielle. A woman like Penelope was the type of woman men married and not just spent a few sweaty hours with. But she couldn't tell Addie that she feared Penelope would steal Maxwell away from her before she even got a chance to really have him.

"You know what you need?" Addie asked as she set a glass of freshly squeezed lemonade and a slice of pound cake in front of her at the kitchen island. "You need to do something with your hair besides wearing ponytails. Put on a pretty dress and have yourself some fun on a date. I have told you so many times that you need to live life. Do something with yourself besides sitting around baby-sitting a grown man."

Gabrielle picked up her fork, but she just poked and played with the dessert. As she looked down at the cake, the only thing she saw was Penelope in Maxwell's bed. Frowning, she stabbed her fork into the vision until it evaporated and nothing remained but a torn-up piece of cake.

She looked up, and Addie had stepped back to stare at her oddly.

Gabrielle smiled weakly. "I'm fine, Addie."

Addie looked pointedly down at the cake and back to Gabrielle's face. "That's what your mouth say."

"I'm not really hungry, Addie. If Maxwell calls, tell him I went home."

"If Maxwell calls. When Maxwell calls. Has Maxwell called? That's all that comes out of your mouth whenever he's away," Addie told her with just a bit of annoyance. "Listen, I love Maxwell to death, just like he was my own son. But I love you too, Gabrielle, and you have got to stop putting your life on hold to be here waiting on Maxwell's beck and call when he wants a Tic-Tac, a Q-Tip, or something else he can damn well get for himself."

"That's my job, Addie," Gabrielle insisted.

"It's my job to cook and clean, but I sure ain't gone feed him too. Do you understand what I'm saying?"

Gabrielle nodded. It was the same exact thing her sister had been telling her for years.

"Maxwell's off in Los Angeles with that barracuda, and you're here with an old woman, making plans to go home and read."

"There is nothing wrong with reading. It stimulates the brain and helps ward off Alzheimer's in later years," Gabrielle told her, rising from the stool.

"You need a life, and I'm going to help you get one," Addie insisted as she danced a little jig over to the telephone.

Gabrielle looked alarmed. "What are you doing, Addie?"

"Helping somebody get rid of some cobwebs, hopefully."

Gabrielle watched as the older woman began to dial someone's phone number.

"Hello, Terrence? Hi there. This is Sister Givens. How are you? And your mother? Good. Just good." Addie gave Gabrielle a meaningful look and wink before turning her back to the younger woman.

"This is a wonderful coincidence. I was just calling your mother to get your phone number and you're there visiting. What a good son you are."

Gabrielle's blind-date alarms went screeching off and she rushed over to Addie, frantically shaking her head and waving her hands. "Don't you do it, Addie," she mouthed.

"Here's why I called you. Your mother and I were talking about how you haven't really dated since you moved to Virginia. Well, I know a beautiful young girl who's so busy with her job that she doesn't date much either. And well, Terrence, I was thinking that you two should meet and maybe have dinner tonight."

Gabrielle didn't want to be disrespectful to Addie, but right then she felt like wrestling the phone from the older woman's hands. Instead she walked to the door. "Goodbye, Addie. I'm not going on a blind date, Addie," she sang, leaving the house without another word.

Gabrielle rushed home. She was initially glad to get inside her cozy cottage. But as soon as she settled down onto the sofa with a novel, she felt loneliness nearly strangle her. All she could think of was Penelope and Maxwell, Penelope on Maxwell, or worse—Maxwell *in* Penelope. She released a frustrated cry and flung the book away as she pulled her knees up to her chest and hugged her legs. She felt near to kicking and screaming like a child who had lost her toy.

The front door opened and in came Addie. Gabrielle watched as the older woman waved to her briefly and walked right past her to the bedroom, humming a little medley. She didn't even bother to follow her and see what she was up to. All she could think of was Maxwell and Penelope marrying and having a bunch of keen-faced little children.

Gabrielle punched one of her throw pillows in frustration. *If he marries that wench, I'll quit,* she vowed.

Addie walked back into the living room, carrying some of Gabrielle's clothing over her arm. "I started you a bath and plugged in your curling iron because there is more to life than a ponytail or a French braid."

"I'm not going on a date, Addie," Gabrielle said calmly, reaching for another book from the coffee table.

"I tried to find you something pretty to wear, but these were the best I could find," Addie continued as if she didn't hear Gabrielle, laying the three dresses on the back of the couch.

"I don't need a dress to do what I'm doing," Gabrielle told her, holding up the hardcover book for Addie to notice.

"You really need to go shopping. I haven't seen dresses like these since Minnie Pearl," Addie complained, picking up one flowered multicolored dress with a white round collar and long sleeves. "Okay, I'll even give Minnie Pearl some credit. I ain't seen a dress this ugly since *Little House on the Prairie.*"

Gabrielle dropped her book and frowned. "Addie!" she gasped in reprimand.

"The truth is the truth. I would say you dress like an old woman but even *I* wouldn't wear this," Addie told her with a frown, picking up another dress that was pale pink. "And *this* one is the best of the bunch."

"Just what I need. My own sad version of *What Not to Wear,*" Gabrielle drawled.

"There's no time to shop, and Terrence will be here in an hour," Addie said. "He's a head doctor who just opened his own practice downtown."

"A head doctor?" Gabrielle shook her head and looked at Addie. "Is he a *psychiatrist*?"

"Yeah, one of those, so you can get some free

therapy while you at it. Ask him why you dress like
a senior citizen and try so hard *not* to be cute,"
Addie teased, picking up the other two dresses to
carry back into Gabrielle's bedroom.

"You really make a girl feel special," Gabrielle
hollered behind her.

"Your bath's waiting, but I couldn't find any Victoria's Secret or that Bath & Body Works to scent
up the water," Addie told her as she walked back
into the room.

Gabrielle looked astonished. "And what exactly
do you know about Victoria's Secret and Bath &
Body Works?"

"Just remember where there's smoke"—she
began, pointing at her gray hair—"there's fire,
baby. And Ms. Addie know you need something
sweet to draw the bees."

Gabrielle settled back on the sofa and again pretended to read her book. "I'm not going on a date,
Addie."

The older woman came to sit down on the sofa at
Gabrielle's feet. "Why not?"

Because I love Maxwell, she thought.

"Come on, Gabrielle. It's just one date. Have
some fun. You deserve it," Addie pleaded with a sad
face. "Do it for an old lady?"

Gabrielle laughed out loud at Addie's act and was
rewarded when Addie too broke out with laughter.
"If you promise to kill the sad old lady bit, especially
when you was just bragging about all your fire, I'll
go. Deal?"

Addie winked. "Deal."

* * *

Maxwell smoothed his hands over his closely shaved chin as he turned to observe his artwork on display. He actually began to feel excited about the reception tomorrow night. The gallery was unique in design, with the entire front of the store made up of large panes of glass that allowed even those who strolled by on the street to view his work. He was glad that Gabby had talked him into having his latest exhibition there.

The Art of Art Gallery was located in the Leimert Park section of Los Angeles, heart of the African-American art community. Jazz clubs, coffeehouses, photo studios, and art galleries could be found, all within walking distance of each other.

As he supervised the gallery's staff setting up his work, many of the local business owners and their clientele had stopped by to congratulate him on his latest collection. They were drawn by the color and vibrancy of his art. They understood and spoke to the sadness or joy depicted in the eyes of the people in the paintings. People whose skin was as deeply bronzed and beautiful as their own.

Yes, it was a warmer reception than he received at the larger, more established art galleries where he usually exhibited his work. Just like Gabby said it would be.

Maxwell reached into the back pocket of his jeans and pulled out his cell phone, quickly dialing his house. He checked his watch as the phone rang. *Three hours difference, so it's nine o'clock there.*

He got no answer at his house or Gabby's. Next, he called Addie at her townhouse in a senior citizen community just fifteen minutes from his house. "Addie? Hey, this is Max. Where's—"

"Hey, how's L.A.? Don't forget to bring me a shot glass for my collection this time."

"I won't forget. Look, where's—"

"That barracuda in silk ain't digging them claws too deeply into you, is she?"

Maxwell's eyes darted to Penelope as she talked to the gallery owner. "Be nice, Addie."

"Ms. High and Mighty wants to be the queen of this castle, so don't you be *too* nice, Maxwell Bennett."

Penelope looked over at him and smiled. Maxwell smiled weakly in return before turning his back to her. "My relationship with Penelope is strictly professional, Addie."

"Don't send the memo to me. I got a clue. It's Ms. High and Mighty that's not hip to the facts, baby."

Maxwell looked to the mirrored ceiling in exasperation. There was no stopping Addie when she was on a roll.

"She gone tell me the house needs a woman's touch. What do she think Gabby and me are, men in drag? Now you tell me what's wrong with the way the house is decorated, Maxwell?"

"I love the house just the way it is," Maxwell told her in a coaxing voice.

"She wanna play so high and mighty, so fine and fabulous, so good and glorious, and those shoes she had on look like a pit bull had ahold of the heel."

Maxwell actually smiled. "Are you done, Addie?"

"I'm just sayin', Max, she's new to all this. Check her . . . before I wreck her."

"I will, Addie,"

"Good. Now what were you trying to ask me?"

"Where's Gabby?"

"Out."

"Maxwell frowned. "Out where? It's nine o'clock there."

"Twenty-eight years old and she got a curfew?"

Maxwell became annoyed. "Out where? Addie?"

"On a date."

"With who?" he bawled loudly, not even noticing the eyes that were now on him.

"A nice head doctor whose mother attends my church."

"What in the world is a head doctor? Do you even know him? Does *he* attend your church?"

"No, he does not attend my church, Maxwell. He just moved back home, and he's a fine young man. And when I say fine, I *mean* fine."

Maxwell began to pace as he envisioned his little Gabby trying to beat off a big, horny stranger who saw the innocence written all over her face. "So you let her go on a date with some nut you don't even know."

"Gabrielle is a grown woman—"

Penelope walked up to him and lightly touched his back. "Max?"

"Gabrielle doesn't know how to handle a man who steps out of line," Maxwell insisted, jerking his shoulder to remove Penelope's annoying hand.

Penelope touched his arm. "Max?"

"Maybe she'll want him to get out of line," said Addie.

"Say what?" Maxwell roared.

"Maxwell?" Penelope asked sharply.

He whirled on her with angry eyes. "What? What do you want?" he snapped loudly in frustration.

Penelope's spine stiffened and for a moment her

eyes were cold as the Arctic. She quickly blinked away any show of anger and forced her lips into a smile. "You're drawing attention to yourself, and I thought perhaps you should finish your call in the owner's office or outside," she told him softly, as if concerned. Really, she hated that he was showing such distress over his assistant being on a date. *What man would want her anyway?*

It finally registered to Maxwell that almost every eye in the gallery was resting on him with open curiosity. "Addie," he said, walking out of the gallery. "I gotta go. I'll call her on her cell."

"Don't hate the player. Hate the game, baby."

Maxwell frowned. "Bye, Addie."

He disconnected the line and dialed Gabby's number. Her voice mail came on, and he clenched his jaw. "Gabby, this is Max. Call me as soon as you get this; it's an emergency. No matter what time," he added in a stern voice that he just prayed she would obey.

Okay, I lied. Sue me.

Gabrielle sat across from Terrence at Soulful Restaurant in downtown Richmond, thinking of ways to slowly and deliberately punish Addie without being disrespectful. *Maybe I could hide her dentures,* she thought without delight, knowing she would never really do such a thing.

Terrence was a playa, and as innocent as Gabrielle was, she could smell his sorry game a mile away—from his fried, died, and laid-to-the-side hair and green eyes that were too glassy not to be cheap contacts, to his little red convertible with the tag that read 4PLAY.

"Hello, Gabrielle."

Gabrielle looked up at Simone Love, a well-known celebrity event planner, who had brilliantly coordinated several of Maxwell's bigger art exhibits in the Richmond area. "Hello, Love," she greeted her warmly, calling her by her surname the way she preferred.

"Yes, *hello*, Love," Terrence chimed in, his glassy eyes racing like a pervert up and down Love's full-figured and shapely body.

Love forced a smile that quickly became a frown and then excused herself to return to her table.

Gabrielle looked at the man as he continued to watch Love's retreat. *Ooh, Addie, Addie, Addie.* "And *you're* a psychiatrist?" she asked, trying to hide the disbelief in her voice as she watched him eat a barbecued pork chop with his fingers.

Terrence was as shocked as she was. "No. What made you think that?"

"Addie said that you were a head doctor."

He loudly smacked the sauce from each of his fingers before answering. "No, I work for *Hedge* Doctors. We do lawn care."

"But she said you just opened up your practice downtown."

Terrence let out a soft belch. "My boss's new office is downtown."

Gabrielle felt a nerve over her left eye jump. "Oh. Okay, well, there's nothing wrong with that. These days it's hard to find a job."

Terrence leaned forward. "I don't know about

that, this is my third one in six months. There's *plenty* of jobs out there."

Gabrielle noticed that one of his contacts had shifted, exposing part of his true eye color—brown. She tried her hardest not to stare at it. "But not lucky enough to stay on one," Gabrielle let slip before she could catch herself. "I'm sorry, that's none of my business."

"No problem. If we're gone hook up, you can ask me about anything."

The piece of chicken Gabrielle was swallowing froze in her throat. "Hook up?" she asked. Her voice strangled as she reached for a glass of water to drink heavily from until the meat dislodged itself.

Terrence reached for her hand and kissed the back of it with the wettest and stickiest lips ever. Gabrielle felt herself actually shiver in disgust. "You look like a girl who needs a little pipe work done. Just call me your plumber, baby, 'cause I lay nothing but pipe."

Gabrielle was quite positive now that she could actually coat Addie's dentures with hot sauce and not feel so awfully bad about it.

Only my second date in four years and this is the luck I have, she thought, politely pulling her hand from his embrace. She smiled stiffly at him as she put her hand under the table and wiped the saliva and barbecue sauce from it with the tablecloth.

Terrence began to rattle on about his two ex-wives and how alimony should be against the law. Gabrielle tuned his behind out and looked around the restaurant. She instantly recognized several of the art pieces adorning the walls and a few sculptures as Maxwell's. She smiled softly as her eyes froze on *Trouble Can't Last Always?*—a painting.

It depicted the gradual transition of the depressing grays of urban decay with all its troubles—drug abuse, poverty, unemployment, and violence—into the vibrant colors of urban splendor without the liquor stores on every corner and drug addicts nodding through their highs on porch stoops, and with children playing peacefully without the threat of violence.

She remembered that when she first saw the completed work, she had truly gotten insight into the depths of the man she worked for. "What's the name of this one?" she had asked as she walked up behind Maxwell in his loft.

He was standing back a bit, surveying his work with an always critical eye. Turning his head, he looked at her over his shoulder, and his eyes showed he was startled by her sudden presence. "You said something, Gabby?" he asked, turning back to face his painting.

Gabrielle hadn't felt offended or even surprised. Maxwell always became so engrossed in his work that she could be in the loft with him and he wouldn't say one word to her all day.

"What are you going to name it?" she asked again, impressed as always by his skills.

"Growing up in Richmond I saw a lot of good in the city, but I would have to be blind to ignore the bad," he began, crossing his arms over his chest. "Thing was, my mother always told me that we as people knew better, could do better, and should want to live better. She never allowed us to throw trash in the streets or disrespect other people's property."

He laughed at his memories. "We lived in a three-family apartment building, and every Saturday my mama got us all up to go clean the backyard and sweep in front of the house. Plant flowers. Rinse the gutters. Do whatever it took to make it feel more like home than just a place to lay our heads, you know? She taught us pride in ourselves and in our home, our environment. So as a little boy I never looked at my neighborhood the way that it really was. I envisioned it the way it could and should be. No liquor stores on every corner. No graffiti on people's homes. No trash in the streets. No people loitering on the corner and blocking the entrance into the stores."

Gabrielle came around Maxwell to study the meaning of his painting as he described the story behind it.

"I told my mama how I pictured the world as a seven-year-old child, and she told me, 'Son, trouble don't last always.' So now when I go back to that area of Richmond and I volunteer at the Boys' Club or talk to kids at the schools, I see that it's almost thirty years later, and some of the neighborhoods are worse than they were when I was a child. I get so frustrated that we as a people have lost our pride. We don't give a damn anymore."

He spoke with such conviction.

"I think of what my mama said and how I believed her. I believed that trouble don't last always, but I was a child then. Now I'm not so sure. So the statement has become a question, an uncertainty, like . . . damn, man, trouble can't last always?"

He turned to her and looked down at her. "You understand what I'm saying, Gabby?" he asked, his eyes troubled.

Tonight she hoped that the very fact that his painting hung on the wall of one of the most renowned businesses in the area, locally owned and operated by a savvy African-American couple, meant that change had come.

"I thought when I invited you to dinner that we would actually have a conversation and not just eat, Max."

Maxwell's eyes darted from his watch to Penelope, sitting across from him in the upscale restaurant. "I'm just thinking about something else. Sorry," he said, sounding like he was anything but.

Penelope raised her flute of champagne. "How about a toast?" she asked huskily, smiling at him beguilingly.

Maxwell quickly checked for the hundredth time that his phone was on, the signal strength strong, and that he had no voice-mail messages before he too lifted his flute. All he could think of was Gabby.

He was a man. He knew the way men thought and what their ulterior motives were. Since he was fifteen and first enjoyed the intimate treasures of females, he had perfected how to woo every type of woman into his bed. Those who were quiet and shy. Those who were bold and outspoken. And every kind in between. He was sure that at that moment Gabrielle might very well be in the middle of a one-night stand and probably thought the man was her one true love. His grip on the flute tightened until he thought it would snap in his very grasp.

"Here's to an enjoyable reception tomorrow night, a great opening day after tomorrow, a successful exhibit for the next month, and the beginning of a wonderful relationship between you and me." Penelope told him huskily, lightly licking her lips as she touched her flute to his with a *ding*.

Maxwell forced a smile, swallowing his champagne in one gulp before looking down at his watch again.

Gabrielle rolled her eyes heavenward as Terrence again pretended to look for something in his glove compartment and let his hand rub across her thigh in the small confines of his car. *God, why didn't I drive my own car?*

When he pulled to a stop before the estate, Gabrielle already had her hand on the door, ready to be free of his offending breath, hands, and cologne—in that order. "Well goodnight, Terrence. It's been . . . something."

Terrence reached out as quick as a pouncing tiger and grabbed her arm. "Don't I get a goodnight kiss?" he asked, licking his lips twice to make them gleam wetly in the dim interior of the vehicle.

Gabrielle swallowed back a wave of revulsion. "I don't kiss on the first date," she told him kindly.

"So I guess a little bed hopping is out then?" he asked crassly.

Gabrielle rushed out of the vehicle and slammed the door shut behind her. "Good night, Terrence. I'll tell Addie to tell your mama that we had a nice time. Good-bye," she said over her shoulder, as she used her electronic key card to swipe the walk-in gate. She didn't feel the beating of her heart slow until the gate closed securely behind her.

"Call me," he hollered through his driver's side window.

Gabrielle began walking to her cottage, not even bothering to acknowledge him or his absurd request. As soon as she passed through the front door her eyes fell on her cell phone plugged into the charger. She felt relieved. During the date she couldn't remember if she'd left it home or lost it. She didn't bother to check if she had any calls.

She removed her glasses and undressed as she walked to her bedroom, leaving a trail of clothes. In the bathroom, she pulled her hair up into a loose topknot before taking a quick shower. All she wanted to do was sleep and try to forget how horrible the day had been, starting with Penelope and ending with Terrence the Terror.

Squinting, Gabrielle dried off after her shower and walked nude into her bedroom, feeling her way as she went. She pulled on one of her beloved nightgowns and literally fell between the sheets. Her head had just hit the pillow when the phone rang.

Gabrielle wanted to ignore it, but whoever was calling her, was persistent. She reached over, put her glasses on, and turned on the bedside lamp before picking up the cordless phone from the base. The caller ID showed Maxwell's cell phone number. "Yes, Maxwell," she said into the phone.

"Where have you been all night? Is your cell phone turned off? Did you just get home? Did your date try anything with you? Is he still there?"

Gabrielle's head felt like it was spinning from all his questions. "On a date. Yes. Yes. No. And hell no," Gabrielle told him, answering his questions in order. "Now goodnight, Maxwell."

"Gabby—"

"I know you haven't noticed Maxwell, but I'm a big girl and I can take care of myself. You're my boss, not my big brother, okay?" she said, her voice soft because she knew that his concern had nothing at all to do with jealousy.

"I just feel like I should watch out for you, Gabby, that's all."

Gabrielle felt swamped with so many emotions. "Goodnight, Maxwell," she told him wearily before hanging up the phone.

Chapter Four

"Rise and shine, sleepyhead. Come on, wake up and tell me all about your date."

Gabrielle dug herself out from beneath the mound of pillows and flopped over onto her back on the bed. She opened first one eye and then the other to scowl at Addie's blurry face. "What are you so happy about?"

Addie leaned back a little at the look Gabrielle shot at her. "Didn't go so well, huh?"

"It would have went well if I didn't discover that Terrence is not a *head* doctor but he works at *Hedge* Doctors. It would have went well if his breath didn't smell like three-week-old cabbage. It would have went well if I didn't have to pay my share of the dinner. It would have went well if he didn't offer to lay some pipe."

Gabrielle's voice rose with each sentence. Addie's face dropped until she too scowled by the end of Gabrielle's tirade.

"Needless to say, Addie, I know that you meant well, but I beg of you, do not offer to hook me up with any more of the sons of your little church ladies again."

Addie did have the decency to look chagrined.

"Well, he was fine though," she insisted, looking for some reprieve.

Gabrielle reached for her glasses and slipped them on so that Addie wouldn't be such a big blur. "Yeah, he was fine *until* his Duke curl frizzed out to a dry Afro during dinner. Then one contact slipped so I had to look at one green eye all night."

Addie frowned. "Oh. So I guess now wouldn't be a good time to tell you that he called, huh?"

The look on Gabrielle's face was unbelieving.

Addie waved her hands. "Just forget I said anything."

"It's forgotten. Burned and then buried into the deepest recesses of my mind."

Addie began to straighten the covers at the foot of Gabrielle's bed.

Gabrielle was busy trying not to let thoughts of Penelope and her Maxwell fry her brain.

"I know," Addie said suddenly.

Gabrielle looked at her with a wary expression.

"Let's get the keys to Maxwell's little sports car out there and go to IHOP for some pancakes."

"Now *that* sounds like a plan," Gabrielle said, kicking away the covers to leap out of bed.

"Mr. Bennett. Mr. Bennett."

Maxwell was just about to step into the elevator of the hotel. He stopped and turned in the direction of the woman calling his name. The front-desk clerk rushed over to him. "Yes?" he asked.

"You have several messages," she said, breathless.

With bags in both hands, Maxwell slid his shopping bag handles onto his wrist so that he could take the messages from her. "Thanks"—he glanced at her name badge—"Erika."

She placed them in his palm, but her hand lingered a few seconds longer.

Maxwell looked at her and saw the intent in her eyes. She was a pretty girl with a dark complexion that reminded him of coffee. She was tall but thick in build, and her short hairstyle suited her round face and large eyes perfectly. She was just his type of woman, and Maxwell knew right then that he could have her in bed if he chose to.

"If I can help you with *anything* else, let a sister know, Mr. Bennett," Erika told him, batting lashes at him that were so long that he wondered if they were real.

"Maxwell," he told her with a smile. *Maybe a little female companionship wouldn't be such a bad thing.*

"Like the singer with those tiny braids?" she asked.

No, like the artist who grossed more money last year than the singer with the tiny braids, he thought. Shaking his head he just said, "Yeah."

A woman whose breast size is bigger than her IQ is hardly a challenge, Maxwell.

Maxwell looked around him. Gabrielle's words had sounded so clearly in his head that he could swear that she was near him. "I have to attend the reception for my art exhibition tomorrow, but if you give me your number, we can hook up later."

"A reception? Ooh, who's getting married? I wonder if it's somebody I know?" she said, reaching out to lightly touch his chest.

I think a real woman scares you, Maxwell.

Again he heard Gabby's voice repeating words she had said to him a million times over the years. He knew there was truth in what she always said, but he certainly didn't need her serving as his conscience or adviser on what women to deal with.

"Something wrong?" Erika asked, looking around as well to see what had caught his attention.

"Everything's fine," Maxwell told her with a smile. "Listen, would you like to attend my exhibit? It's at The Art of Art Gallery over in Leimert Park."

Erika frowned in distaste. "No, no. You go ahead and we'll hook up after, okay. I'm not going to spend my night looking at paintings on a wall."

Oh, yeah, Max. This one's a keeper.

Erika pulled one of the hotel business cards from the pocket of her uniform jacket. "My home number's on the back," she said as she handed it to him. "I can't wait for your call."

Max accepted the card in the same hand that he held his messages. "I have to run, but I'll call you later, all right?" he said, pushing the button for the elevator.

"See you later, Maxwell."

He stepped backward into the elevator, and eventually the doors shut her from his view. He looked down at the six messages in his hand and scowled when he realized that every one of them was from Penelope. "What in the hell?" he asked as classical music played in the background.

The next morning Maxwell got up early and decided to spend his Saturday sightseeing and enjoying everything Los Angeles had to offer. Back home they were just transitioning into fall, but L.A. was alive with the summer season. He enjoyed breakfast at an outside café, visited some of the local art galleries and museums, and then went shopping.

Maxwell found three unique shot glasses for Addie, a wooden sculpture of a mother figure that he purchased for himself, and for Gabby a signed first edition of Langston Hughes's poetry that he discovered in a bookstore carrying rare works of fiction. He wanted to make up for the bossy way he had treated her and he knew that this would do just the trick.

Back in the hotel, he stepped off the elevator and nearly jumped back into it when he saw Penelope leaning against the wall near his door, talking on her cell phone. He was beginning to think that Addie was right. Penelope was laying a trap for him that would be hard to free himself of like a mouse on a glue trap.

She caught sight of him and headed straight in his direction. Maxwell knew it was too late to flee. "Max, I've been looking for you."

He strode past her, setting his bags down as he reached into his pocket for the key card to swipe and unlock the door. "I know you were. I got all of your messages," he told her over his shoulder as he entered the living room of the suite.

Penelope followed him in, closing the door behind herself. "Well? Where were you yesterday?"

Maxwell shrugged as if trying to free her from his neck. He felt as crowded as a shopaholic's closet. "What can I do for you, Penelope? I already know we're meeting downstairs at six."

Penelope watched as he placed his packages on the sofa, swallowing back her irritation at his constant aloofness toward her. "Actually, I was able to pull some strings and get you an interview with a local jazz station this morning. Since you were AWOL—"

"Since when did I enlist?" Maxwell asked dryly.

"I couldn't reach you, but the deejays ran some good promos all day promoting the opening," she told him, looking around the room and spotting his cellular phone on the bar. "Funny thing about a cell phone. It only works if you carry it with you wherever you go."

"Huh?" he asked, looking up from the room service menu with a distracted air. He seemed to be surprised to still see her there.

"Never mind."

"Thanks, Penelope," he told her, walking into the bedroom. "Just let yourself out."

"Actually, I wanted to discuss some things with you," she told him, quickly walking to the bedroom door as it slowly began to swing closed.

"We'll talk on the ride over to the gallery," he yelled just before the door shut.

Penelope stomped her foot in frustration. The man was actually making her begin to question her ability to catch a man. She'd tried every trick in her book, and he still remained distant and aloof. "That arrogant, preoccupied, but oh so sexy son of a bitch," she whispered aloud.

"A dress cut down to here." She motioned to her breasts. "And up to here." She motioned mid-thigh as she spoke to her reflection in the mirror on the wall in front of her. "That will do the trick. Just got to let him see what he's been ignoring, that's all." Penelope leaned forward in the mirror to inspect her flawless make-up. "He's handsome, wealthy, and nearly famous. He's worth all this hassle, right? Right."

Curious, she strolled over to the sofa. She looked down in the shopping bags he had left there. With one quick glance at the closed bedroom door, she searched them. There were gift-wrapped packages. "Couple for the old maid and one for the little assistant, huh?"

There was a note attached to Gabby's, and Penelope read it aloud:

> *Sorry about the way I acted, Gabby.*
> *Forgive me?*
>
> > *Maxwell*

Her face became reflective. She figured that something was getting in her way. Something that would explain why Maxwell was avoiding her subtle advances. She turned and looked at herself again in the mirror. "Why else would he deny all of this?" she asked her reflection.

Penelope replaced the package. Her thoughts were filled with the nondescript woman who worked for Maxwell. There was no way they were involved sexually. She refused to even consider that idea.

Gabby Dutton was the antiwoman. Her clothes were hideous in style, color, and fit. Her body was thin and lacking of any curves, and her glasses were so big and awkward on her face that no one could tell what she really looked like. The woman had never progressed out of her awkward teens. She seemed to be frozen in time.

No, they weren't involved, but Penelope had recognized the crush little Gabby had on Maxwell. The woman stared at him when he wasn't looking, and she protected him better than a mother did her own child.

Penelope was picking up her purse and keys when she heard Max's cell phone vibrate on the top of the bar. Again she eyed the bedroom door before walking over to the bar and lifting the phone. The caller ID displayed Max's home number, and Penelope figured that it was Gabby. She smiled devilishly as she answered the call.

"Hello," she said huskily, as if awakening from sleep.

The line remained quiet, and Penelope smiled in delight.

"I don't know who it is, Maxy, baby. Just go back to sleep," Penelope said, holding the phone away from her mouth just enough to make it seem as if she was in fact talking to someone else in the room.

"Ms. Tillman?" Gabby asked.

Penelope moved away from Max's door with the cell phone. "Yes, who is this? Mr. Bennett and I are . . . busy at the moment."

"This is Gabrielle. I need to speak to Maxwell."

Penelope feigned a yawn. "Oh, hi, Gabby. He's sleeping, and I'd hate to wake him," she said, speaking in a whisper. "Is there something I can help you with?"

The line went quiet for a few moments again.

"Gabby?" Penelope prompted.

"Uh, um, yeah, could you tell Maxwell that I need to talk to him?"

"Of course, and Gabrielle—"

The line disconnected.

Penelope smiled in delight as she placed the phone back on the bar and left the suite. "Now it's time to go shopping."

Gabrielle slammed the phone down on its base. Penelope had succeeded in bedding Maxwell. So many emotions twirled in the pit of Gabrielle's stomach that she felt ill.

She looked down at the invoices on her desk. Work. Work that she didn't feel like doing all of a sudden. She couldn't focus on the numbers in front of her. All she could see were images of *her* Maxwell and Penelope as frolicking lovers in L.A.

Needing a distraction, Gabrielle picked up the cordless phone and dialed her sister's number. She was a little nervous as the phone rang. Their last call had ended less than politely.

"Hello."

"Still mad at me?" Gabrielle asked, biting on her fingernail with a vengeance.

"Gabrielle," April said with pleasure. "You know you and me, we all we got with Mama and Daddy gone. It's gone take more than you throwing my man problems up in my face for me to stay mad at you."

Gabrielle felt relieved. "So what's been up?"

"Nothing much *except* I met a guy last night at

the club," April squealed with pleasure. "And before you say a word, I'm not in love or nothing. He's just real cool, you know."

"I'm happy for you, Ape. I hope it works out."

The line went quiet.

Gabrielle frowned. "Ape?"

"You mean you don't have anything negative to say?"

Gabrielle set her chin in her hand and gazed off at another one of Maxwell's works that she loved. The painting was of an oversized pair of eyes. In the eyes was the love he imagined could be seen in the eyes of a woman who truly loved her man. *Why can't he see the love in mine?* "If you're happy, I'm happy," she finally said, fighting back the tears that threatened to fall.

"Uh-oh. What's wrong, Gabrielle?"

"Nothing's wrong," Gabrielle insisted, forcing energy into her tone. "But let me tell you about this loser I went on a date with."

"You went on a date?" April asked, thoroughly astonished.

"You make it seem like world peace is more believable than me going on a date."

"No, I just thought the only man for you was the great Maxwell."

Gabrielle sat up straighter in her chair. "What makes you think that?" she asked.

"For six years he is the only man you have had more than two words to talk about. I'm in another state, not on another planet," April told her dryly.

"Well, you're mistaken."

"Good. I'm more than happy to be wrong, believe me."

Gabrielle froze. "Now why do you say *that?*"

"For six years you've been sitting right under Maxwell's nose, and if he's too blind to see what a beautiful woman you are—inside and out—then he doesn't deserve you, Gabrielle."

Gabrielle's eyes locked with those in the painting again. She thought of loving Maxwell and never having him. "Max and I are just friends," she told her sister, picking up a pencil to tap upon a notepad on her desk.

"I hope so."

Gabrielle started to doodle on the pad as she began to fill her sister in on every gross detail on her date. She drew a large heart and then wrote inside it: Gabrielle loves Maxwell. She didn't even realize she was crying until a tear hit the pad and smeared the ink of the words inside the heart.

"Ape, I'll call you back," she said suddenly, fighting to keep her tone neutral.

She ended the call, putting the phone on the desk as she dropped her head in her hands and let the tears fall from her eyes like spring rain.

Maxwell growled in frustration as he yanked the bow tie from around his neck. He never could do a bow tie, and Gabby usually handled it for him when he was home. He didn't dare ask Penelope because he was trying his best to keep his distance from her.

When she came back to his room an hour ago, he didn't even answer the door but watched her from the peephole until she finally got back into the elevator. He was already regretting agreeing to ride to the gallery with her for the opening of his show.

Maxwell glanced at the phone on the mahogany nightstand and then at his watch. It was just around eight back in Virginia. He strode across the room and picked up the phone, dialing his house first.

"Hello."

"Gabby? Hey, this is Max," he said, glad to hear her voice.

The line remained quiet.

"Gabby?"

"Hey, Maxwell. It's about time for your opening, isn't it?"

Maxwell frowned in concern at the soft, muffled sound of her voice. "Gabby, you okay?"

"I'm fine, Maxwell. How did the setup go? Is everything just the way you wanted?" she asked, sounding like she had purposely changed the subject.

"Everything's fine except I can't fix my tie, but other than that everything's cool I guess," he answered.

"Penelope's not there to tie it for you?"

"Nope."

Gabrielle laughed, but it sounded lifeless. "Are you wearing the black Calvin Klein tux I packed?"

Maxwell turned and looked at his reflection in the mirror hanging on the inside of the open closet door. "What else would I wear, Gabby?"

"I thought maybe Ms. Tillman chose something else for you, that's all," she answered, her voice tight.

"Penelope's here to help sell my art, not me.

She's my consultant, not my stylist," he drawled, still confused by her behavior.

"Well, I'm not there to get updated on the status of your relationship, so I didn't know what her duties were," she snapped.

"What's going on, Gabby?" Maxwell asked again, annoyed by her vagueness.

"Nothing. Look, I gotta go, Maxwell," she told him. "Oh, and if it's okay with Ms. Tillman just wear your shirt open and leave off the tie. "'Bye, Maxwell, and good luck."

The line disconnected, and Maxwell looked down at it in surprise before placing it back on its base. It was obvious Gabrielle felt her position was threatened by Penelope. "Might be time to talk raise with Gabby," he said to his reflection as he stepped closer to the mirror.

He loosened the top two buttons of his shirt and smoothed the jacket. Gabby was right again. It looked just fine.

Having made a quick decision that he felt good about, he grabbed his room key. Quickly, he walked to the door.

What he was planning was probably a little impolite if not downright rude. He shrugged as he stepped into the empty elevator. "What the hell?" he said to himself.

In the main lobby he stepped out and made his way to the front desk. "Damn," he swore when he saw Erika. He had decided not to even call her. In fact he had torn up the card with her number on it.

Not having any other choice, he continued on to the front desk and placed his best smile on his face as he looked down at her. "Erika, could you give me a piece of paper?"

She licked her lips as she smiled at him. "Looking good. Damn good. Maybe I shoulda went to that reception thing," she said as she pushed a pad and pen toward him.

"It's very boring, actually. Lots of speeches and reading," Maxwell responded, his eyes darting over to the elevator as he scribbled a quick note.

She frowned in distaste. "You right, it does sound boring, but don't forget the fun that'll come later when we hook up, a'right?"

Maxwell winked at her, folding the note in half. "I can't wait," he lied. "Listen, give this to Ms. Tillman for me when she comes down to catch the limo, please."

Erika took the note and actually opened it. After giving her approval she nodded. "Thought, she was your chick or something. Just checking 'cause I ain't trying to be nobody's undercover trick, ya heard me?"

"I'm running late," he told her, turning to walk out of the foyer.

"Call me," she hollered behind him.

She's got a better chance of winning the lottery than of me calling her, he thought, as he motioned to the doorman to hail a cab.

Maxwell reached into his pocket and pulled out his gold money clip. He pulled off a ten and handed it to the doorman just before stepping into the waiting cab with ease.

Gabrielle dug to the bottom of the ice cream bucket and scraped the sides until she had the last of the rocky road ice cream on her spoon. She had dragged herself home from Maxwell's house and fallen into any and every snack she could find in her kitchen.

She went through such drama every time Maxwell had a new lady in his life.

For six years you've been sitting right under Maxwell's nose, and if he's too blind to see what a beautiful woman you are—inside and out—then he doesn't deserve you, Gabrielle. Translation: Max doesn't view you as a woman.

Gabrielle dropped the empty ice cream container on the floor along with the empty doughnut bag, cookie tray, and soda bottle already down there. She reached for the jar of pickles she had placed on the coffee table and let out an unladylike belch. "What does it matter? Max doesn't even know I'm a woman, so why be a lady?" she muttered darkly as she fought to loosen the top of the jar.

It was her own little pity party.

All these years it had never really crossed her mind that Max wasn't sexually attracted to her. She honestly thought three or four years ago that the man would probably try to mate with a log with a hole in it, but never once did he even look twice at her with a hint of desire. She had always assumed that their work relationship, and more importantly their friendship, had discounted her as a possible bedmate.

Her self-esteem sank lower than a fat woman on a seesaw.

Gabrielle yelled out in victory as the jar finally

went *pop* and she was able to extract a large dill pickle that was just a bit on the vulgar side.

She lay back on the couch, using her arm to knock the remnants of her hog fest onto the floor. She took a large bite of the pickle and crunched on it as she used the remote to flip through her cable channels.

Her answering machine was on in case Maxwell called back. Her front door was locked in case Addie felt like visiting before she left the estate for the night. And her baseball bat was by the chair in case Terrence the Terror felt like climbing the electronic fence.

"Congratulations, Max. I got a few previews from some of the art critics, and you should be pleased," Penelope told him with delight after the opening as they walked outside to the waiting limo.

"Good," he said shortly, before covering his hand with his mouth to stifle a yawn.

"When I get back to New York I should have a few sample press kits ready for you to choose from. We will strike while the iron is hot and continue getting your name out there to build an even bigger fan base," she told him eagerly, once they were settled in the limo.

Maxwell let his head fall back against the seat and closed his eyes. "Just mail them to me. I'll have Gabby look over them for me and choose the best one."

Penelope's mouth thinned in exasperation. "Really, Max, this is a decision that you should make, not your assistant. If you don't want to choose *I'll* pick the best."

"That's fine."

They rode in silence and Penelope watched him in the dim interior of the vehicle. "Max?"

Maxwell opened one eye and looked over at her. "Penelope," he said, as if trying to remain patient. "I know you don't know this, but after an opening I just like to chill and reflect on the night. It's a ritual for me."

Penelope crossed her legs and blinked rapidly. "No, I didn't know that, but I just wanted a moment of your time to discuss something very important with you. After that you can . . . uh, *chill* as much as you want."

Maxwell rubbed his hands over his eyes, releasing a heavy and frustrated breath. "If you insist."

"It's about Gabby."

Maxwell opened both eyes to look at her this time. "What about her?"

"I think you should consider replacing her and finding a more efficient assistant. Her records are unorganized. Her behavior at times is insolent, and she has already made some serious mistakes concerning your career," Penelope exaggerated.

Maxwell laughed loud and vibrantly in the back of the limo before sitting up to stare over at her. "Are you suggesting I fire Gabby?"

"For the betterment of your career, yes, I am," she said softly.

"Penelope, if you want to remain serving as my art consultant, I'd advise you to continue consulting me on those things on which your opinion is desired," Maxwell told her coolly, leaning back against the seat to close his eyes.

Penelope released her own heavy breath. *Okay, Plan B,* she thought.

Chapter Five

"The temperature is dropping out there," Gabrielle said, hurrying to shut the door behind her as she entered the kitchen.

"Yeah, and just last week it was steaming hot. Everybody better start praying around here 'cause I'd hate for the end of the world to catch everybody off guard," Addie told her, turning away from the television Maxwell had installed in the kitchen so that she could watch her soaps.

"Well, it seems it doesn't matter what the weather is for Maxwell. The partying must continue," Gabrielle told Addie as she poured herself a cup of coffee.

She knew Max wished he could warm the cold shoulder she'd been giving him since he returned from L.A. two weeks ago.

The days of her hanging around the loft while he painted were over. She no longer entered his bedroom for any reason, and she tried to keep their conversations strictly professional. She was never rude or disrespectful, but she had dropped the casual air that once existed between them. It was hard being near him when she thought he viewed her as appealing as chop liver.

Besides, Penelope was hanging around enough to fill any void that Gabrielle's absence made. The more time her face floated about the estate, the less Gabrielle wanted to be there. As much time as the woman spent there, Gabrielle seriously doubted that she had any other clients.

As of late the woman was actually pretending to be nice to her. Gone were the catty comments and disdainful looks. Gabrielle didn't buy it for a second, but what could she do, run and complain to Maxwell that Penelope the Pit Bull was being *too* nice to her?

Gabrielle opened the morning newspaper to the comics section, pushing up the sleeves of her favorite tan argyle sweater.

"How are my girls?" Maxwell yawned as he walked into the kitchen, dressed in pajama bottoms that Gabrielle knew he'd put on just before coming downstairs because he slept in the nude.

"Good morning," Gabrielle said shortly, turning her attention back to the paper.

"Morning, Maxwell." Addie smiled at him as she set a bowl of oatmeal in front of each of them. "Eat up, you two."

Maxwell sat down beside Gabrielle and frowned when she turned slightly so that her back was to him. He looked at Addie, and the old woman just shrugged, and he said, "You know Gabby, when my sister, brothers, and I were coming up, oatmeal was all that my mother would feed us for breakfast. It was cheap but filling. She wouldn't even let us go to school early and eat free breakfast. She said there was no need to get up earlier to go and eat cold cereal."

"I remember you told me that before," was all that Gabrielle said in a bored tone.

"I made it with lots of cinnamon, brown sugar, raisins, and walnuts just the way you said your mama used to," Addie told him, sitting down at the island with her own heaping bowl.

They both watched Gabrielle continue to read as she reached for her cup of coffee. One sleeve worked its way back down her slender arm and fell into the top of her oatmeal. She never even noticed.

Maxwell picked up his linen napkin and reached for her wrist.

Gabrielle jumped at his touch, hating her reaction to the warmth of his hand against her skin. She tried to pull her wrist from his grasp and looked up at him when he resisted.

Maxwell smiled. "You have oatmeal on your sleeve," he told her, using his napkin to wipe it away. "You know if you'd stop buying your clothes so big they might actually fit."

"I told her she needed to burn all her clothes and start fresh," Addie added teasingly.

Gabrielle's cinnamon complexion flushed with embarrassment as they jokingly critiqued her. "I didn't mean to offend anyone with my appearance. Why don't I just go and shrivel up in a corner somewhere, and then you both can enjoy the daily fashion show Penelope the Putrid puts on when she drops by for absolutely *nothing* every . . . single . . . day," she snapped, reaching up with her index finger to push her glasses up on her nose. She missed the glasses and forcefully poked herself in the forehead with a wince.

Addie looked hurt. "We were just teasing, Gabrielle, like we always do," she told her softly.

"Well, it's not very funny when everybody's laughing *at* you and not *with* you." Gabrielle gathered up her portfolio and the section of the paper she was reading. "I'll be back later. I have some errands to run."

When she was gone Addie and Maxwell looked at each other in confusion.

"Has Gabby been acting different to you lately?" Maxwell asked, stirring more sugar into his oatmeal.

Addie eyed him. "Would you like more oatmeal with your sugar?" she asked dryly.

He smiled at her boyishly.

As far as Addie was concerned the matter was instantly settled. "Charming devil, you. And to answer your question about Gabrielle, she's been a little testy, but nothing to suggest invasion of the body snatchers."

Where does the woman get the things that she says?

"Testy?" he asked, his tone disbelieving. "She's been downright rude to me."

"Why don't you ask what you did wrong?" Addie offered.

Maxwell's spoon dropped into his oatmeal just as his mouth dropped open in astonishment. "What makes you think *I* did something wrong?" he balked.

Addie waved her hand dismissively. "Gabrielle's an angel, a feisty one sometimes, but an angel nonetheless. So ask her straight out: 'Gabrielle, what did I do to make you mad this time?'"

"So she can bite my head off?" Maxwell responded. "I don't know if you've ever seen it, but your little angel has quite a temper when she wants to. Hell, I still remember the first time I saw it. It shocked the hell out of me." He had mistakenly written a rather large check out of his business account and not his personal account. That one check sent a series of checks bouncing for days, including Gabrielle's paycheck. The little woman had been madder than a bear woken out of hibernation.

"No, I'll let her cool off, and things will go back to normal," he told Addie, silently wishing that his words would come to fruition.

Gabrielle picked up a pale pink sweater and held it against her in the mirror of the department store. She envisioned herself in it and could see nothing but her small breasts actually poking through the thin wool like a twelve-year-old girl with her first tiny buds. Sighing, she refolded the sweater and set it back on the table with the rest.

Gabrielle knew absolutely nothing about all the girly things like fashion and make-up. Things that most women were skilled or, at the very least, knowledgeable about. So she pulled her hair into a ponytail, wore her oversized clothing, and left her face completely free of make-up. She bought clothes more for function than beauty, and her make-up was limited to cherry-flavored Chapstick.

She had always wanted to be one of those thick, size-ten girls who could fill out a pair of jeans and make a sweater sing. Like the girls in the hip-hop videos. Her body looked like that of a child compared to them. But, alas, her metabolism wasn't having it. She could eat a man under the table, and she still hadn't gained an ounce over her 115 pounds since high school. She hadn't even gained the "freshman twenty" during her first year of college. Gabrielle was destined and predetermined by genetics to remain slender. Her father had been a tall and lean man whose Adam's apple was almost as large as his head. Her sister April, on the other hand, had inherited their mother's soft, curvaceous frame.

To this day Gabrielle remembered having an awful crush on a boy in their Georgia neighborhood when she was just thirteen. One day she was walking toward the little neighborhood candy store, which was nothing more than Old Man Wilson's garage, when all the local boys were gathered outside. She had worked up the nerve to meet the boy's eyes and felt like a million dollars when he smiled at her. But as she entered the shop she heard him say, "Damn, she ain't got no booty. Flatter than the wall." The boys all laughed, and Gabrielle felt ashamed. It took every bit of her spunk to walk out of that shop with her head held high.

During her impressionable early teens his words had affected her self-image. Having always felt awkward about her slim frame, Gabrielle had taken to wearing clothes that were slightly large so that every bony elbow, knee, shoulder, and less-than-bodacious behind didn't protrude quite so much. She didn't even know what size she truly wore in clothes anymore. She automatically grabbed a size ten.

Gabrielle sighed as she moved along in the department store. After running from the house in anger, even though she knew Addie and Maxwell

had not meant to hurt her feelings, she had foolishly decided to go shopping. She now knew that
coming to the mall had been an absurd idea.

Gabrielle was just perusing some cardigans when
her cell phone rang. She pulled it out of her purse
and flipped it open. "Hello."

"Gabby?"

Maxwell. *Why does my heart jump at the sound of his
voice?* "Yes," she snapped, feeling irritable.

"Are you on your way home? I can't find the catalog you did of the paintings."

Gabrielle knew as sure as the sun would rise in
the morning that he hadn't even bothered to look
for it. "It's in the file cabinet under 'C' for, that's
right, you guessed it, catalog."

The line went quiet.

"I found it, Gabby, what would I do without you?"
Continue to paint, party, and be happy, that's what.

"I gotta go, Maxwell," she told him.

"Gabby?" he called out to get her attention.

"Yes, Maxwell?"

"Nothing. Never mind."

The line disconnected.

Gabrielle replaced the cell in her purse and continued to wander through the department store.

Feeling as frustrated and overwhelmed by shopping as she always did, Gabrielle left the department
store and walked out into the mall. She found a store
with a beautiful wood interior and baskets of colorful bottles strategically positioned by the door. She
stepped back to look at the sign. BATH & BODY WORKS.

Gabrielle had never gone into the place before,
but how could she let a senior citizen outdo her?

One hour later, she left the store, laden with

bags, and headed home with her heavenly scented goodies. She pulled up to the drive-in gate and reached out the driver's window to swipe her card. She frowned to see that several of Maxwell's friends had already arrived in preparation for the night's festivities.

Leaving her purchases in the trunk of her VW Cabrio, she pulled out the tiny shopping bag of items she had purchased for Addie before walking over to the entrance leading into the kitchen. Instead of finding the older woman, she saw Maxwell and three of his closest friends sitting around the island, eating spaghetti. "Hello, Dwayne. Martin. Alex. Hey, Maxwell."

"Hey, Gabby," they all greeted her around mouthfuls of food.

Gabrielle shrieked as Martin stood, took two large steps over to her, and picked her up in a massive bear hug. When he put her down she smelled strongly of his overpowering cologne. "Just what I needed, a back breaking," she said smartly as she massaged her lower back. "Maxwell, is Addie around?"

"She's already gone home. You know how she is on party night," he told her, using the last of his Italian bread to sop up the sauce left on his plate.

"I too shall be hightailing it from here. Just as soon as I get some of this spaghetti to go with me," Gabrielle said, reaching up into the cupboard for a small Tupperware bowl. The hairs on the back of her neck stood on end and she felt a presence behind her. She knew without turning that it was Maxwell.

"You okay, Gabby?" he whispered close to her ear

with obvious concern before bending to place his plate in the dishwasher.

Gabrielle shivered. *Will I ever get used to him being near me?* "I'm cool, Maxwell," she lied, as she pushed the lid down on her more than full bowl.

"Are *we* cool?" he asked, looking down at her.

Remaining aloof, she look up to meet his gaze very briefly. "Sure."

Maxwell studied her face and then smiled at her in a way that weakened her knees. "Sure you don't want to stay for the party? Alex is gonna grill."

"Cool as it gets at night?" she balked.

"Hey, it's never too anything for barbecue, Gabby," Alex shouted from across the room, standing up to show her his apron that stated KISS THE CHEF.

Gabby just laughed. "Well, you all enjoy yourselves," she said, moving to the door with Addie's gift bag in one hand and her supper in the other.

"Hello, all," Penelope greeted, as she breezed into the kitchen as if she lived there.

Gabby rolled her eyes heavenward.

"Who is this, Max?" Dwayne asked, rising to eye Penelope appreciatively.

"Yeah, Max, who's the pretty lady?" Alex chimed in.

"Now tell me you'll be at the party," Martin insisted, flexing his muscles through his shirt for Penelope.

"Fellas, this beautiful lady is Penelope Tillman, my new consultant. Penelope, this is Alex, Dwayne, and Martin."

Penelope preened under their attention. "Hello, guys."

Sure is different from how they greeted me, Gabby thought, disgruntled. She left through the kitchen door without saying another world.

* * *

Three hours later, Maxwell stood in the middle of the kitchen flipping through the television channels as his party went on. Earlier that night, searching in his walk-in closet for something to wear, he wondered why he was even bothering having the party at all.

Maybe if we get some family up and through here you won't feel the need to surround yourself with people who are just looking for free liquor and food for the night. He literally shook his head to free it of Gabby's insightful words.

When he first began to truly see the fruits of his labor, Maxwell had been young and anxious to have a good time in life. All he wanted to do was party and paint. These regular gatherings of his had eventually become more habit than anything. At the last few parties he hadn't even been in attendance the entire night, preferring to walk the grounds, go up to the loft and create, or hang out in the kitchen, seeking a reprieve from the loud music and louder friends.

He had felt lonely being the only one of his siblings to remain in the area. The parties had been a way to surround himself with a crowd. The older and more mature he became, however, the less he felt the need to show off his wealth and party like it was going out of style. His taste for alcohol was waning, and his refusal to call Erika in Los Angeles was proof that his choice in fast women was slacking as well. He was growing up and it was about damn time.

He knew that his friendship with Gabby had a lot

to do with it. She never forced her opinion on him, but she always had a way of stating it that sank through to him. She was his levity, his reasoning, his conscience.

And now she was treating him like he had the plague. She hadn't worked at her desk in the loft in weeks, and anytime he tried to strike up a conversation about anything besides work, she brushed him off politely. He was used to her quiet presence when he worked, even if his focus was his art. He loved to stop painting and ask her opinion. Or just take a break too so that she could make him laugh. He missed her.

"You are missing one heck of a party, Max," Penelope sighed, as she strolled into the kitchen, holding a Cosmopolitan in her hand.

Maxwell's eyes shifted from the TV to her. He had to admit that she looked pretty in the pale silk halter she wore with wide-leg pants. "Just needed a break," he told her, leaning against the island as he continued to flip through the channels.

Penelope went to stand beside him, and he was engulfed by her strong perfume. "You have some crazy friends,"

"Acquaintances," he told her, fighting the urge to move as she pressed the side of her body close to his.

"Touché," she said softly, looking down into her drink before she took a sip.

"This will probably be my last throwdown with this crew for a while," he told her, moving to the door.

"Where are you going?" she asked, having just built up the nerve to lay her amorous feelings for Maxwell out on the table.

He glanced over at her as he pulled on a jean

jacket that looked ridiculous with the black silk shirt and slacks that he wore. "I need to talk to Gabby," he informed her over his shoulder as he left the house.

Maxwell was glad to see that Gabrielle's lights were still on. He wanted to get things right between them again. *Now's as good a time as any.*

Gabrielle tried her best to tune out the music as she poured two luscious capfuls of Cucumber Melon bath gel under the running water filling her claw-foot bathtub. It was part of the set that she'd purchased, along with aromatherapy candles and some essential oils. Soon her skin would have the same delicious scent as the rest of her house now had from the candles she was burning.

She was just about to step into the steaming water when her doorbell rang. Frowning, she grabbed her housecoat, stepping into it before she zipped it straight up to her neck. "Who is it?" she yelled from the bathroom as she slid her glasses back on.

"It's Maxwell. Open up," he yelled back through the door.

Gabrielle's face was confused as she closed the bathroom door and made her way to the front of the cottage. Even though her heart raced, she fixed her face into a cool mask as she opened the door. "Something I can get for you?" she asked, hiding her body behind the front door.

Maxwell pushed the door open slightly and walked into the cottage.

"I know this is your house, Maxwell, but as long as I am living here as part of my pay, you really should wait for me to invite you in," she said in a voice that was lifeless.

Maxwell stared at her long and hard. "What's going with you lately, Gabby?" he asked her. "Are you still mad at me about how I acted about your date?"

Despite her best wishes, Gabrielle's eyes darted down to take in the hard confines of Maxwell's chest that peeked through his shirt. She would love to just lie in his arms and run her fingers through the soft, flat hairs there. "I'm not mad about anything, Maxwell," she lied, swallowing hard as she diverted her face from him.

He walked toward her, reaching out to lightly grab her chin so that she would look up at him. "Don't you like the 'forgive me' present I got you?"

Gabrielle actually felt bad about her distant behavior as she thought of the Langston Hughes poetry book, which she treasured. "I'm just tripping. Everything's fine. I promise," she said with a weak smile. "Must be PMS."

Maxwell nodded as if he understood and tweaked her nose playfully. "Get better, kiddo. I need my Gabby back."

"Don't worry, I'll always do my job," she told him dryly, crossing her arms over her chest and sitting down on the arm of the sofa.

Maxwell paused in his perusal of the living room to look over at her. "That's not what I meant, Gabby."

"I know," she said with honesty. *He wants to make sure we're still friends. Surprise, surprise.*

"Smells good in here. Is it all the candles?"

Gabrielle nodded, quite sure that he was stalling. "Why aren't you at your party?" she asked, tilting her head to the side to look up at him.

Maxwell shrugged and picked up a novel from one of the bookshelves occupying every bit of wall on all sides of the television. "Just don't feel like it, I guess. I've actually been thinking about the re-union thing. Let's do it. Is next month too soon?"

Gabrielle laughed as she rose to walk over to grab Maxwell by the shoulders and steer him toward the front door. "Yes, a month is too soon. Most people have a thing called a job where they have to request time off and not just hop on a plane at a whim."

"Are you putting me out?" he asked, looking down over his shoulder at her.

Gabrielle reached around him to pull the door open. "I have a bath and some serious aromatherapy awaiting me. You have a room full of loud, drunken people and even louder music. And don't forget the barbecue. Go and enjoy your evening, Maxwell. I know I will."

He turned on the stoop to face her. "But—"

"Bye, Maxwell," she sang, before closing the door in his face.

Gabrielle unzipped her robe as she walked to the bathroom, opening the door and kicking the garment from around her feet. She stepped into the tub, sighing at the smell and the feel of the water as it caressed her skin. "Now for some me time," she whispered aloud as she removed her glasses and let her eyes drift close.

"Gabrielle."

Her eyes flew open and she shrieked as Maxwell stepped into the bathroom. She frantically sank lower beneath the bubbles. "Maxwell, get out of here," she gasped harshly as he kneeled by the tub.

"I just had an idea about the reunion I thought we could discuss before I forgot," he said.

Gabrielle gave him her best Aunt Esther from *Sanford & Son* one-eyed glare. "Maxwell, you are the most insufferable, arrogant, and selfish person I think I have ever met. I am *bathing*, this is not the time to discuss your reunion . . . or anything else, for that matter," she told him, her tone constantly rising and filled with exasperation.

Maxwell tilted his head to the side as he reached into the bubbles to extract a handful. "Come on, Gabrielle, you know you don't want me to go," he said calmly, before raising his hand to blow the bubbles into the air.

"What?" she shrieked in disbelief.

"I thought about it, and I finally know what's really wrong with you," he said matter-of-factly as he rose and began to remove his clothing.

Gabrielle's mouth dropped open as she watched him. "Maxwell, I am sorry if you are bored with your party, but I am not your entertainment for the night."

Maxwell kicked his pants from his ankles and smiled at her as he dropped his boxers. "You think that I don't think you're beautiful," he continued.

Gabrielle gulped as the undergarment momentarily caught on his lengthy arousal before it finally fell down his long, muscled legs.

"Of course I know that you're beautiful, Gabrielle," he told her, as if the very notion that he didn't was foolish.

Gabrielle opened and shut her eyes rapidly, desperately trying to awaken from yet another dream.

"That's why I really was so mad about your date."

At the closeness of his voice, Gabrielle's eyes flew open to find him kneeling by the tub. She looked down over the side and gasped as his thick erection pointed up at her from between his strong thighs. Speechless, she watched his hand go over the side of the tub until his whole arm disappeared beneath the water. He lifted first one of her legs and then the other until both were flung over each side of the tub.

Gabrielle gasped suddenly as his fingers began to caress the throbbing pink bud between her legs. "Maxwell," she sighed, letting her head fall back as she gave in to the pleasure he created.

"Tell me you love it," he ordered strongly in her ear as he plunged first one and then another of his solid fingers into her core.

"I love it. Ooh, I love it. Love it, love it, love it," Gabrielle gasped hotly, clenching her eyes shut as the first waves of her climax began to rise. Her feet became warm, and her hips arched off the bathtub to meet his hand as she grasped her own breasts and teased her nipples with eager fingers.

"Maxwell! Yes, Maxwell!" she cried out as delicious wave after delicious wave of her release took control of her jerking body, sending water splashing out of the tub onto the floor.

Her heart pounded hard and fast as she slumped down into the tub with weakness. "Maxwell?" she called out to him softly. "Maxwell?"

She slowly opened her heavy eyes to find she was in the bathroom alone.

Chapter Six

Gabrielle made a rather rash decision. It was made strictly on emotion, and that emotion was frustration. She was fed up to her glasses with Penelope Tillman. Gabrielle was quite positive that she had taken as much of the woman as she could stand.

When Penelope arrived at the estate the next morning, complaining of lower back pain and insisting on using Maxwell's Jacuzzi, Gabrielle had become annoyed. Then the woman pulled a bikini out of her purse that looked small enough to fit a toddler.

Gabrielle decided right then to pull herself out of the ongoing circus Maxwell called a life. If he wanted to spend his free time with a manhunter like Penelope Tillman on his trail, that was just fine, but she didn't have to sit around and watch.

"I'm going on vacation."

Maxwell looked up from his sketch pad at Gabby standing over him. Even though he thought they had repaired the break in their relationship on the night of his party, Maxwell had felt the coolness remain. He nodded slowly. "For how long?"

"Two, maybe three weeks. I haven't taken any

time off in six years, and I think I'm owed that," she said stiffly.

"Look, Gabby," Maxwell told her, closing the sketch with angry movements as he rose to tower over her. "I've been walking on eggshells around you for the past few weeks. Why all the attitude?"

She wanted to tear into him for getting involved with Penelope, but what could she say without revealing her own jealousy and deep feelings for him? All she could think of was the sleepy and sated tone of Penelope's voice when she answered Maxwell's cell while they were in Los Angeles. It pained her deeply that he'd fallen into the barracuda's trap. No, she would never let on to Max that she was in love with him, even if it meant sitting by while the manhunter dragged him right down to the altar.

"I just need a break, that's all," she said.

"Fine, Gabby, but I hope when you return you've dealt with whatever is going on with you," he told her, retaking his window seat in the living room.

"I doubt it as long as Penelope's hanging around," she mumbled under her breath as she turned to leave the room.

"What was that?" he asked.

"Nothing," Gabrielle threw over her shoulder and continued out of the room.

One week later, Gabrielle waited for her sister to pick her up at the airport.

"Gabrielle!"

She turned as her sister shouted her name and she saw a shorter, more curvaceous version of herself running shamelessly toward her. "Hey, Ape," she sighed as she felt her sister's arms surround her with love.

"Look how little you still are. Girl, I wish I could stay so thin," April exclaimed, circling her sister.

Gabrielle did an eye roll, taking in her sister's thick frame, which all the brothers, including Maxwell, loved. There was no way for April to hide all of the legs and bottom she had, and there was no reason for her to do so. "I have the body of a twelve-year-old while you look gorgeous."

"As always, Gabrielle, you haven't got a clue," April told her. "You're beautiful, big glasses and all."

Gabrielle looked unsure. "You think I'm pretty?"

April grabbed both of Gabrielle's hands. "I think you're beautiful," she exclaimed.

"You're just saying that 'cause you're my sister."

April put a hand on her hip. "No, I say it because you are. I mean, you don't do much to accentuate your looks, but they can't be denied."

Gabrielle just shrugged. *Then why doesn't Maxwell think so?*

"Why do you care what Maxwell thinks?" April asked.

Gabrielle froze. "Did I say that aloud?"

April smiled. "Sure did."

Gabrielle dropped her head in her hands as she covered her face.

"I don't know who you think you fooling. A blind man can see you got a thing for your boss. Don't worry, I'm not gone get all up in your business. Not now anyway. But later. Oh, later . . . it's on."

* * *

"Now, let me get this straight, baby sister."

Gabrielle nodded at April as she took a deep sip of her wine cooler. "Okay. Go on."

"Maxwell hired this Penelope to be his consultant," April began, ticking the facts off on her fingers. "Penelope let on to you and Addie, his housekeeper/cook who doesn't really clean and cooks when she wants to, that she wants to be the lady of the manor. I got it so far?"

Gabrielle nodded again and took another healthy swig.

"Now, Penelope went with Max to L.A., and she answered his phone, giving you the impression that they were . . . intimate. They return from L.A., and although you haven't seen anything that shows that they are really involved, this Penelope been hanging around like white on rice. Plus, she accuses you of wanting Max for yourself, which you deny."

"You hit the nail on the head," Gabrielle said, her voice slurring just a bit.

April rose from where she was sitting cross-legged in front of her coffee table while they ate their dinner of Chinese take-out. "Hold on, little sister, let me think this through. Don't take this the wrong way, but I been playing this game with men a lot longer than you."

"There's nothing to think through. I mean, just because he's not slobbing her down in front of me doesn't mean they not doing the . . . the . . . the *hokeypokey*," she ended on a dramatic wail.

April pulled the wine cooler from her sister's hand. "That's enough of this for you."

Gabrielle shrugged and reached for an egg roll.

"Has she ever spent the night?"

"Nope."

"Does she always have an excuse every time she comes over?"

"Yup."

"Sounds like she ain't got no more headway in getting Maxwell into bed than you have," April concluded, plopping down on her leather sofa and tucking her bare feet beneath her. "And on top of it she feels threatened by you, so she's trying to make you believe she's got 'em when she ain't."

Gabrielle attempted to rise from the floor but felt lightheaded and just plopped back down. "No, this woman is gorgeous, and she's got plenty of—" she cupped her hands in front of her chest, motioning how big Penelope's breasts were.

April reached for a fried chicken wing. "Look here, little sister, big breasts ain't everything. Remember anything over a mouthful is a waste, okay," she ended with a laugh. "You got a picture of this Maxwell? Let me see what two grown, educated women are fighting over."

Gabrielle pointed to the table by the door as she let her body relax on the floor. "In my wallet," she slurred.

April bit into her chicken while rising from the couch to grab her sister's purse. She reached in and pulled out her wallet. When she opened it, there was a photo of their parents, one of her graduation, and the next one had to be the great Maxwell.

"Damn!" April exclaimed. The brother looked like a caramel version of Morris Chestnut. "Girl, no wonder you sprung. Brother man is *fine*."

The only thing she heard in return was a snore.

April looked down at her sister to find that she

had fallen asleep right on the floor. Grabbing a throw pillow and an afghan, she pushed the pillow under Gabrielle's head and threw the afghan over her sleeping form. "Sleep good, baby sister, 'cause tomorrow we gone work on getting you your man. I promise you that."

Gabrielle grimaced as she awakened. From the unrelenting hardness beneath her, she knew without opening her eyes that she had slept on the floor. She smacked her lips, hating the taste in her mouth. Morning breath was bad enough. Morning breath after a night of drinking was way worse.

She rolled onto her back and looked right up into her sister's smiling face.

"Rise and shine, sleepyhead. We've got work to do," April said, reaching out a hand to help her up.

Gabrielle accepted her sister's assistance and winced as she pulled to her feet. "Next time I get drunk, send me to bed before I pass out on the floor again, huh?"

April laughed. "Who knew three wine coolers would knock you out like a light?"

Gabrielle tossed a throw pillow in her sister's direction before she turned to go into the guest bedroom of April's two-bedroom apartment. "What are we getting into today?" she called out to her sister.

"It's a surprise," April called back.

Gabrielle grabbed her toiletry kit and made her way to the bathroom, emerging ten minutes later invigorated from a shower with her new Bath & Body Works bath gel. She wasn't quite sure of how to dress since April was being vague, so she just went for what was comfortable, a pair of baggy jeans and a sweatshirt. She pulled her hair up into a ponytail, put on her glasses, and she was all set for anything April had to throw at her.

She grabbed her tapestry purse and headed for the living room. "All set, Ape."

"Oh Lord, you *can't* be serious," a male voice said.

Gabrielle's eyes locked with one of the most beautiful men she had ever seen in her life. Everything about him was perfect: his closely shaven head, his groomed brows and beard, his clear, unblemished complexion, and his noble features. His clothes were perfectly tailored to his tall, muscular frame, and the natural color palette blended with his mocha complexion.

To Gabrielle, Maxwell was I-T it, but even he had flaws. There was the faded scar on his chin from when he fell off the monkey bars as a child, and then there was his slight overbite that was very Denzellike but an overbite nonetheless.

This man, though was unreal, unmarred . . . unnerving.

"Gabrielle, this is Clayton Wilkes. Clayton, this is my sister Gabrielle."

Clayton slid his hands into the pockets of his pants and circled Gabrielle with a critiquing eye. He reached up casually, but quickly, and removed the band from her hair.

"Hey," Gabrielle shrieked, turning to face him as her hair fell down around her shoulders.

Clayton strode over to April. "She's a challenge. This will be interesting."

April looked up at the gorgeous man with pleasure. "So you'll help?"

Gabrielle's eyebrows shot up. "Help do what?"

Clayton handed Gabrielle her rubberband before reaching onto his belt for a tiny silver flip phone. "Excuse me, ladies. I got a call."

He turned and left the apartment.

"Is that your new boyfriend?" Gabrielle asked, pulling her hair back into its ponytail.

"Clayton? Oh, God no. Clayton's gay," April said matter-of-factly as she turned to walk into her brightly lit kitchen.

"No!" Gabrielle gasped in disbelief, following behind her sister.

"Yes, girl. He lives in the apartment next door."

Gabrielle watched as her sister poured them both a cup of coffee. "He's gorgeous."

"Tell me about it," April drawled. "When I first moved into this apartment complex, it was summer, and I was carrying a box of plates up the back staircase. Well, I look over to my right and there he is in the community pool outside. Girl, I almost dropped that box when I saw him climb out the pool in this skimpy little black bikini with that body and that— Well, let's just say he's . . . *blessed.*"

Gabrielle's cheeks warmed.

April reached into the fridge and pulled out a carton of French vanilla creamer and handed it to her sister. "I tried everything to get his attention. He was always friendly and polite, but he never once made a pass at me. Well, one night I did the ultimate. I put on my naughtiest lingerie, hid my front-door key under my breasts, and then walked right out of my apartment, letting the door lock behind me. I went straight over to his apartment and lied and told him that I accidentally locked myself out of my apartment," she continued, accepting the creamer so that she could pour some in her own cup.

"Ape, you didn't," Gabrielle cringed.

"All I could think of was finding out for myself whether he was as good as he looked. I was shameless."

"Well? What happened?"

April took a sip of her coffee. "He let me in his apartment, which looks like a photo out of some home interior magazine I might add, and he immediately retrieved a robe for me to put on."

"Weren't you embarrassed?" Gabrielle asked, too caught up in her sister's tale to even sip from the cup she held in her hands.

"Somebody could've bought me for a nickel, especially when he told me that I'd have a better chance of meeting God than getting him hard."

Gabrielle was shocked when April actually laughed.

"He told me he was quite aware and even impressed by my little antics to get his attention but advised me to, and I quote: 'Not waste your time on a homosexual man who could find you nothing more than amusing.'"

"Weren't you offended?"

"Nope. But he did tell me that if he was straight, or at least a lane switcher, that he would give me *exactly* what I was plotting for."

"Lane switcher?" Gabrielle asked with a look of confusion.

"You know, bisexual, going both ways, living on the down low."

"He sure doesn't look or sound or act gay," Gabrielle said, still amazed that that man was loving nothing but men.

"Not all homosexual men are of the two-snaps-up variety," Clayton informed her with a smile as he strolled into the kitchen.

"I'm sorry," Gabrielle said, reaching out to touch his hand.

"No offense taken."

April picked up Gabrielle's coffee cup and poured it down the drain.

"Hey, I wasn't finished," Gabrielle complained.

"No time for coffee, baby sister. I got a promise to keep."

"What does that have to do with me?"

April and Clayton exchanged a long look before she turned to face Gabrielle with a big smile. "It has everything to do with you."

"Huh?"

"Clayton's a fashion visionary, and he's gone to help me give you a makeover."

"Oh, no," Gabrielle said with dread.

"Oh, yes," April answered with excitement. "We're going to help you get Maxwell's attention."

"Shouldn't he be interested in me just the way I am? Why should I change for him or anybody?"

April started to say something but Clayton placed a hand on her arm to halt her. "Nothing about you says 'I am interested in having a man in my life.' No offense, but that's the gospel. You have to present yourself seriously if you want to be taken seriously," he told her.

Gabrielle looked unsure but found herself agreeing nonetheless.

Gabrielle looked with horror at the silk sweater Clayton handed her. "I am entirely too bony to wear that. I'll look like a crackhead or something with that all tight up on me."

Two hours and three stores later, Gabrielle had not accepted one of Clayton's suggestion. His frustration with this woman had nearly strangled him until he felt like strangling her. "April, I need to talk to you," he told her over his shoulder as he turned to walk a short distance away from Gabrielle.

April gave Gabrielle a murderous look before she walked over. "I'm sorry, Clayton, she's new to all this."

Clayton crossed his arms over his massive chest. "Your sister's problem goes a lot deeper than choosing the wrong clothes. I'm not a therapist, but she had body image issues. So you can force her into those new clothes, but if she doesn't get over her issues, she's either going to wear the clothes and feel uncomfortable, or just go back to shop for clothes three times too big."

April knew that he was right. She cringed when she turned to look over her shoulder and found Gabrielle holding a sweater up to her body that was obviously not her size. She said, "She's so busy trying to hide that she doesn't realize she's only making herself look even smaller in those awful clothes."

"Thing is, I caught a glimpse of your sister when she was coming out of the shower this morning with her little towel. She has one helluva body," Clayton said.

April turned to him in shock. "You're kidding," she gasped.

He shook his head. "Nope. I honestly believe that she doesn't even know it. And she isn't as skinny as she thinks. Poor thing is so afraid to look at her own body that she probably hasn't noticed that she's a lot curvier than she was at eighteen."

April got an enlightened look on her face. "Wait here. I got an idea."

Gabrielle looked up and saw her sister coming toward her with a determined look on her face. *Oh no, now what?*

April grabbed Gabrielle's hand and pulled her behind her into one of the dressing rooms. "Okay, baby sister. Strip."

"What?"

"You heard me. Strip. It's time you took a good hard look at yourself."

"I am not going to stand half naked in front of a mirror in a department store like a perv, Ape," Gabrielle protested.

"Fine," April said, moving behind her.

Gabrielle eyes widened as April snatched her sweatshirt by the hem and pulled it upward, entangling her arms. "Ape!"

"Are you two okay in there?" Clayton's voice came through the slats of the wooden door.

"Just fine, Clayton. Just fine," April told him with determination as she stepped up onto the bench in the room and continued working her sister's arms out of the shirt.

Gabrielle couldn't see a thing because the shirt

covered her entire head. Blindly she flailed her arms. "I'm going to kill you, Ape," came her muffled voice.

April just nodded as she finally yanked the shirt over her sister's head and then flung it over the door. "Hold on to this for me, Clayton."

"Done deal," was his reply.

Gabrielle's arms flew up to cover her brassiere-covered breasts as she eyed April viciously. "I can't believe you just did that."

"Believe it," April told her. "Now are you going to get the pants or am I?"

Gabrielle saw so much determination in eyes so like her own that she loosened her belt and stepped out of the jeans before April wrestled her to the floor of the dressing room.

"Hand me that last outfit, Clayton, and make it a size six," April hollered out to him.

Gabrielle caught a glimpse of herself in the mirror and did a double take as she eyed her long shapely legs. "When on earth did I get these?" she asked in amazement as she turned, letting her arms fall to her side.

"This heifer been complaining for years about being bony and the whole time she's hiding a perfect size six under all those ugly clothes," April muttered as Clayton handed the outfit over the top of the door.

Gabrielle still thought she was a little on the slender side, but gone was the gawkiness of her earlier years. Her shoulders were soft and rounded, her hips even shapely above long legs with knees that no longer were quite so knobby. Her breasts were small, but full and pert in the white cotton bra she wore.

"Here, put this on," April told her, removing the sweater from the hanger and handing it to her.

Gabrielle pulled on the beautiful garment quickly, eager to see the silk V-neck on. "Wow," she exclaimed softly, touching the point of the V neck where it rested in her cleavage.

"Now the pants," April urged.

Gabrielle slipped them on, initially nervous about how closely they fit her bottom and thighs until she turned to study her reflection. The flowing material accentuated her long legs and shapely hips.

"Okay, I'm coming in," Clayton warned, before the door opened and he stepped into the room.

"It does look okay, right?" Gabrielle asked, turning to face him.

He loved the burnt orange against her complexion, and the outfit was perfect for the smooth, shapely lines of her slender frame. "It looks perfect," he told her honestly.

Gabrielle was emotional. "I mean I still wish I had a bigger booty, but I just can't believe that this is me," she said softly as she turned to study her reflection again.

"Oh, no, Gabrielle we've only just begun," Clayton promised.

"Is this really necessary?" Gabrielle asked, her voice shaky as she felt herself lowered back into a chair.

Clayton placed his hands in his pockets and looked down at Gabrielle in the salon. "Your eyebrows look like you're trying to win a Groucho

Marx look-alike contest. Oh, it's very necessary," he drawled, and then smiled that perfect smile at her again to soften his insult.

April unsuccessfully stifled a laugh.

"Um, April. I wouldn't laugh so quick if I were you," he told her, looking pointedly at her own slightly unruly brows.

April lowered her head and covered her forehead with her hand. "Oh."

Gabrielle watched in mock horror as the female technician began to stir the honey-looking mixture with a wooden stick. "Won't that burn?" she asked uneasily, shrinking down farther into her seat.

"Not at all," the technician, Tamara, answered.

"I'll hold your hand, you big baby," April told her, stepping past Clayton to do just that.

"If it hurts, can I squeeze your hand?" Gabrielle asked, lying deathly still as the woman smoothed on the first of the wax.

"Sure can."

"Ooh, that's not so bad," Gabrielle offered, even relaxing a little.

"Close your eyes," Tamara prodded softly.

"Just what are you doing so that I can't see?" Gabrielle asked, tensing again.

"I'm going to take this strip and smooth it against the wax and then remove it," Tamara explained patiently.

"You wouldn't lie to a sista would you, Tamara?" Gabrielle asked again, only half teasing.

Tamara smiled. "I got you, girl," she told her jokingly.

Gabrielle acquiesced, letting her eyes close as she tightened her grip on April's hand just a little.

Tamara lifted the edge of the strip and then pulled it away in one swipe.

Gabrielle's eyes and mouth popped open. "Ooooooooooooh!" she hollered, squeezing her sister's hand.

April buckled to the floor with a grimace.

"Just wait until the bikini wax," Clayton mused dryly.

Gabrielle shot everyone a round of daggers with her eyes as she finally released April's hand. "Bikini wax?" she snapped.

Clayton looked pointedly down at that intimate area between Gabrielle's thighs.

Her face became a look of horror as she crossed her legs in the chair.

Later that night, Gabrielle was glad to finally have a moment alone. Things were moving so quickly, and it was all a little disconcerting. It was more than the new clothes and her newfound confidence. Everyone just assumed that she was going to proclaim her love to Maxwell when she returned to Virginia.

Sure, she'd bought some clothes that showed off her surprisingly nice figure, but that didn't automatically mean Maxwell was going to fall magically in love with her, like a fairy tale. Even she was not that naive.

Gabrielle sat on the middle of her bed in her nightgown and held her cell phone in her hands. Maxwell had left two voice mail messages, and she was contemplating whether to call him back.

She smiled as she thought of the messages. First:

"Hey, Gabby. I hate to bother you on your vacation, but I can't find the art supplies you ordered for me. Um, call me when you get this, and I hope you're having fun. Tell your sister I said hello." And then: "Gabby, I thought maybe you'd call to let us know you arrived safe. Addie's worried sick about you. Okay, I am too. Call me."

April said to give Maxwell a chance to miss her. "Don't call him, and when he calls you, pretend you're too busy to talk," her sister had advised her over dinner earlier that evening.

There were too many games that she was expected to play. She didn't want to become another Penelope, throwing herself at Maxwell or trying to manipulate him. Besides, she'd rather stay his friend than admit she loved him and ruin their friendship.

Giving in to temptation, she dialed Maxwell's phone number. When his answering machine came on she just hung up without leaving a message.

After she turned off the lights and snuggled down deep under the covers, she couldn't help but wonder what Maxwell would say about the new and improved Gabrielle.

Chapter Seven

Two Weeks Later

"Gabby!" Maxwell roared, before he remembered that Gabrielle wasn't there to answer his bellowing, solve his problems, talk to him about nothing, and fix what he messed up.

The past two weeks had been the most frustrating of his adult life.

He knew his sanity was too wrapped up in Gabrielle being there.

Well, she was gone, and he didn't like it one damn bit. Particularly since he wasn't quite sure what she was doing in Georgia.

Last week he had called to check on his assistant with the true intention of getting a firm date on her return. Imagine his surprise when her sister answered her cell phone and told him that Gabrielle was out with someone by the name of Clayton.

"Who is Clayton?" Maxwell had asked, his ire obvious in his tone.

"Oh, just a friend," April had replied vaguely, even sounding amused.

"When will she be back?" he asked.

"Oh, sometime later on . . . I guess."

"April, could you ask Gabby to give me a call? It's important."

Needless to say, Maxwell had ended the useless conversation very soon after that.

Frustrated and unable to concentrate on his painting, Maxwell flung his paintbrush against the wall and stormed out of his loft. He took the stairs two at a time until he reached the bottom and strode down into the kitchen where Addie was busy watching *All My Children.*

"Boy, I just love me some Erica Kane," Addie told Maxwell, smiling until she saw the look on his face. "What's eating at you now? You been in the worst mood ever since Gabrielle left. She deserves a life too. And I mean a life not filled with babying your big, rusty behind."

"And I actually pay you for this wonderful advice," Maxwell commented dryly, as he walked over to the refrigerator.

"Whatever is wrong with you, you'll be okay 'cause you don't have no other choice *but* to be okay," Addie told him dismissively.

Maxwell yanked open the refrigerator door and pulled out a can of apple juice, which he wrenched open, and took a healthy swig of it. "Nothing's wrong with me," he answered tightly.

"Any word from Gabrielle?"

The can in Maxwell's hand crumpled as he made a fist. "No, she's too busy flitting around Georgia with *Clayton,*" he muttered darkly.

The doorbell rang.

"I'll get it," Addie volunteered, glad to be out of the way of Maxwell and his bad mood.

Addie strode through the foyer and pulled the

front door open to look directly into Penelope's smiling face. "Don't you have a home?" she snapped irritably.

Penelope walked past her into the house. "Don't you?" she answered easily, handing her lightweight trench coat to Addie with ease as she strode away.

Addie took the coat and tossed it into the living room, not sure, and not caring, if it landed on the floor or a chair.

"Maxwell, there you are," she heard Penelope sigh.

Addie made a face. "Oh, Maxwell there you are," she mimicked the other woman. "Where else he gone be, this is *his* house."

Addie walked into the kitchen and purposefully used her remote to turn up the volume as Penelope was explaining something to Maxwell.

Penelope shot the older woman an agitated look. "Maybe we should talk somewhere—"

Brrrrnnnggg.

"I got it," Addie sang, moving to pick up the cordless phone from where it sat on the island. "Hello, Maxwell Bennett's residence."

"Maxwell, I was able to acquire a deal with Art Work Gallery in Washington," Penelope told him, removing a contract from her portfolio. "In fact they are interested—"

"Gabrielle? Well, long time no hear from," Addie exclaimed.

Maxwell's head shot up. "Is that Gabby?" he asked.

At Addie's excited nod, he brushed briskly past Penelope to stride over to the phone.

"Maxwell? Oh, he's fine physically, but he's been in the worst mood lately," Addie was saying.

"Let me talk to her," Maxwell whispered to Addie.

She waved her hand and turned her back to him. "Now don't forget to bring me a shot glass or two from Georgia for my collection."

Maxwell tried to grab the phone, but Addie held her hand up. "Addie, give me that phone," he demanded, using his most stern voice.

Addie just laughed. "What did you say, Gabrielle? Okay, I'll hold."

"Could you at least ask her who Clayton is?" Maxwell asked, trying not to lose his patience with the elderly woman.

Addie frowned. "Who in the world is this Clayton you keep going on about?"

Maxwell closed his eyes, dropped his head, and counted to five. "That's what I would like to know."

"Gabrielle? Okay. Now when are you headed back this way?"

Maxwell tried again to reach for the phone, but the older woman was quicker than he thought.

"Uh-huh. Okay. Yes, yes. All right. Bye-bye."

"No, I need to talk to her," Max said, just as Addie hung up the phone.

Addie moved back over to her television. "Said she was on her way out and she would call us back."

"Did she say when she was getting back?"

Addie shrugged. "I think she said not for another two weeks."

"Damn," he swore, before turning to walk out of the kitchen.

"Max?" Penelope called out to him.

"Later, Penelope," he threw over his shoulder as he raced up the stairs.

"But, I have to let—"

"Later."

Addie strolled out of the kitchen to stand beside the woman. "Since Maxwell ain't got time for you and *I* don't want to look in your face, why don't you go and reacquaint yourself with where it is you live."

Penelope clutched her portfolio to her chest as she gave the older woman a withering look. "If you'll just get my coat, I do have some other appointments to tend to today."

"Do tell," Addie said sarcastically before walking back into the kitchen. "Your coat's in the living room."

Penelope swallowed her annoyance and walked into the living room, almost tripping on her trench where it lay in a pile on the floor. She swore that when, not if, she got to be lady of the manor that the first item on her to-do list would be sending Addie back to whatever senior citizen home or crazy hospital she had sneaked out of.

Two days later, Maxwell felt as if he had completely lost his muse. With his ability to paint, and sleep for that matter, now faltering, he put his energy into cleaning the loft. He threw away old supplies, stocked new ones, and then got to work moving the majority of the paintings from the floor to hang on the walls the way Gabby had been suggesting for years.

At the thought of her, he looked down the long length of the loft to her desk. Right now she would be busy at work, with her little head nearly bent to the desk as she organized and kept his life straight for him. She gave him the freedom to do nothing but paint.

Now that he was mentally blocked from doing that, Maxwell moved toward her desk and sat down behind it. His eyes lighted upon Gabrielle's "To Do" list for his reunion. Quickly, he skimmed her plans and saw that the first item was to contact his family for a possible date.

He decided to get the ball rolling and start calling them himself. "Not like I'm busy," he mused, pulling her Rolodex toward him. Maxwell saw all of his business contacts and even his creditors but none of his family. Gabrielle had the addresses and phone numbers, though, because she was the one who wrote the checks and she was the one they called for emergencies like a car about to be repossessed.

Five minutes later, after searching her desk, Maxwell still had no clue where to find the numbers. Plus, it gave him a reason to call Gabrielle. He picked up the cordless phone and dialed her cell phone since he didn't have her sister's home number. It rang just once. "Hey, Gabby."

"This isn't Gabrielle."

Maxwell frowned at the masculine voice on the phone. It was deeper than his own. *What the hell?* "Sorry, man, I must have the wrong number."

"This is her cell phone."

Max scowled. "Well, can I talk to her?" he asked shortly.

"Hold on."

Max leaned back in his chair as he heard muffled voices in the background.

"Gabrielle wants to know who's calling," the Barry White–sounding voice said.

"Max," he replied tightly, swiveling the chair to look out the window at the sweeping landscape of his estate.

"Hold on."

Again the muffled talking.

Maxwell felt his ire rise. Since when did Gabrielle have her calls screened, and who was the deep throat on the line anyway? Clayton?

"Hey, Maxwell."

He sat up straight at the sound of her voice. "Hey to you. I think it's easier to get through to the president," he teased, his anger immediately dissipating.

"Oh, that was just Clayton."

The tension in his neck returned swiftly. "Clayton?" he asked, forcing his voice to be light. "Who's he?"

"Just a friend," she answered vaguely.

A boyfriend? Are you two dating? Is that why you suddenly went on vacation? Is he the reason you're too busy to call? All those questions and more whizzed through Maxwell's head, but he didn't ask them. What right did he have to grill her on her personal life?

"I was going to start calling my family about the reunion. I haven't spoken to most of them in awhile anyway. Except for Darlene's, I don't know the numbers by heart," he said, using his fingers to rub his eyelids.

"They're in my personal phone book, and that's over at my house. Just grab the key from inside the potted plant by the front door, and you should see it on my nightstand," she offered.

"That's too far to walk. I'll just get the numbers from Darlene when I call her."

Gabrielle sucked air between her teeth. "You are so lazy, Maxwell," she told him.

Maxwell nodded, but all he could think of was a big eight-foot-tall Shaquille O'Neal–looking brother courting Gabby.

"Maxwell?" she prompted softly as he remained quiet.

"Are you enjoying your vacation?" he asked, not wanting to end the call.

"I'm having fun, Maxwell. I'm glad I came," she told him. "As a matter of fact we were just headed out for the night."

"You and Clayton, I guess?" he asked, his face pensive.

"Ape and her boyfriend are going too."

"Oh, okay."

"Maxwell?"

"Yeah," he answered, leaning forward to place his elbows on the desk.

"Everything's okay?"

"Yeah! Shoot, everything's cool. Everything's good," he told her, forcing joviality into his tone.

"That's good. Well, they're waiting for me. I gotta go."

Maxwell nodded, rubbing his hand over his chin. "Okay. See you next week."

"Yup, next Sunday."

"That's the same day of this dinner party Penelope is throwing here for a bunch of bigwigs in the art community. She wants to get me maximum exposure."

Even though April had finally convinced her that

there was nothing between Maxwell and Penelope, Gabrielle was still sensitive about the possibility of him becoming involved with her.

"It's at eight. Will you be back in time to attend?" he asked, hating the eagerness that crept into his voice.

"If you want me to attend, I'll make it back just in time."

"Good," Maxwell said with the first real smile he had had in weeks. "Bye, Gabby," he said reluctantly.

"Good-bye, Maxwell."

He hung up the phone and then picked up a piece of paper that he balled up and shot toward the wastepaper basket in the corner. It missed. For some reason Gabrielle's good-bye had seemed so final to him. *But she was just on vacation, right?*

Maxwell picked up the cordless phone and dialed his sister's house in Boston. Darlene had met her husband, Kwame, while attending Boston University and decided to remain in the area after she graduated. Of all his siblings, Darlene and he were closest in age and thick as thieves.

"Hello."

Maxwell smiled broadly. "Hey, Kwame. How you doing, man?"

"What's the good word, brother-in-law?"

"Nothing much, nothing much. Where's that wife of yours?"

"She went to run some errands. You want me to tell her to call you back?"

Maxwell frowned in disappointment. "Yeah, tell her to call me. I'm thinking about having a big reunion bashe here in Virginia around our mama's birthday. I was just calling to see if y'all would be down."

"Now Maxwell, that sounds like a damn good idea. I was just telling Baby Girl that you all really should get together more," Kwame answered in a serious tone.

"Y'all talk it over and let me know, okay?"

"Sure thing, brother-in-law. And I'll tell her to call you as soon as she gets in."

Maxwell hung up the phone.

He had to find something to do. Moving on an impulse, he grabbed his workout bag. Flinging the strap over his shoulder, he left the room and jogged down the stairs.

"Addie, I'm going to the gym," he told the woman as he crossed the kitchen.

She just waved her hand and leaned closer to her television.

Maxwell left the house and crossed to the Land Rover parked in front of the garage. He climbed in and twenty minutes later was pulling into the parking lot of his favorite muscle gym.

Two hours later, Maxwell stood sweaty and exhausted in front of a punching bag.

I'm jealous.

He honestly didn't know where the emotion had come from so suddenly, but he certainly couldn't deny it, for it nearly strangled him. His stomach was in knots, and he felt a serious lack of control over the entire situation. At first he hadn't known what his problem was, but eventually the feelings in him had a face and a name. The face was that of the green-eyed monster and its name was jealousy.

"Damn it," he swore, as he swung hard at the punching bag.

Bam! Bam!

As he had since he first entered the gym, Maxwell was trying to come to grips with his newfound emotions. "What the hell is wrong with me?" he asked himself aloud.

Bam! Bam!

Still nothing.

Bam! Bam! Bam!

No answer.

Exhausted, he caught the punching bag with his gloved hands as he breathed deeply and let his heart rate decelerate. He leaned his body into the bag as sweat dripped from every sinewy muscle of his bare chest.

Jealousy was not an emotion that sat well with him, especially jealousy concerning a woman he had no intentions of getting involved with. It was none of his business who she dated or what they did on their dates. He had no right to dwell on her activities until he had lost his desire to paint. He should care less.

But he didn't. He stood upright and then pushed the bag away. "Get it together, Bennett," he warned himself as he swung viciously at the bag.

Bam! Bam! Bam!

"You know, there are other ways to break a sweat."

Maxwell switched his boxing stance and paused in his motion to look over at a beautiful woman who stared at him in open invitation. "This one has fewer consequences," he said pointedly, focusing his eyes back on his swinging target.

Bam! Bam! Bam! Bam! Bam!

"Yes, but it's not as much fun," she countered, holding both ends of the towel hanging around her neck.

Maxwell paused again and turned his head slightly in her direction to briefly let his eyes take in all that she was offering. She was tall and thick, but firm, just the way he usually liked his women. The leotard was fitting her like a second skin, and she knew it. She was inviting and enticing, but he simply wasn't interested.

"I'm Yvonne," she offered softly, stepping toward him with her hand extended. "And you?"

"Oh, no. I've got enough drama with the females in my life, and I don't need to add more fire to the flame, but it was nice meeting you anyway." He hit the bag one last time before walking away.

"Ms. Tillman, Mr. Bennett to see you."

Penelope smoothly reached into her desk for her hand mirror, quickly but unnecessarily checking her flawless hair and make-up before replacing it in the drawer. She hit the intercom button. "Send him in."

Penelope watched as Maxwell strolled into her office wearing all black, and she actually had to push her chair back a little and cross her legs to stop the quivering he caused between her legs. *This man is just too damn fine for his own good.* "Good afternoon, Max. I wasn't expecting you. What can I help you with?" she asked, waving a hand at one of the seats in front of her elaborate glass desk.

"I just left my attorney's office, and he looked over the contract from the gallery," he offered as his eyes locked on an early work of his own hanging over the fireplace on the far wall of her office. "*You* purchased *The Love Below*?"

Penelope leaned back in her chair and swiveled slightly to eye the erotic abstract painting. "I have been a big fan of yours, Maxwell, well before the rest of America finally recognized your skill and talent," she told him. "This was a piece from your first showing, I believe. I was just completing my graduate studies in art history when I saw it. As soon as I laid eyes on you and the painting I decided I wanted to have it." *And you,* she added in her thoughts.

Maxwell rose and walked over to study the massive painting more closely. "Ah, my horny stage," he sighed jokingly.

Penelope let her eyes size him up from behind. She could so clearly see herself locking her office door, laying him across the mink rug on the floor, and riding him like he was a stallion on which she wanted to win a race. She rose, her eyes on him constantly as she did. "Not a bad stage at all, Maxwell," she offered huskily, coming to stand behind him.

Maxwell tensed at the now husky timbre of her voice as the scent of her perfume thickened around him, letting him know she was near.

"Actually, I think your erotic work has always been your best. It really reflects the raw sexuality and passion that you contain. You make a woman feel like a woman and a man feel like a man."

He felt her hands lightly graze his back.

"Sex is a common denominator for males and females. It is the only level on which we can all relate," Penelope said as she moved around his body to stand closely in front of him. "Who doesn't like it and want it? I know I do."

Maxwell looked down into her hot eyes and saw the lust she had for him there. He could lay her on the floor, strip her, and do with her as he wished. Her eyes begged him to accept what she had to offer.

"Don't you like sex, Max?" she asked provocatively.

Maxwell watched her open, panting mouth as she lightly licked her lips. Maybe sweaty, hot sex with Penelope would free him of his absurd and confusing emotions about Gabrielle. Maybe he was just horny and in need of release.

Ms. High and Mighty wants to be the queen of this castle, so don't you be too nice, Maxwell Bennett.

This would be nothing but sex to Maxwell. A release. Physical contact with a woman who could be nameless and faceless. It would be much more for her, so he couldn't stroke her down on the floor of her office, because he knew he never had any intention of anything serious with her.

"We're not going to do this, Penelope," he told her huskily.

"One day we will. Why wait? Isn't sooner always better than later?" she asked him, reaching her chin up to lightly graze his lips with her own.

"You're a beautiful woman—"

Penelope laughed softly. "Oh, so you have noticed?" she asked teasingly.

"You're a beautiful woman," he began again. "But I don't mix business with pleasure."

An Important Message From The ARABESQUE Publisher

Dear Arabesque Reader,

I invite you to join the club! The Arabesque book club delivers four novels each month right to your front door! It's easy, and you will never miss a romance by one of our award-winning authors!

With upcoming novels featuring strong, sexy women, and African-American heroes that are charming, loving and true… you won't want to miss a single release. Our authors fill each page with exceptional dialogue, exciting plot twists, and enough sizzling romance to keep you riveted until the satisfying end! To receive novels by bestselling authors such as Gwynne Forster, Janice Sims, Angela Winters and others, I encourage you to join now!

Read about the men we love… in the pages of Arabesque!

Linda Gill
PUBLISHER, ARABESQUE ROMANCE NOVELS

P.S. Watch out for the next Summer Series **"Ports Of Call"** *that will take you to the exotic locales of Venice, Fiji, the Caribbean and Ghana! You won't need a passport to travel, just collect all four novels to enjoy romance around the world! For more details, visit us at www.BET.com.*

SPECIAL OFFER!
4 BOOKS FREE!

BET BOOKS

www.BET.com

A SPECIAL "THANK YOU" FROM ARABESQUE JUST FOR YOU!

Send this card back and you'll receive 4 FREE Arabesque Novels—a $25.96 value—absolutely FREE!

The introductory 4 Arabesque Romance books are yours FREE (plus $1.99 shipping & handling). If you wish to continue to receive 4 books every month, do nothing. Each month, we will send you 4 New Arabesque Romance Novels for your free examination. If you wish to keep them, pay just $18* (plus, $1.99 shipping & handling). If you decide not to continue, you owe nothing!

- Send no money now.
- Never an obligation.
- Books delivered to your door!

We hope that after receiving your FREE books you'll want to remain an Arabesque subscriber, but the choice is yours! So why not take advantage of this Arabesque offer, with no risk of any kind. You'll be glad you did!

In fact, we're so sure you will love your Arabesque novels, that we will send you an Arabesque Tote Bag FREE with your first paid shipment.

* PRICES SUBJECT TO CHANGE.

YOU'LL GET 4 SELECT ROMANCES PLUS THIS FABULOUS TOTE BAG!

ARABESQUE

Visit us at: www.BET.com

THE "THANK YOU" GIFT INCLUDES:

- 4 books absolutely FREE (plus $1.99 for shipping and handling).
- A FREE newsletter, *Arabesque Romance News*, filled with author interviews, book previews, special offers, and more!
- No risks or obligations. You're free to cancel whenever you wish with no questions asked.

INTRODUCTORY OFFER CERTIFICATE

Yes! Please send me 4 FREE Arabesque novels (plus $1.99 for shipping & handling). I understand I am under no obligation to purchase any books, as explained on the back of this card. Send my free tote bag after my first regular paid shipment.

NAME _____

ADDRESS _____ APT. _____

CITY _____ STATE _____ ZIP _____

TELEPHONE (___) _____

E-MAIL _____

SIGNATURE _____

Offer limited to one per household and not valid to current subscribers. All orders subject to approval. Terms, offer, & price subject to change. Tote bags available while supplies last.

Thank You!

AN035A

ARABESQUE

Accepting the four introductory books for FREE (plus $1.99 to offset the cost of shipping & handling) places you under no obligation to buy anything. You may keep the books and return the shipping statement marked "cancelled". If you do not cancel, about a month later we will send 4 additional Arabesque novels, and you will be billed the preferred subscriber's price of just $4.50 per title. That's $18.00* for all 4 books for a savings of almost 30% off the cover price (Plus $1.99 for shipping and handling). You may cancel at any time, but if you choose to continue, every month we'll send you 4 more books, which you may either purchase at the preferred discount price. . . or return to us and cancel your subscription.

THE ARABESQUE ROMANCE BOOK CLUB
P.O. BOX 5214
CLIFTON NJ 07015-5214

PLACE
STAMP
HERE

"I quit as your consultant effective immediately," she said jokingly as she pressed her body closer to his.

Maxwell laughed. "Penelope," he drawled in a warning tone.

She nodded slowly, as if in understanding, and stepped away. "Later than sooner if you prefer," she said, expressing her belief in their eventual hookup.

He didn't bother to correct her.

"So if you're not here to make me scream the Lord's name like I was in church, what can I do for you Max?"

He turned and moved back to her desk. "I want to visit the gallery before I sign a semi-exclusive contract. Of course," he finished with a smile.

Penelope looked down at her calendar. "I'm free for a couple of hours. Let me just call and let them know—"

Maxwell grabbed her hand. "No calling. Let's just go and catch them off guard."

Penelope grabbed her purse with her free hand, and Maxwell pulled her out of the office behind him.

"Oh, God, Maxwell, yes. Yes," she whispered from beneath him as he stroked deeply inside her.

He nuzzled his head into the softness of her neck and suckled a spot there that caused her to tighten her walls against the length of him with a deep-throated purr. He felt near his release and ceased his movement so that their interlude would not end too soon.

"Don't stop, Maxwell. Please," she begged with

no shame as she massaged the strong muscles of his buttocks with eager hands.

"I want to ride you," she whispered in his ear before licking the lobe playfully. "Roll over."

Maxwell did as she bid, holding her securely with his arm around her waist so that he stayed deeply implanted inside her. He shivered as she suckled deeply at his nipple and began to move her hips in a rhythmic up-and-down motion that pulled deeply on the throbbing tip of his shaft. His toes curled and his legs stiffened as he tightened his grasp on her buttocks.

"Good?" she asked him teasingly in his ear, leaning up slightly so that her breasts were at his mouth.

He followed her cue and deeply suckled the hardened nipple, flicking the bud with the tip of his tongue just like he knew she loved.

She groaned in the back of her throat and leaned closer to him as one hand moved to clasp wildly at the back of his head. She pushed her other hand under his body to grip his hard buttocks while the pace of her hips quickened. "Who's the best?" she asked throatily as he winced with pleasure.

"You are, baby. You're the best."

She laughed in triumph.

Maxwell reached for both of her hands, moving them to his chest. "Sit up," he ordered her softly.

She sat up straight, now working her hips in a circular motion as she teased his nipples with her fingertips.

Maxwell opened his eyes and looked at his lover. She flung her hair back from her face and smiled down at him softly. "I love you, Maxwell."

Maxwell shot up in bed and looked wildly around

the dark room as his heart pounded a furious pace. He was in bed alone, but there was no denying the erection tenting the thin cover of his bed. And he couldn't deny that the woman in his dream had been Gabby!

Chapter Eight

One Week Later

Addie's normally sedate kitchen bustled with activity as the caterer Penelope had hired, along with is five servers, took over. Addie wrinkled her nose at one of the trays of food that a server carried out of the kitchen. She couldn't identify it so she wasn't going to eat it. *Mess around and have the runs,* Addie thought spitefully, more than annoyed that Penelope hadn't thought it would be best for *her* to do the cooking. Not that she was enthusiastic about cooking for a large dinner party. Still, she was Maxwell's cook, and the choice should have been hers.

So Addie sat in the corner watching her television and making sure that everybody understood that this was *her* kitchen and she wasn't leaving it until every last person and their mess was cleaned out of there.

"Holding down the fort, Addie?" Maxwell asked as he stepped into the kitchen, pushing his back against the swinging door leading into the next room as a server whizzed past him with yet another tray.

"No diggety, no doubt," she answered, pointedly looking across the room at Antoine, the chef.

"Good evening, Mr. Bennett," Antoine said, his Italian accent heavy as he stirred a steaming pot. "I was just finishing your main course."

"Which is?" Addie asked, still perched on her stool.

Antoine looked amused by her proprietary behavior. "It's *cassoeula*," he said with relish, leaning over the pot to inhale deeply of the aroma.

Maxwell crossed his arms over his chest and nodded. "Sounds delicious."

"Boy, please. He could be feeding you sautéed rats, you wouldn't know," Addie snapped.

Maxwell turned his back to Addie and looked at the chef apologetically.

Antoine nodded in understanding. "*Cassoeula* is a stew of pork ribs and sausages, Ms. Addie."

"Well, la-di-da," she sighed sarcastically, turning up the volume on her television.

Antoine laughed good-naturedly, pausing to stop one of the servers and sprinkle fresh Parmesan cheese on yet another appetizer tray before they carried it in to the guests.

Maxwell strolled over to the back door and looked down toward Gabrielle's cottage.

"A watched pot don't boil," Addie said, catching him out of the corner of her eye. "She's not back yet, Maxwell."

He looked at his watch. "It thought she would be here by now. She said she would be back in time for this dinner party. Why wouldn't she let me pick her up at the airport?"

Addie shrugged.

Penelope walked into the kitchen. "Antoine, everything is just delicious. Those rice dumplings are perfect."

"Ah, the *suppli' di riso,*" he said with pride.

"We're all going to be too full for the main course," she teased, lightly touching his arm.

"Good food is like good sex, you never can get too much."

Penelope looked directly at Maxwell, locking her eyes with his. "Now I can drink to that. How 'bout you, Max?"

Maxwell said nothing as he forced a smile, lifted the glass of wine he held in a mock toast to her, and then took a healthy swig of it.

Addie shot daggers at Penelope with her eyes. "Hey Antoine, is that your pork ribs I smell or is it desperation?"

Penelope shot daggers right back at Addie.

Maxwell smiled into his glass as he took another drink.

Antoine laughed. "Ah, she reminds me of my mama."

Maxwell saw Penelope about to head in Addie's direction and he quickly walked toward her. "Let's not forget all of these people we have waiting, Penelope," he told her, grabbing her elbow to lightly steer her out of the kitchen.

Gabrielle was nervous as she used her key to unlock her cottage. She set her two suitcases near the sofa, beginning to remove the casual clothes she'd traveled home in even as she reached back with her foot to nudge the front door closed.

Everything was not going as planned. Her plane had been delayed and the cab she caught at the airport got a flat tire. *What next, Gabrielle?*

She was attempting to pull her shirt over her head without ruining her hair when she heard the telephone ringing. "Aw, hell," she drawled, letting the shirt swing around her neck as she raced to pick up the cordless phone.

"Hello."

"How's it going?"

"Awful. My plane was late, the cab got a flat on the way home, and I'm about thirty minutes late for the dinner party," Gabrielle told her sister, settling onto the bed as she reached with her free hand to turn on the bedside lamp. "This big reveal of the new me is not going off on the right foot."

"Are you dressed?" April asked.

"Nope. I haven't even showered."

"First off, take a bath so that the steam of the shower doesn't knock out your curls. Then you won't have to worry about your hair."

Gabrielle's shoulders slumped. "I don't even know why I'm bothering. It's not like I'm planning on declaring my love for Maxwell."

April sighed. "It's not just about Max. It's about you, too. This is your night to shine, and if you get the guy in the meanwhile, then it's a nice bonus."

Gabrielle did feel more confident. In just three weeks Clayton and her sister had helped her find the pretty girl in the mirror she'd never quite seen when she looked at her reflection. "I do look more like one of the ladies on *Girlfriends* and not so much like Ally McBeal."

"Better," April told her with honesty.

Could Maxwell be hers? Would the swan she had become finally open his eyes?

"All right now. So are you gonna do this or what?"

Gabrielle stood and looked at herself in the full-length mirror on the back of her bathroom door. "I'm gonna do it."

Maxwell was working on his second Cosmopolitan as his guests milled around his den. Usually the parties he threw in the room were loud and boisterous, with hip-hop music bouncing over the dancing and gyrating bodies. Nothing at all like the sedate classical music playing softly in the background as people spoke to each other in dulcet tones.

He was bored out of his mind.

"You're supposed to mingle, Max, that's the purpose of this little soiree," Penelope said as she walked up to him in her strapless tea-length dress of crimson red.

"I did the meet-and-greet with everyone. I've even circled the room once to make sure I briefly held an intellectual discussion with them all. I've had my fill of the rounds for the night, Penelope," he told her with finality.

"You look good in black," she told him, quickly switching gears before he left the event altogether. "Bet you look better naked."

"Is it called sexual harassment if lewd comments are made only by an employer to an employee?" he mused as he looked at her over the rim of his drink.

"I'm not harassing," she insisted, reaching out with her free hand to smooth down the lapel of his tailored Gucci blazer. "I'm propositioning, and there is a difference. I think we'd make a good team, in and out of bed."

Maxwell just shook his head. She had no idea that her aggressiveness in bedding him was a turnoff. He didn't bother to tell her because he knew she'd simply switch gears and come at him from a whole new angle.

"Why don't we move dinner up so that we get this night rolling along?" he asked.

"Dinner is not scheduled to begin for another thirty minutes, Maxwell," she chided him.

Penelope began to fill him in on the newest offer the owner of the Art of Art Gallery in Los Angeles had made. She wanted to extend his exhibition to another gallery she owned in the Gaslamp Quarter of San Diego.

The offer was intriguing to Maxwell, for his impromptu visit to the gallery in D.C. had been less than pleasurable. He hadn't liked the superior attitude of the owner, the setup of the gallery's interior, or its locale. Maxwell actually believed that if the owner saw him on the street and knew nothing about him, she would clutch her purse and accuse him of attempting to mug her.

"You'll probably need to fly out to Cali this week sometime," Penelope was telling him.

Maxwell happened to look over at the entrance to the den. He did a double take when his eyes lit upon Gabrielle as she sauntered into the room. Or at least he thought it was Gabrielle. A more sophisticated version of his little assistant.

Gone were the childish bangs and ponytail, oversized misshapen clothing, and gawky tortoise-shell glasses. Her hair fell in supple, curly waves that soft-

ened her face. Without the spectacles she was open
and beautiful with make-up that only accentuated
her wide-set eyes and regal cheekbones. A high-
sheen gloss emphasized the fullness of her mouth.
A clinging white sheath perfectly reflected the curvaceous lines of her tall frame as the V-neck top
plunged daringly in the valley of her plump-sized
breasts and the flirty skirt fell above shapely legs.

Maxwell's eyes widened in shock. "Gabby?" he
asked in a strangled voice that reminded him of his
harrowing puberty-ridden days.

Penelope's words froze in her throat as she
turned to follow Maxwell's line of vision. Her initial
surprise quickly transformed to envy and then
worry as she eyed the all-new Gabrielle from her
styled hair to her perfectly pedicured toenails.

"Who kissed the frog?" Penelope said snidely.

Maxwell brushed past Penelope to snatch Gabrielle
up into a tight embrace. "Welcome home, Gabby. Look
at you!" he exclaimed.

Gabrielle hugged Maxwell back and allowed herself the pleasure of snuggling her face into the
warmth of his neck as she inhaled deeply of his scent.

Maxwell's eyes widened as he felt his body instantly react to having Gabrielle in his arms, her
body pressed closely to his own. Before she could
feel his lengthening erection, he sat her down, suddenly remembering his erotic dream. That was
something he had yet to come to grips with.

Even before she stood so beautifully before him,
he had desired her and felt jealousy over her possibly
being with another man. His newfound feelings were
odd and unsettling because as far as he was concerned he would never ever, never-ever ever cross

that line with Gabrielle. But with the way she looked tonight, restraining himself would be a battle.

"You look beautiful, Gabby," Maxwell told her honestly.

Gabrielle warmed under his compliments as she looked for the signs that Clayton and April had taught her to tell whether Maxwell was attracted to her.

"He'll keep staring at you."

"He'll keep touching you."

"He won't let you out of his eye sight."

"He'll keep complimenting you."

"Trust me," Clayton had finished. "You'll know."

Gabrielle stood up and twirled in front of her boss and friend, not caring at all how many eyes were on her in the room. "You like?" she asked, actually flirting as she licked her lips lightly.

Maxwell's eyes caught the move, and he felt his body warm to her yet again. He knew as he looked down at her that he was in big-time trouble.

"Welcome to the ball, *Cinderella*."

Gabrielle's eyes shifted in the mirror to Penelope's reflection as the woman walked into the guest bathroom. "I came in to check my make-up and tinkle, not to have a cat fight," she told the other woman lightly.

"You know," Penelope began, walking behind Gabrielle to stand on her other side in the mirror. "It's going to take more than a little make-up and a new dress to win Max from me."

Gabrielle finished touching up her lip gloss and then dropped the slender MAC container into her tiny clutch purse before turning sideways to face her. "Didn't know he was yours, and funny thing, Penelope the Putrid, I don't think he knows that either."

"Oh, I think if you'd ask him he'd say something very different," Penelope tested her.

Gabrielle laughed. "Penelope, I don't want Maxwell in that way, but I'm pretty sure Maxwell doesn't want you either. So all of the little tricks you try to pull to convince me otherwise are not working. But of course if I'm mistaken, then by all means let's go to Maxwell and get me straight with a quickness."

"You'll just make a fool of yourself, little girl," Penelope taunted, completely threatened by the woman who stood before her.

"Well, I'd guess if I did make a fool of myself, then you and I would *finally* have something in common. What do you think?"

Penelope stepped closer to Gabrielle, some of her urban upraising seeping out of her sophisticated shell. "Don't test me, *Gabby.*"

Gabrielle released a sigh, letting Penelope know she was completely bored with her, before turning and walking to the door. "Oh, and Penelope," Gabrielle began, standing in the archway with the doorknob in hand as she looked back over her shoulder. "It's a very thin line between pursuing a man and stalking him. You're walking the line, dear, and trust me . . . it's not a pretty sight."

Gabrielle left the bathroom on that note.

"There you are. I've been looking all over for you."

Gabrielle looked up and saw Maxwell jogging down the stairs toward her. "Something wrong?"

she asked, tucking her clutch under her arm as she turned to face him.

"No, I just wanted you to tell me all about Georgia and you know, your visit with your sister, and all this prettiness you got going on, and . . . and Clayton," he finished with a huge smile.

Gabrielle cocked her head to one side. "Clayton?" she said vaguely before leading him down the brightly lit hallway.

Maxwell reached for her wrist, his hand accidentally brushing against the softness of her breast. He instantly pulled his hand away as he felt his loins rev up like a motor. *This is Gabby, man. Calm the hell down.*

Gabrielle saw the bathroom door open behind Maxwell. "Here comes your girlfriend," she teased lightly, wanting so badly for Maxwell to officially deny that he was involved with Penelope.

Maxwell's face became a mask of confusion before he turned to look over his shoulders at Penelope, who was quickly walking toward them. He turned back to Gabrielle. "Penelope? We're not—"

"Maxwell, isn't it time for dinner?" Penelope asked loudly, obviously meaning to interrupt as she came to stand next to him.

He frowned and looked at his watch. "Already? Ten minutes ago you said not for thirty minutes."

Penelope laughed nervously. "I was wrong. Sue me."

Maxwell shrugged, glanced at Gabrielle, and had to avert his eyes at the sight of the delicate swell of her breasts.

"Gabby, why don't you go in and escort the guests

to the dining room?" Penelope offered, wanting Maxwell out of the other woman's company.

Maxwell made a face as he stared at Penelope. "Gabby's a guest tonight just like everyone else. This is *your* event."

"Of course," Penelope said tightly.

"Come on, Gabby, I want you to sit next to me," he told her.

Penelope stepped in their path as they headed for the dining room. "Actually, Maxwell, I have you seated next to the art critic for the *Star Gazette* and myself."

Maxwell nodded and continued on into the empty dining room. Both Gabrielle and Penelope followed, watching Max as he changed the place cards. "Now no one's the wiser."

"But Max," Penelope began to protest.

He walked over to the swinging door leading to the kitchen. "Antoine? Would you ask one of your servers to escort the guests to dinner, please? Thanks."

Penelope's face was hard enough to crack, but she forced a smile to her thinned lips.

The guests began to file into the room as Gabrielle took the seat to Maxwell's right. "Who's Antoine?" she asked him.

"The chef Penelope hired," Maxwell told her.

"Oh," Gabrielle said in surprise as she placed her silk napkin in her lap. "I assumed Addie was cooking."

Maxwell smiled a little. "So did she."

"Oh."

Penelope was mad enough to spit. Once everyone was seated, she finally realized that it was her place card that Maxwell had switched so that she now sat at the other end of the table from him. With cold eyes she turned her head to watch Maxwell and Gabrielle's heads huddled close together at the head of the table.

Little Gabby wants to play with the grown-ups, huh? We'll see.

"You know, Clayton would love these honey balls," Gabrielle told Maxwell as she enjoyed the sweet dessert they'd been served at the end of the meal.

Maxwell's smile was as false as dentures. "And just who *is* this Clayton?" he asked.

Gabrielle shrugged. "Just a friend I met while in Georgia."

"Is he the reason for the change?"

Gabrielle scooped the homemade almond ice cream up with her spoon, leisurely licking the contents onto her tongue. "Just thought it was time I grew up. I'm a big girl you know, Maxwell. So that means you're going to have to stop treating me like a kid, right?"

Maxwell's mouth was slightly open and he leaned forward, drawn by the sight of her tongue seeming to French-kiss her spoon. Right then his thoughts certainly were of a man and a woman. When Gabrielle looked up at him and licked the spoon again, a subtle move, Maxwell was again surprised. Was he so aroused by her that he imagined that she was deliberately flirting with him?

"Right, Maxwell?" she asked him again as he dipped a honey ball directly into her ice cream.

"Yeah, right," he answered, not even sure of what

he had agreed to because he couldn't think straight as he watched Gabrielle suck the ice cream from the spoon. When her eyes cut up at him again, Maxwell knew for sure that she was definitely throwing him some rhythm. *Don't play with fire, Gabby,* his eyes warned.

All his alarms went off and he had to stop himself from actually propositioning her. *This is Gabby. Slow your damn roll, man. Think with the right head.* "You'll have to invite your new boyfriend to Virginia for a visit," he said, clearing his throat and diverting his eyes from hers.

"Clayton's not my boyfriend. He's gay," she stated, very matter of fact.

"Oh, really?" was all that he said. Why did he feel so relieved? *Because you want to be the only man to make love to her, that's why.*

Needing a diversion and feeling guilty about his thoughts, Maxwell turned his attention to the art critic to the left of him at the table. He knew that he had to put a stop to the madness in his trousers before he did something they both would regret.

Penelope watched Maxwell as he watched Gabrielle. The man couldn't keep his eyes off of her even though they were on opposite sides of the den. When their endless conversation at the dinner table had finally ceased, Penelope had been initially pleased to see Maxwell spend the rest of the meal talking to the art critic. She mistakenly thought his obvious fixation on the new and improved Gabrielle had waned as the two entered the den and moved in opposite directions.

But she had been watching, and no matter how much he pretended not to, Maxwell had barely let Gabrielle out of his line of vision. He was overly curious when she talked a little too long with a young, attractive man. His stance had become stiff, only softening when Gabrielle moved on to chat with someone else.

Maxwell was damn near undressing the woman with his eyes, and Penelope knew that if she didn't step in soon, it would be his hands doing the undressing.

Pieces of Max's artwork were displayed on easels around the room and Gabrielle was standing in front of *Desire*, a painting depicting a man's fixation on a woman, when she felt one contact lens flip out. She tried not to panic as her vision began to blur horribly. *Okay, Gabrielle, keep calm.*

Tonight had been her first time putting the lenses in by herself, and she felt a little nervous about what she viewed as sticking her fingers into her eyes. Obviously, she hadn't done a good job of it.

She froze where she stood as everything before her blended into hazy layers of fuzzy colors. She should have known when the flight was late and the taxi had a flat tire that some other mishap was going to happen tonight. *Think, Gabby, think.*

Gabrielle began walking forward, closing her lens-less eye so that she could try to focus out of the one with the contact still in place. A white blur suddenly appeared in front of her, and she felt herself collide with it full force.

She fell backward and was unable to stop herself as the floor welcomed her back and rear end with a thud. Seconds later she felt cool liquid falling on her, followed by what she knew to be two glasses. *A damn server.*

"Gabby? Are you okay?"

She heard Maxwell's voice above her. "My contact fell out," she admitted, sitting up as she reached in her purse and pulled out her contact container. She carefully replaced the missing one and soon was rewarded with clear vision again, only to look down and see that her beautiful new white outfit was splashed with red wine. Then she looked up from the floor to see that everyone in the room circled her and stared openly.

"Must be after twelve, Cinderella," Penelope teased crudely.

Gabrielle turned to find the woman stooping beside her.

Swamped with embarrassment, Gabrielle rose quickly, pushed through the crowd, and fled out the door into the cold winter night.

Chapter Nine

Great move, Gabrielle. Just great.

Gabrielle was mortified at the spectacle she'd put on. At that moment she felt that Penelope had hit the nail on the head. She was just a fake Cinderella, and the midnight bell had certainly chimed for her, except there was no slipper to leave behind for Prince Maxwell to use to find her. If he even wanted to.

Gabrielle sank onto her couch and pulled the throw cover around her shoulders as she leaned back against the plush pillows.

What would she tell April when she called for an update? *Oh, I was pretty as can be—until I lost a contact, bumped into a waiter, spilled wine on my dress, and made a complete and total ass of myself.* Gabrielle felt tears of embarrassment, disappointment, and frustration gathering in her eyes.

On top of everything else, at one point during dinner Maxwell had started avoiding her for the rest of the night. Had she scared him away with her boldness? She had only flirted because she thought she'd picked up on cues that let her know he was attracted to her.

"I'm going to strangle both April and Clayton,"

she muttered darkly, enjoying a rather vivid vision of doing just that.

What a night. She pulled the throw over her head, wishing she could pray the whole night away. She had to just face the facts. As much as she loved Maxwell and desired Maxwell and wanted to do the hokey-pokey with Maxwell, he didn't feel the same way about her. She had to move on with her life. The daydreams of fairy-tale weddings and the hot erotic fantasies of long nights of wicked sex all had to cease.

Better said than done. Surrounded by the darkness of her home and swamped by the memories of her embarrassing evening, Gabrielle was glad when sleep finally made her lids heavy. *Maybe in my dreams I won't be such a dork.*

"Gabby?"

Her eyes shot open beneath the throw. Frowning at the sound of Maxwell's voice, she pulled the cover down slightly and looked into his face, which was highlighted by moonlight gleaming through the window. "Maxwell? Why aren't you at your party?"

"To hell with that party. I left Addie to escort them all out," he told her with a huge grin that made him even more sexy.

Gabrielle actually smiled as she pictured *that* going down.

"Hey, why are you crying?" Maxwell asked softly, reaching out to wipe away the track of her tears with his thumb.

"Oh, I don't know, maybe because I just made a fool of myself," she answered, hating that tears were welling up in her eyes again. Tears that she couldn't stop from falling for the life of her. All her insecurities came washing back in tidal waves that she felt herself drowning in.

"Aw, damn, don't cry, Gabby," Maxwell told her huskily, as he sat down on the couch and pulled her upper body into a comforting embrace. "It was just an accident. No big deal. And don't worry, the ones who laughed were the first ones I let Addie give the boot."

Gabrielle actually smiled at his serious tone. "Even Penelope?"

"*Especially* Penelope."

Gabrielle was overcome by Maxwell's scent, and his face caressed her nape as he pressed her against his chest. It was all just too much, and she tried to pull away. "I'm fine, Maxwell, but thanks for checking on me."

"You stopped crying?" he asked, looking down at her as he tilted her chin up to inspect her face.

Their mouths were just inches apart, and when his eyes dropped to her lips, Gabrielle's heart actually surged. That was definitely another of those cues. Maxwell wanted to kiss her!

Oh, what the hell. I'm going for it.

"Kiss me, Maxwell," she begged sweetly as she felt his heart pound against her hand.

"Gabby—" he began.

She lifted her head and captured his mouth with hers, using her tongue to trace his bottom lip before she sucked it deeply. "Kiss me," she begged again throatily, not wanting her boldness to be for naught.

Seconds later he took the lead, capturing her

tongue with his own. "Gabby," he moaned into her mouth.

Gabrielle felt desire and happiness nearly float her into the air as she sat up to place her hands on his handsome face and stroke him as his tongue caressed hers.

They both moaned in pleasure as Maxwell lifted her easily with one strong arm and flung the throw cover from her with a *whoosh*. The white of her dress glowed in the darkness as Maxwell gently placed her back on the couch and then lay beside her, bending his head down to claim her mouth once again.

Gabrielle groped blindly for a hand and pressed it against her chest. "Touch me," she ordered hotly.

His hands slipped inside the plunging V-neck of her top and massaged her full breast before he used skillful fingertips to tease her hardened nipple. She broke the kiss to gasp deeply at the pleasure he brought as she began to unbutton his shirt with shaky hands.

When his head lowered farther to suck deeply at her breast through the material, Gabrielle wanted more. "Take it off," she demanded hoarsely, lifting up so that they both could work the barrier up and over her head.

The first feel of his lips and tongue and teeth on her breast made Gabrielle's bud swell and pulsate like a rapid heartbeat between her legs. She pulled Maxwell down on top of her and wrapped her legs around his waist as she ground against the long length of his erection.

"Gabrielle. God, Gabrielle," he moaned against her breast, working his hands down under her buttocks to grind back against her.

She kissed his temple and massaged his back as she felt her climax near. "I'm gonna come, Maxwell," she gasped hotly, arching her back.

Maxwell shifted his hands to lean on his elbows and looked down into her face as he continued to grind into her. "You're beautiful," he whispered softly, lowering his head to lightly kiss her lips as his eyes devoured the sight of her perfectly formed breasts before shifting to watch her face become transformed as she came.

"I'm coming, Maxwell. Baby, I'm coming," Gabrielle cried out hoarsely as her body became hot with her release, causing her hips to jerk up against his. When she felt his lips suck deeply at her breasts she nearly passed out as she clawed his back with her hands.

"Come for me, girl. Come on," he ordered her huskily as he licked a trail from one breast to the other to claim the mound hotly in his mouth.

Gabrielle breathed heavily and felt her body slacken as the tidal waves finally stopped washing over her body. It was like nothing she had ever experienced, but she wasn't done and she wanted more.

Maxwell raised his head to look down into her face. "You get it?" he asked playfully, tenderly placing kisses over her entire face.

Gabrielle opened her eyes and gave him a "Say what!" look that caused them both to laugh.

She reached up with her hands and pulled his face down to trace his whole mouth with her tongue. She reveled as his body shivered, and it made her more bold. She pushed him off of her and stood to slowly remove her skirt. Feeling confident and sexy, she bent to turn on the lamp on the coffee table, wanting him to see her stand before him in nothing but her black lace thong and heels.

Gabrielle stepped out of the thong and then kicked it away. "It's a little wet," she said with a coy smile.

Maxwell sat up on the couch, his eyes massaging her as he seemed spellbound by the very sight of her body. Gabrielle was slender, true enough, but there were curves where curves mattered.

She flipped her hair away from her face as she moved to straddle his lap. She placed her hands under his open shirt and wildly teased his nipples with her fingertips as his own hands rose to massage her buttocks. "Here, let me take this off," she told him, working the shirt down his arms to fling behind her.

Gabrielle leaned forward, placing one hand on each side of his head, as she lightly jiggled her breasts in his face. When he lifted his head to taste of one, she teasingly leaned back from him several times until Maxwell wrapped his arms around her waist and jerked her forward to suck deeply at her breasts. "Damn," she moaned, closing her eyes as she caressed his neck and let the side of her face rest on top of his head.

Her eyelashes fluttered slightly as she felt him place one of his fingers deep inside her. She winced in pleasure as her thighs quivered.

"Damn, it's wet," he moaned, kissing a trail up to claim her mouth.

Gabrielle gasped into Maxwell's mouth as he began to stroke her slickly wet bud with skillful fingers. Warmth began to spread from her toes to the pit of her stomach as he continued his relentless pursuit of yet another climax for her.

She moved her hands down between her legs to unbuckle his pants, wanting his heat in her hands. She unzipped him and reached inside his black boxers to pull his hardness out. It slipped from her hand and fell against his rigid abdomen with a slight thud.

Gabrielle broke the kiss to get her first sight of the tool she had dreamed of. She swallowed over a sudden lump in her throat and felt her first bit of apprehension. It was thick, dark, and so long that it passed his navel easily.

"Touch it," he ordered, extracting his finger from her core to suck deeply of her juices with a grunt of pleasure.

Gabrielle took him in her hands and his hips arched as she did. She massaged the length of him, having to use both hands. Slowly she began, circling her hands around him to rise and stroke the throbbing tip.

She looked at Maxwell's face and was pleased as he tilted his head back and let his mouth fall open in pleasure. Wanting to please him, she quickened her pace, never once taking her eager eyes from him.

Maxwell stretched out his legs, holding her by her buttocks so that she wouldn't slip down his legs.

Gabrielle wanted to taste him, feel him throb against her lips and tongue, but she wasn't quite that bold yet. Instead she used the trickle of released to lubricate her hands as she continued to work him.

When Maxwell grabbed her hands suddenly, she

thought she had done something wrong and looked at him in question.

At her look of distress he shook his head. "You gone make me come, baby," he told her, shifting her hands up to his chest as he pulled her face down to kiss away her concern.

Gabrielle's tension eased as she kissed Maxwell with all the passion she'd held for the last six years. This was the night she'd dreamt of so many times that she wondered if this too was an all-too-vivid dream. Was Maxwell really here on her couch making love to her with an energy that was going to make her explode?

Gabrielle's face was confused as Maxwell placed his hands on her hips and easily lifted her up above his head.

"Put your knees on the back of the couch," he instructed her, as he tilted her head back and lowered her down onto his face.

"Hold on," he warned her with a wicked smile, before he nuzzled his face up under her and opened the lips that led into her with his tongue.

Gabrielle was precariously perched above him and nearly teetered over when she buckled at the first feel of his tongue lightly plucking at her bud. She placed her hand on his shoulders for support and held on for dear life while she enjoyed his work. "Maxwell," she sighed, sitting up straight and arching her back as she felt heat infuse her.

He was dogged as he wildly sucked all of her into his mouth.

Gabrielle trembled uncontrollably and a fine sheen of perspiration coated her body. "Maxwell," she moaned coarsely, shifting one of her hands to press his head closer to her.

He stiffened his tongue and plunged it inside her walls. Gabrielle cried out freely as her body contracted. "Sweet Jesus," she gasped when he made love to her with it.

Maxwell used his skillful tongue to open her further and suck deeply on the sensitive bud buried deep beneath the lips of her womanhood.

Gabrielle nearly fell again but tightened her grasp before she did. Loving what he was doing, she began to grind against his tongue in wild abandon and to cry out unashamedly.

Maxwell sucked on her bud even deeper.

Gabrielle felt her eyes roll up in her head and her heart pounded frantically while she quivered. "Don't stop. You better not stop," she warned him, grimacing as she felt her release fill Maxwell's mouth.

He swallowed greedily and sucked and sucked on her as if his very life depended on it. Gabrielle sighed and whimpered when he lowered her to straddle his lap again. Her body was damp with perspiration and weak from exhaustion. She circled her arms around his neck and held him tightly.

He kissed the side of her face, both his hands lightly playing in the wetness he had created between her legs. "Good?" he asked.

Gabrielle nuzzled her face into his neck and nodded. "The best," she answered him honestly.

Maxwell shifted his wet fingers to her back and he stood up. His pants dropped down around his shoes as she wrapped her legs around his waist. Massaging her back, he carried her into her bedroom, his erection stiff and awkwardly hanging from his body.

Standing by the side of the bed, he slowly lowered both of them upon the mattress, using his feet to kick off his shoes and work his pants onto the floor. Gabrielle still clung to his body like she was afraid he was going to leave, but Maxwell wasn't going anywhere. The night had just begun for them.

She sighed as she reached between them to massage the long length of his hardness. Maxwell tensed at the feel of her soft hands on his body and deepened his pulling motion on her hard nipples.

"God, your body feels so good," he told her.

Gabrielle lifted her face and enjoyed being blessed by his lips. "Yours too," she whispered against his face.

Maxwell gave her one final kiss before he moved down her body to kneel by her feet. With the most enticing circular motions he began to massage her calves and toes, smiling as she stretched leisurely like a feline. His eyes locked with hers as he lifted one foot and suckled each of her toes.

Gabrielle was surprised and her face showed it as she looked at him with her mouth agape. "Oh, that . . . feels . . . *so* good," she sighed.

He lifted her other leg and repeated his massage technique before lifting her foot to suckle deep into his mouth, his tongue tickling her toes.

Gabrielle literally purred and stretched her arms languidly above her head.

Maxwell came closer now, deeply working his fingers into her shapely thighs. She propped her other foot on his shoulder, and he switched to her other thigh, enjoying the feel of the silken skin beneath his fingertips. And he didn't stop until he had massaged her entire body, including her fingertips. "Turn over," he demanded softly, massaging the length of his erection as she did as he bid.

On her stomach, Gabrielle buried the side of her face into the pillow as Maxwell kiss, bit, and licked his way up the back of both her legs before she felt him take a deep and delicious bite of her left butt cheek. She sighed and smiled into the pillow as he did the same to the other. She thought he was done, but he proceeded to cover every expanse of her derriere with his kisses.

"I guess now if I get mad and tell you to kiss my butt, you can say you have," she teased. She yelped as he bit down playfully into her flesh, but then he made up for it by deeply massaging the spot with his tongue.

Maxwell moved his magic hands up to massage her lower back as her buttocks sweetly cupped the length of his hardness.

"Not only can you paint but you give one hell of a massage. God has truly blessed those hands," she mumbled into her pillow.

"That's not all he blessed me with," Maxwell teased, as he used one hand to lightly tap her buttocks with his shaft.

Gabrielle flipped onto her back and then bent her legs to open wide in front of him. "Now why don't you bless me?" she asked boldly.

Maxwell reached over the side of the bed to retrieve a Magnum condom from his wallet. His hands were shaking as he tore the package and quickly rolled the tight-fitting latex down the length of himself. It only reached two-thirds of the way, but he was used to that.

He rubbed the tip of his manhood up the middle of her core, coating himself with her juices, before he lay down upon her and gently probed her. Gabrielle winced slightly at the feel of him as he slowly pushed inside the heat and warmth of her womanhood. He kissed her deeply, shivering as he inched inside her.

"God, it's so tight, Gabrielle," he moaned, dropping his forehead to lightly rest on top of her own.

Gabrielle held her breath when she felt him reach the point of no return.

Maxwell froze and looked down at her in shock. "You're a vir—"

She kissed him, swallowing his words, just before she clasped his buttocks with her hands and lifted her hips off the bed to slide more of him inside her. Tears filled her eyes, but it was mostly from the pleasure of having Maxwell's shaft planted so deeply inside her. He was her first lover, and there was no one else she wanted to share her gift with.

"Are you sure?" he asked, his voice shaky.

Maxwell remained still, struggling to ease his climax. His jaw was clenched tightly and his body shivered uncontrollably while she suckled his tongue with a skill that was now surprising to him.

Gabrielle lowered her legs beneath his and began to work her hips in an up-and-down motion that pulled on the length of him.

Maxwell again looked down at her in surprise, unable to stop himself as he met her stroke for delicious stroke. "Damn, Gabrielle. Damn. Oh, damn it, girl."

He plunged his shaft into her but was careful not to lose control and mate with her too roughly. He was sure to plant only a portion of himself inside her tight sheath for fear he would hurt her with all of it.

Gabrielle reached up to lick furiously at his nipples, loving the feel of his soft hairs against her tongue.

"Suck harder," he begged, moving up so she could reach them easier.

She pulled the whole nipple into her mouth and enjoyed the feel of his body jerking in pleasure.

"Gabrielle, what the hell are you doing to me?" he cried out just as he felt his own climax near. He was able to control himself until the world became a blur and his body felt like an inferno. "It's gon' come, baby."

Feeling her own release and wanting to increase his pleasure, she worked her hips even harder, increasing the pace as they both clutched each other strongly and held on for dear life.

Wave after delicious wave coursed over their entwined bodies as they both stiffened and then hollered out hoarsely as they came together for long delicious moments that blew them away.

Hours later, Maxwell sat in a chair beside the bed and watched Gabrielle sleep. She looked so peaceful and rested, so beautiful and serene. Making love with her had been one of the best experiences of his life. She had given him everything he ever longed for in a bedmate: excitement, fun, and passion. She had fulfilled him and completed him, but now he wanted her again.

She had been such a temptress, kissing him first and then standing before him nude, and later opening herself up to him and ordering him to "bless her." Never in a million years would he have guessed that the temptress was truly a virgin.

Maxwell leaned forward in the chair. She had a different hairstyle and no longer wore glasses, but this was Gabby. *His* Gabby—the innocent young woman he had promised himself he would watch over so that no unscrupulous men could take advantage of her. In the end he had been the one to take her virginity.

He hated himself for it. Gabrielle deserved the whole picture: the courtship, the ring, the fabulous wedding, and a good husband who deserved the gift of her virginity. *Damn, I messed up.*

Gabrielle shifted in her sleep and reached out for her lover. When she felt nothing but the coolness of the sheets, she actually thought she had dreamt it all until she opened her eyes and saw him sitting in the chair beside the bed and then felt the tenderness between her legs.

Maxwell's lovemaking had been everything she'd dreamt of and more. She had been pleasured over and over again until she thought she had to be the luckiest girl in the world to have been blessed with his lovemaking. It had been so good that it was almost unreal. And she wanted him again.

She reached out her hand to him from under the covers, smiling as he rose to take it and sit down in his boxers on the edge of the bed. At the grim look on his face her smile faded. "What's wrong, Maxwell?" she asked, feeling alarmed.

Gabrielle sat up in bed and pulled him into her arms. She frowned when he pulled back from her.

"Maxwell, what's wrong?" she asked sharply as tears welled up in her own eyes.

He wiped his face and looked over at her with an expression that she would never forget. "I'm so sorry. I . . . last night . . . I . . . um," he said, struggling for the words to explain.

Gabrielle's face closed up as she pulled the sheet over her breasts. All of her insecurities came back to her in a rush. "You're . . . you're . . . um, you're regretting that we . . . we made love—I mean had sex. Right?"

Maxwell reached out his hand to touch her face and felt pained when she drew back from him like he was fire. "Gabby?"

"Gabby?" she snapped and then laughed hysterically, wiping her tears away with shaking hands. "I'm Gabby again. Okay, I got you. That's cool."

Maxwell felt his own anger at himself rise. "Gabby, I didn't know that you were a . . . uh . . . a virgin. I should've guessed that you were—"

"Why? Because the way I looked before, no man would want a dog like me?" she said, her voice low and cold.

No, I wanted you even then, he thought, remembering his dream. He shook his head before dropping it into his hands. "You're taking this all the wrong way, Gabby."

She smiled sarcastically as she looked about her bedroom at anything and nothing. "Well, why don't you explain it to me, Maxwell? Huh? Go ahead, give me a clue."

He released a heavy breath before shifting on the bed to face her. "Girls like you—"

"I'm a woman, Maxwell. I think I've finally proved that point to you, haven't I?" she snapped disparagingly.

His guilt rose. "I just took your virginity, and that was something you should have saved for your wedding night with your husband. And I'm sorry for that."

Gabrielle closed her eyes and tried her best not to let Maxwell know how much pain his words brought to her. He had in fact just let her know that his feelings for her were not emotional but physical. He did not intend to marry her. He had only wanted to bed her.

Loving him so completely the way that she did, that hurt her deeply. Part of her had actually thought that she and Maxwell were on their way to a happily ever-after.

"Get out, Maxwell," she said softly, turning her head away from him.

"Gabby."

"I just want to get some sleep, Maxwell. Go home. We'll talk tomorrow," she told him wearily before lying back down and turning her back to him.

Long after he had gathered his clothes and quietly shut the bedroom door behind himself, Gabrielle wept until she was empty of tears.

Chapter Ten

Gabrielle walked into the kitchen out of the light drizzle and hung her raincoat on the rack by the door.

Addie entered the room and then did a double take as she spotted Gabrielle. "Well, what fashion truck hit you?" she exclaimed, rushing across the kitchen to circle the younger woman.

The warm smile she gave Addie didn't quite reach her eyes, and she was glad the older woman didn't notice. "My sister decided I needed an updated look," Gabrielle told her, feeling pretty in the sleeveless pale pink cowl-neck shirt she wore with fitted jeans and stiletto boots.

Even though she had cried like a baby nearly all night as her hopes of being Mrs. Maxwell Bennett were crushed, she refused to let him see that he had hurt her. So she'd got up, made sure her hair was still a riot of curls, applied her make-up the way April had taught her, and pulled on a sexy but casual outfit.

"You always were a beautiful girl, but now no one has to look twice to see it behind Mister Magoo glasses and underneath those childish clothes."

Gabrielle walked over to the counter and poured

herself a cup of coffee. "Maxwell up yet?" she asked, trying to sound casual.

"Funny, bossman didn't sleep in his bed last night, must have got lucky with someone at the party. Probably that barracuda Penelope," Addie told her as she stirred a pot. "I made his favorite oatmeal again, and he's not even here to eat it."

Gabrielle's grip tightened around the handle of the cup until she thought it would snap off in her hand. She kept her back to Addie and forced herself to take a sip of the brew as she fought for composure. *Where was he? Surely he didn't go to another woman after we made love last night? No, he wouldn't dare.* Gabrielle carried her cup out of the kitchen.

"You don't want breakfast, Gabby?" Addie called behind her.

"I'm not hungry. Just the coffee is fine," she told her with a weak smile, hurrying up the stairs before Addie went into full motherly mode and forced her to start the day off right with a heaping bowl of oatmeal.

Once in the loft, Gabrielle cradled the warm cup as she walked over to examine the paintings now neatly hung on the walls. *Someone's been busy,* she thought as she nodded in approval. She had been nagging Maxwell for years to display his work and not just leave the canvases leaning against the wall like posters.

She couldn't help but be nervous about seeing him again after the night they had shared. Their sex had been wild and uninhibited, and loving—at least on her part. Oh, she knew Maxwell cared about her, even loved her as a friend, but he wasn't *in* love with her. He'd made that painfully clear last night.

Would they be able to put it behind them? Should they?

Her first time making love had been memorable. The only thing that would have made it more divine was if Maxwell had been her husband and it had been their wedding night. But she didn't blame Maxwell because all he could provide was the physical aspect of her fantasy. The body but not the heart.

Gabrielle loved her job as his assistant. It paid well, and she had a free place to stay and as much free time as she wanted. But today the job felt like a troublesome burden. Before last night her love of Maxwell had been yet another reason to keep the job. Now her emotions were a hindrance since she knew that they were not ever going to be returned on the same intense level.

Gabrielle lost her desire to reacquaint herself with Maxwell's paintings and turned halfway down the loft to return to her desk. She set her coffee cup down and she took her seat. Swiveling in the chair, she let her eyes caress the sun as she tried to fight the sadness she felt weighing down her slender shoulders. *Where is he?*

She was replaying their steamy moments on the couch in her head when the phone rang, breaking the silence. Reaching behind her, she picked up the cordless. "Maxwell Bennett's. Gabrielle speaking. May I help you?"

"Gabby? This is Darlene. How are you doing?"

Gabrielle actually smiled at the sound of Maxwell's

older sister's voice. "I'm good," she lied. "How are you?"

"I'm great. I was just trying to reach that brother of mine. Is he there?"

"No, he didn't stay home last night."

Darlene laughed. "Who's he messing 'round with now? That man knows he loves him some women. Always did. His nature is so high. Even when he was just a toddler he would walk up and touch women's breasts. Mama used to be so ashamed."

Gabrielle smiled again as she pictured Maxwell as a little boy. "Well, the ladies love him too," Gabrielle told her, swiveling back around in her chair to let her head fall in her hand.

"I was calling to tell him that I was able to put in for the time off and come to the reunion. So will you tell him May is good for me?"

So he did make the calls, Gabrielle thought as she pulled out her planner. "Okay, I'll let him know."

"And tell him I said to give those skirts a break."

Gabrielle forced a laugh. "I will."

She hung up the phone, placing it back on its base. No sooner had she pulled her hand away than it rang again. "Maxwell Bennett's. Gabrielle speaking."

"So how did it go?"

Gabrielle instantly recognized her sister's animated voice. "It all worked. Maxwell and I did the do."

April howled into the phone.

Gabrielle winced and pulled it away from her ear a little.

"Okay, tell me all about it and don't leave out a single nasty, freaky deaky little detail."

Gabrielle retold April everything, even about

knocking the server and herself off their feet and Maxwell coming to the house to check on her. "Girl, I was so ashamed."

"And I feel your pain. I swear I do, but get to the nitty-gritty, girl," April urged.

Gabrielle's eyes got a faraway look in them. "It was good. It was better than good. That brother turned me every which way but loose."

"No!" April exclaimed in mock disbelief.

"Yes," Gabrielle sighed.

"So what happened next?"

"I woke up and—"

"He put you to sleep, huh?"

The door to the loft opened. Gabrielle shifted her eyes to watch Maxwell and Penelope walk in together. "April, I gotta go," she told her, shooting Maxwell daggers before she pointedly looked away from him.

"Now I know you not gone leave me hanging like that," April complained.

"April, I *have* to go."

"Is he there?"

"Yes."

"Time for round two? Girl, call me."

Gabrielle hung up the phone and placed it back on its base. "Good morning, Maxwell. Penelope."

"Morning, Gabby—"

She shot him a sharp look.

"Gabrielle," he amended, shifting his eyes away from hers. "I didn't know you were up yet. Penelope and I were going to select a couple of pieces to ship to Los Angeles for the exhibit."

"I thought it was over last week?" Gabrielle asked, opening her day planner to double-check.

"It was, but I was able to secure a new contract with the owner for a bigger and even better exhibit in San Diego," Penelope said, stepping up to the desk to hand her the signed contracts.

She accepted them and then began to look through them. "Did the attorney review these before you signed them?"

Penelope raised an eyebrow. "I wanted you to file Max's copy, not review them."

"Penelope," Maxwell said sharply. "And yes, I took them by his office myself."

If looks could kill, both Gabrielle and Penelope would have dropped each other on the spot.

"Gabrielle, you and I need to talk," Maxwell reminded her. "Just let us go through these paintings first, okay?"

She looked up to meet his eyes and hated that her heart swelled with love for him. "Actually I have an appointment today," she lied. "Can we talk later?"

Maxwell frowned. "Can't it wait? I think this is important. Don't you?"

Gabrielle just shrugged as she shifted papers on her desk unnecessarily. "Not really," she said, successfully sounding blasé.

"What?" he asked, shocked.

Gabrielle picked up her cordless phone. "Your sister called and she's fine for May for the reunion," she told him as she dialed numbers.

"Which one?"

"Huh?" Gabrielle asked, looking confused.

Maxwell released an exasperated sigh. "Which sister?"

"Oh, Darlene."

"Are you still going to plan the reunion for me?" he asked, his voice low.

"Hey, this is Gabrielle Dutton. Could you hold for one sec?" Gabrielle placed her hand over the mouthpiece as she looked up at him with a blank face. "Of course. That's my job."

Maxwell stared at her hard for long seconds that drew a curious glance from Penelope before he turned and walked to the other end of the loft.

Penelope stepped close to Gabrielle's chair and leaned down to whisper in her ear. "Were you able to get that wine off your pretty little dress, Cinderella?" she taunted, glaring at Gabrielle with devilish eyes.

Gabrielle hung up the phone, not even sure who she'd called, gathered her keys, and left the loft, slamming the door behind herself.

She was almost to the lower level when Maxwell caught up with her.

"Gabrielle, we need to talk," he told her, reaching out to grab her wrist and halting her further descent down the stairs.

"What is there to talk about, Maxwell?" she asked, turning to look up at him as she pulled her wrist from his all-too-warm grasp.

"Last night."

Gabrielle shrugged. "What's to talk about?" she asked again.

"Gabrielle, I took your virginity last night," he whispered harshly as his eyes darted over her face.

"No, I *gave* you my virginity. You didn't take anything," she told him as she played with the keys in her hand. "It's really not that big of a deal."

Maxwell dropped his head and shoved his hands

into his pockets. "Gabrielle, I don't want things between us to change."

Gabrielle felt victorious as she swallowed back the pain she felt at his words. "Don't worry, Maxwell. You're a good boss and a cool friend, but you'd make a lousy boyfriend, and no one knows that better than me. You change women like most people change drawers."

He leaned against the wall as he looked down at her with sad eyes. "I feel like I took advantage of you, Gab—I mean, Gabrielle."

"I wanted to lose my virginity and get it out of the way. I chose to have you as my first lover because of our friendship, not because I wanted you as a boyfriend. That type of drama I don't need okay?"

Maxwell's face was filled with disbelief.

"Look, Maxwell. I have a date so I really need to go," she lied, continuing down the stairs.

Again he reached for her wrist and stopped her. "After last night you have a *date* this morning?" he balked.

"That's right."

"I don't believe you, and I don't believe your jive about wanting to get rid of your virginity, either."

Gabrielle just shrugged again. "Is there anything I can bring you from the art supply store? I'll be down that way for my brunch date with Miguel."

"Miguel?" he drawled, disbelieving. "Okay, play your games, Gabby, but when you're ready for us to get everything out in the open with *honesty*, I'll be waiting."

"I *do* have a date," she insisted, stomping her foot in frustration as he turned to climb the stairs.

"Whatever," floated down the stairs.

"And it's Gabrielle, not Gabby," she yelled up at him.

Maxwell bent over the rail to look down at her. "Whatever, *Gabrielle*. Tell Miguel I said *'buenos noches.'*"

"Ooh, he gets on my last nerve," Gabrielle muttered before strolling into the kitchen.

She was glad Addie wasn't in her usual spot on her stool. Gabrielle grabbed her raincoat and left the house.

Penelope quickly shut the door to the loft and tiptoed as fast as she could to the far end to pretend to be looking at the paintings on the wall. When Maxwell walked in seconds later, slamming the door behind him, she turned on her heel to face him. "I really love this one, Max," she said, pointing to an abstract of couples dancing in a 1950s juke joint.

But Maxwell wasn't listening. He walked over to the windows behind Gabrielle's desk and watched with narrowing eyes as she drove through the open gate to leave the estate.

He thought of what they had shared last night and shivered, remembering sucking deeply of her juices as she came in his mouth. The way she worked him until his entire body became hot as he reached his climax. He'd had good sex before, great sex even, but never had he felt his whole body burn like he'd stood in front of an oven. Little Gabby had given him the best night of his life. And he wanted her again. He felt his groin aflame and his maleness harden from just the very memory of being buried so deeply inside her.

It all spelled trouble with a capital *T*. He knew that he had to put some distance between himself and her before he gave in again to his desire to stroke inside of her so deeply that he got lost.

"Max?" Penelope asked, walking up behind him to lightly touch his back.

He looked over his shoulder at her with a questioning look.

"I was thinking that the painting *Hell Up in Harlem* would be good for the exhibit," she told him as she massaged the small of his back.

Maxwell moved away from her touch, turning to stride to the other end of the loft. "That is a good one. I'll get it down today and make sure it's shipped."

"You look tired. Rough night?" she asked, walking over to him again and reaching her hands up to massage his broad shoulders.

"I was up here all night working on a new painting," he told her, pointing to an easel with a cover draped over it as he again stepped away from her probing hands.

"Can I see it?" she asked eagerly, strutting toward it.

Maxwell shook his head adamantly. "No, it's for my personal collection," he said with finality.

Penelope's steps halted and she turned back to face him. "Okay, that's fine. Listen, I have to get back to Washington, but I definitely like *Hell Up in Harlem* and maybe *Groovin'* for the exhibit. You just need probably one or two more to get shipped out today."

Maxwell nodded as he began to mix paints on his palette. "Got it. And we fly out on Friday, right?"

"Actually, I'm going a day ahead of you. I have to check on some things for another client I have out there."

"See you Friday, then," he told her as he walked over to the easel.

"Get there safely. I wouldn't want a thing to happen to that body," she teased, blowing him a kiss before she left the loft.

Maxwell set his palette down and carefully removed the cloth covering his painting. Gabrielle's face looked back at him with a teasing and seductive smile.

"A pretty lady like you should never eat alone."

Gabrielle released a heavy breath before she looked up from her stack of pancakes at the third gentleman to stop by her table and offer her his company. *Women who were actually looking for a man really should eat alone at their local Friendly's*. She had to hide her irritation at the elderly man standing over her with a grin so white and perfect that she knew his teeth were as false as cubic zirconia earrings. "Actually I'm waiting on my boyfriend. He's running late, but thank you," she told him politely.

"Tell that young buck if he slip, somebody else will beat his time," he said, pushing a business card on the table toward her.

Guess he thinks I'm impressed. Gabrielle picked up the card and looked at it. "Thank you, Mr. Harris, but I don't think I'll need any exterminating services," she told him, pushing the card back and pointedly returning her attention to her breakfast.

"Girl, I could change the way you see the world," he whispered in her ear.

"I guess so, since you're old enough to be my granddaddy," she snapped irritably.

He reached in his pocket and pulled out his wallet, extracting a fifty-dollar bill to fling onto the table. "Pay for your breakfast with that, darling. And give me a call."

Having had her fill, Gabrielle picked up her purse, threw her pale pink raincoat over her arm, and signaled for her waitress.

"I thought you'd change your mind," the man said with satisfaction as he grinned again and nearly blinded her.

The waitress walked over to stand beside him at the table. "Is everything okay?"

"Yes, ma'am," Gabrielle told her, handing her a ten-dollar bill. "This is for my food." She picked up the fifty-dollar bill and handed that to the waitress as well. "And this is your tip."

The waitress's mouth fell open. "Thank you!" she exclaimed excitedly.

The old man looked shocked as Gabrielle pushed past him. "Don't thank me. Thank Pappy the Pervert," Gabrielle told the waitress and left the restaurant.

She ran headfirst into a strong and solid body, yelping as she fell backward onto her butt.

"I didn't even see you, beautiful. Are you all right?" a deeply masculine voice asked.

Gabrielle looked up into a smiling and handsome face. "Are you married?"

"No," he answered, pulling her to her feet.

"Dating? Seriously involved?"

"No and no," he answered again, smiling.

Gabrielle stared at him, her mind going a million miles per minute as she did. "Would you—could you—no, never mind, thank you," she said, strolling away quickly.

She had been about to ask a complete stranger to dinner just to parade him, in all his magnificence, in Maxwell's know-it-all face. The man could be a murderer or at the very least a liar because there was no way a man that fine didn't have someone in his life, be it serious or not.

Have I lost my ever-loving mind?

Gabrielle was standing by the exit to the mall, pulling on her raincoat, when her cell phone rang. She reached in her purse and retrieved it, flipping it open. "Hello."

"I thought you were going to call me back?"

Gabrielle placed the phone between her shoulder and face as she buttoned her coat. "Aren't you working?" she asked her sister, reaching into her totebag for her umbrella.

"I'm on break. Now finish telling me what happened. We left off with him putting you to sleep."

Gabrielle walked out of the mall with her umbrella open, the cell phone still to her ear. "Listen, forget the sex. He told me that he regretted it and gave me this sad face about taking advantage of me because he didn't know that I was a virgin."

"You *are?*" April asked in wonder.

Gabrielle unlocked the car door and slid into the driver's seat, closing the umbrella before she shut the door. "Was."

"Oh, Gabrielle, I didn't know that."

"*Anyway*, this morning I tried to save face and I told him I had a date. Do you know, he flat out told me he didn't believe me?"

"No, he did not."

"Yes, he did," Gabrielle answered, as she started the car and turned on the wipers. "That's not even the half."

Gabrielle filled her sister in on her morning of propositions from odd men and then how she had almost propositioned a complete stranger.

"Little sister, you got more drama going on than all the soap operas combined."

"Tell me about it," Gabrielle drawled.

"Hey, hold on one sec."

Gabrielle groaned as elevator music filled the phone line. She had wasted the entire day walking around the mall, and she was ready to get back to her cottage and out of the wet weather. Adamantly against talking on cell phones while driving, she sat in the parking lot with the motor running as she waited for her crazy sister to remember that she had put her on hold.

"Okay, Gabrielle. Tell me how much you love your big sister," April proclaimed suddenly.

"Unless you're about to ask me to borrow money, you're the best big sister a girl could ask for. Why?" Gabrielle finished suspiciously.

"When this is all said and done, we're both going to owe Clayton some big-time favors."

Maxwell stood back from the painting, amazed at how far along he was with its completion. He looked up at the clock and was surprised to see that it was nearly six. He had passed the day painting and had loved every minute of it. He had become lost in mixing the right hues of silky brown and using the right strokes to represent the woman he painted completely from memory.

His stomach growled, reminding him that he had not eaten since the dinner party the night before. He didn't regret it though. Something was driving him to finish the painting he'd named *The Muse*.

Last night after Gabrielle asked him to leave he had gone straight to bed, barely washing away the scent of their lovemaking before he climbed between the sheets. But sleep had eluded him. His mind became a chaotic blur of guilt over his actions and visions of how perfectly proportioned Gabrielle's frame had been. Curves where curves belonged and sleek long lines that were a testament to her fitness. She was perfection personified as she stood naked and proud before him. The image of her high breasts with their large chocolate areolas, her flat abdomen, hips and long shapely legs haunted him until he no longer fought the desire to rise and climb the stairs to his loft.

There he had remained long into the night, glorifying and immortalizing Gabrielle's beauty.

Setting his palette down, he took several steps back and surveyed his handiwork. He had painted her lying nude on her side among rose petals that were not nearly as sweet, delicate, and beautiful as she. He had missed no detail of her body. Not the gloss of her auburn-tinted curly hair. Not the tiny mole near her navel. Not the tiny strip of fuzzy hair atop the plump *V* between her legs. Not even the French manicure on her delectable toes.

Who knew that beneath those layers of bulky clothing was one of the most extraordinary bodies he had ever had the pleasure of tasting, touching, and enjoying? Who knew that little innocent Gabrielle had ardor and seduction oozing from her like steam off a hot tin roof? Who knew that he and Gabrielle would make the most passionate, hot, and spicy love?

Certainly not him.

Even now he could taste her juices, smell her unique feminine scent, and feel the softness of her skin. And he wanted her again. A desire for her had been created that he worried would never wane. Painting Gabrielle had been sheer madness, but with the way he felt last night, he would have gone mad *not* painting her.

He returned to the picture and covered it before turning to leave the loft. It wasn't until he spotted Gabrielle's desk that he realized that he hadn't seen her all day. "On a date," he said aloud to himself, shaking his head at her attempt at deceit as he jogged down the stairs two at a time. There was no way Gabrielle was on a date after the night they had shared. He knew she was trying to demonstrate that his seduction of her was nothing for him to feel remorseful about.

Maxwell had just reached the bottom of the steps when the front door opened. His eyes immediately filled with heat at the very sight of Gabrielle in a black V-neck sweaterdress that clung to her curves like a second skin. "Gabby," he began, hating himself for his thoughts of pulling her sweater dress up around her waist and sitting her down atop his hard shaft.

She looked up at him and then stepped aside to allow someone else to enter. "Hi, Maxwell. I'd like you to meet Miguel."

Maxwell's eyes cooled considerably as he sized up the tall Latino helping Gabrielle take off her matching jacket.

"Miguel, this is my boss, Maxwell Bennett," she said, reaching back to lightly grab his hand and pull him forward.

Maxwell's eyes dropped to catch the move and then chilled several degrees further.

What the hell is she up to?

Chapter Eleven

"Oh, *gracias*, Miguel," Gabrielle sighed after he fed her a piece of Addie's pecan pie from his dessert plate with his fingers.

"You are welcome, *excitante*," he told her with the most exquisite Spanish accent.

"What does that mean again, Miguel?" Gabrielle asked, leaning in close to his classically handsome face with lean lines, dark coloring, and supple lips.

"Sexy," he told her with a low growl.

When she looked away from his dreamy hawklike eyes of the deepest ebony, she found both Maxwell and Addie staring at them. Addie's mouth was slightly open as she leaned forward as if she too wished to be fed by a beautiful Latin man, while Maxwell's face was so tight he looked like he just sucked on lemons.

Serves his butt right, Gabrielle thought with pleasure.

"Addie, dinner was delicious as always, but we really have to be getting along," Gabrielle told them, placing her hand on Miguel's shoulder as she rose.

"Where you two headed?"

"We're going to do the forbidden dance at a salsa club in the city," Miguel said, reaching out to lightly caress Gabrielle's cheek.

Maxwell dropped his napkin atop his uneaten food. "Gabrielle, can I talk to you for a second before you go?"

"Sure," she agreed, watching him as he strode out of the kitchen. "Miguel, excuse me for a sec?"

Gabrielle headed out of the kitchen and smiled when she overheard Addie ask her date, "So Miguel, any more like you for a more *mature* lady?"

The door to Maxwell's den was open so Gabrielle headed in that direction. As soon as she stepped into the room, the door slammed shut behind her. Gabrielle whirled. "Maxwell, what on earth is wrong with you? You were rude to Miguel all night long."

"I don't give a damn about Miguel," he told her tightly before grabbing her by the waist and yanking her body close to his and capturing her mouth in a hot kiss.

Gabrielle tried hard to resist him, pushing her hands against his broad chest and leaning back.

Maxwell was relentless. He bent his body to conform to hers as he released all the want and frustration he had for her into the kiss.

Gabrielle weakened when his tongue traced the contours of her lips with slow ease and his hands lowered to pull her dress up around her waist to massage her fleshy buttocks. Unable to deny the heat between them, she opened her mouth and welcomed his tongue with a high-pitched moan, raising one of her legs to circle his legs.

Maxwell pulled her thong aside and delved first one and then another finger into the hot recesses of her core, wincing at her tightness around his fingers. When he used those fingers to stroke up into her, he grunted as Gabrielle began to work her hips against his hand.

Gabrielle took the lead and suckled his tongue with deep motions, rushing her hands under his shirt to tease his hard nipples with eager fingers that drove him wild.

Maxwell used one strong arm to pick Gabrielle up off her feet, and she immediately wrapped her shapely legs around his waist. His other hand fumbled as he clumsily tried to undo his belt. With a swoosh his slacks and silk boxers dropped to become an ebony puddle around his feet. His erection stood out awkward and heavy away from his body.

All Max could think of was burying himself deeply into Gabrielle. He was hooked, and there was no way he could deny it.

"I'm all out of condoms," he whispered harshly against her quivering lips.

Gabrielle froze, her mouth still locked with Maxwell's, but her eyes immediately shot open as she looked frantically about the room. *Gabrielle, what are you doing!* her brain screamed.

"Put me down, Maxwell," she muttered after she'd wrenched her lips from his. She pulled her hands from under his shirt to push against his shoulders with persistence. All she could think of was him being with someone else last night since he had not slept at home.

Maxwell began to cool and felt himself slipping out of her spell when she unwrapped her legs and dropped to her feet before him. He immediately reached down to jerk his boxers and pants up around his waist, being careful of his erection as he zipped them.

"Excuse me, my date's waiting," she said coldly, angry at herself as she walked past him toward the door.

Maxwell turned and grabbed her elbow in his firm grip. "Just what kind of game are you playing, Gabby?"

"What do you mean, Maxwell?"

"One second you're hot and horny in my arms, and the next you're leaving to go on a date," he chewed out, his eyes turbulent.

"It was a weak moment, nothing more," she told him, attempting to pull her elbow from his grasp.

Maxwell tightened his grip. "Is this big show with Miguel all about me saying we wouldn't work out in a relationship?"

"No, that most certainly is not what this is about. I got just what I was looking for last night and nothing more. Am I to forever stay indebted to you, or is it that once a woman is made love to by Maxwell she's spoiled for any other man for all eternity? Get real, Maxwell, and stop acting like a big baby."

"I'll stop acting like a baby if you stop acting like a—"

Gabrielle's eyes chilled. "Like a what, Maxwell? Huh? What am I acting like?"

He released her elbow and walked away from her. "Look, Gabby, I'm just trying to understand what the hell is going on here."

"What's going on is that you are keeping me from my date with Miguel," Gabrielle said as she turned and opened the door. "So if there's nothing else, let me be on my way so I can keep acting like whatever it is you didn't have the balls to say."

She walked out of the room, softly closing the door behind her.

Maxwell poured himself a glass of Crown Royal, sipped from it, and then flung it into the unlit fireplace in frustration.

Gabrielle walked back to the kitchen, hating the angry words that she and Maxwell had just shared. Where would their friendship and work relationship go from here? Every bond between them seemed irrevocably damaged.

"Addie, where's Miguel?" Gabrielle asked as she entered the kitchen.

"He said he would wait in the car."

Gabrielle nodded. "Well, I better go. Get home safely and I'll see you in the morning."

"Hold on there, Gabrielle Dutton," Addie called to her while wiping her hands on a dish towel.

Gabrielle turned. "Yes, ma'am?"

"What's going on with you and Maxwell?"

Gabrielle's eyes became alarmed as she looked over at the older woman. "Me and Maxwell? Nothing, why?"

Addie gave her a one-eyed stare. "Oh, *something* in the milk ain't clean."

Gabrielle grabbed Addie for a hug and a kiss on her soft cheek. "You worry too much, Addie."

"Something in the milk ain't clean," Addie repeated.

Gabrielle pulled on her jacket as she left the house through the front door and ran down the stairs to hop into Miguel's car.

"Thank you so much, Hector. I really appreciate

your pretending to be my new boyfriend," she gushed when the passenger door closed behind her.

"So that's the love of your life?" he asked her as he pulled the car to the gate.

Gabrielle nodded. "Big jerk."

"Big *jealous* jerk," Hector said with a laugh.

"Well, I'm just glad Clayton had a good friend in D.C. who was willing to pretend to be my Miguel. Thank you again."

He did a Z-snap and smiled back at her. "We girls do what we have to get our man, sweetheart."

Gabrielle was able to show him a weak smile while inside her heart was shattering like broken glass. "You know what, Hector, a night of salsa dancing sounds like just the cure for the common heartache. Let's go."

"Girlfriend, you ain't said nothing but a word."

Maxwell was in his bedroom packing for his flight to San Diego the next day when he heard steps pass his room and continue up the stairs to the loft. He paused, folding his boxers, dropping them into the open suitcase on his bed. He strode out of the room and took the stairs to the loft as well. It could only be Gabrielle. The same Gabrielle he hadn't seen for two days straight.

Maxwell entered the loft and found her sitting at her desk looking absolutely gorgeous, with bronze chandelier earrings dangling from her ears down to her shoulders and a matching necklace. "Hello, stranger," he said, going to stand before her desk.

"Hey," she said, seeming distracted as she stared down at her open calendar.

"You know I'm not paying you to gallivant around town with Miguel," he began, angry and not even trying to hide it.

Gabrielle licked her glossy lips and looked up at him, having to divert her eyes because he stood before her sans shirt with his jeans slung low on his narrow hips. "I took two days off to handle some personal business, Maxwell. I left you a note explaining that. I didn't know you would have a problem with it, so I apologize for any inconvenience my absence brought you. If you would like to dock my pay, please do so, although I do believe I am entitled to sick leave." Her words were so cool and calculated, as if prepared, and dismissive, as if he was interrupting her.

"I hardly consider fawning over a new boyfriend as personal business."

Gabrielle leaned in close to him as she folded her hands atop the desk. "What's wrong, Maxwell? Mad because I'm not fawning all over you?"

"I didn't know it was so easy for you to jump from one man to the next."

Gabrielle stood up and swung wildly to slap him. But he caught her wrist, going around her desk to jerk her body close to his. "Does he make you come like I did?" he asked, his voice low as his cool breath fanned against her lips.

Gabrielle hated that she was shivering in response to him.

"Does he make you forget the night we shared so easily?"

Gabrielle stiffened her spine and met his bold

look, her face just inches from his as their hearts pounded in unison together. "Isn't that what you wanted me to do? Forget it?" she asked.

"Yes. But I can't," he admitted roughly, before he captured her lips with his own.

Gabrielle couldn't fight him. She didn't want to. So when his tongue plunged between her lips she freely offered her tongue to him for his doing. And she whimpered as he suckled it like he was trying to free nectar from the sweetest of fruit.

He released her arms to circle her waist and massage her full bottom in the snug khaki capris she wore and then press her lower portion intimately close to his. "You feel that?" he asked her thickly, kissing the length of her soft neck.

Gabrielle nodded, moving her hands between their heated bodies to massage the full length of his erection in his baggy jeans. "God, it's so hard," she whispered against his mouth before hotly licking his full bottom lip while working to unzip his pants and free his hardness of its constraints.

Maxwell used both his hands to pull Gabrielle's white form-fitting T-shirt over her head and to fling it away. He dropped to his knees weakly as he grasped the bottoms of her breasts, which remained covered by a sheer brassiere of delicate yet erotic pale pink. He lowered his head and sucked deeply of one nipple through the material, loving it when she arched her back for more and pressed her hands to his head.

"Yes, Maxwell. Yes," she sighed, feeling so aroused by the feel of his mouth on her throbbing nipple that she lost track of time and space.

"You're like a drug, Gabrielle," he whispered

hoarsely as he worked to undo the clasp of her bra.

Gabrielle frowned through the haze of desire that she was under.

"I can't fight this. I try to, but I can't fight wanting you," he said as he slipped the bra down her arms and flung it over his head.

"Wait a minute. Hold up, hold up. Wait. Just wait," she begged in a whisper, pushing his face from her breasts and then covering both with her forearms.

Maxwell looked up at her, surprised that she was calling a halt to their passion. His eyes were dazed with lust.

And Gabrielle knew that was all it was, just lust and nothing more. Love wasn't part of the equation. *Not for Maxwell, anyway.* "Since you want to fight this and can't, I'll help you," she told him succinctly, moving away to retrieve her bra and blouse. "I'm not here to satisfy your lusts and then listen to your regrets later."

Maxwell stood up and his pants and boxers fell around his waist as his erection hung strong, long, and curved away from his frame. "Are you accusing me of using you?" he asked coldly while reaching down to jerk up his pants and to fight his erection back inside them.

Gabrielle turned her back to him as she pulled on her bra, fastened it, and then pulled her blouse over her head. "What I'm saying is that you're full of you-know-what, Maxwell," she snapped, turning to face him with angry eyes and searching for her jacket. "You want to want me, but you don't want to. So that means you're allowed to give in to your addiction as long as you beg forgiveness later. First the night of your dinner party, then the night I brought Hector—"

"Who?" he frowned.

Gabrielle flushed at her slip. "Miguel's middle name is Hector," she lied. "Like I was saying, Maxwell, grow up, get sane, buy a clue. Do whatever it takes so that you can not act like a jackass."

"Oh, and I guess Miguel is the epitome of a real man?" he bit out, his hands on his hips as the erection continued to bulge against his zipper. "All he wants is to get you into bed."

Gabrielle's face became incredulous. "And that makes him different from you in what way? Listen, if the only thing you're looking for is a piece of tail like a nasty slut puppy, why don't you go running off to Penelope? I'm sure she's more than willing to be your *sexual healing*."

"Maybe I'll do just that," he told her coldly as he strode out of the room and slammed the door behind himself.

Gabrielle took fast steps after him, swinging the door open wide. "Make sure you give Penelope as good as you gave me," she yelled down the stairs, even as tears flowed down her face.

Maxwell didn't pause in his steps. "Believe me I will," he yelled back.

Seconds later his bedroom door slammed.

Gabrielle slammed the door to the loft.

Penelope entered Maxwell's suite in the hotel in San Diego, carrying a basket of goodies with her. Maxwell wouldn't arrive for another hour, and that gave her just enough time to get this thing started between them once and for all. She had begun it by coming on to him in her office that day, and he had almost taken the bait. Now she felt it was time to kick the door off the hinges.

The first thing out of her bag of tricks was a package of tiny tea candles, which she positioned and then lit around the entire suite, including the bedroom and bathroom. Next, she removed the sheets from the bed, replacing them with her personal red satin ones, and laid her black silk teddy atop them. She placed Barry White in the CD player, hit PLAY, turned his sexy music low, and put him on REPEAT. While she waited for the Jacuzzi bathtub to fill, she called room service and ordered up champagne and chocolate-covered fruit. From the bottom of her basket she pulled out her last item, her Kama Sutra kit filled with all kinds of sexual goodies to tease, tantalize, and tame any man. She placed that on the floor by the bed.

"It's time to show Max what a *real* woman can do," she spoke aloud while looking around the bedroom to survey her handiwork.

Penelope overheard snippets of Maxwell and Gabrielle's heated argument on the staircase, so she was quite aware that *something* had happened between them. Whatever it was, it hadn't brought them any closer, and thus she considered it irrelevant.

No, Maxwell was hers to be had.

Maxwell didn't go straight to the hotel after landing in San Diego. His thoughts were filled

with Gabby and he needed a diversion before he
drove himself insane. He caught a cab to the his-
toric Gaslamp Quarter in downtown San Diego
to oversee the setup of his paintings and sculptures at the gallery.

For the rest of the day, he decided to tour the
area, which was an eclectic mix of cultures. He enjoyed a succulent steak during his late lunch at
Greystone on Fifth Avenue before beginning to
cruise the many shops lining the sheets.

When he walked into a shop specializing in cus-
tom-made jewelry, he immediately spotted a
turquoise necklace that would perfectly suit the
white V-neck dress Gabrielle had worn the night
they first made love. Even though they had exchanged angry words, he bought the costly piece
on impulse. She would either accept it or accuse
him of paying for her sexual services. Maxwell
didn't know what to expect from her these days.

As he left the store with his purchase and continued walking, he thought about the roller coaster
of emotions that woman had him on. This was the
first time he actually found himself angry at
Gabrielle, and the truth of the matter was that he
was so pissed because of imagining her making love
to another man. He couldn't get the vision of her
being wild and uninhibited with Miguel out of his
mind.

She was right: just because he himself didn't want
to want her, why was she supposed to put her life on
pause for him? But the question was, if he didn't
want to be the man in Gabrielle's life, why did he
care so much who was?

Penelope stretched on the satin sheets on Maxwell's bed as she awakened from her impromptu nap. She hadn't realized that she'd fallen asleep waiting on him to arrive. She lifted her head from the pillow to look at the clock on the nightstand.

It was nearly four o'clock; Maxwell's plane should have landed around eleven. Alarmed that he might have missed his flight or worse, she scrambled off the bed to pull her cell phone from her purse. First she tried dialing Maxwell's cell phone, but the call went straight to voice mail. She dialed the house phone next.

"Maxwell Bennett's. Gabrielle speaking."

"Gabby, do you know if Max caught his plane to San Diego this morning?"

"Don't worry. He's on his way to you with my blessings," Gabrielle snapped.

"I understand your being upset because Max and you didn't work out, but there's no need to be hostile with me," Penelope said cattily, relaxing back on the bed.

"Who said there was a Maxwell and me at all?"

"Well, Max told me about what happened between you two the night of the dinner party."

"He what!"

"Yes, he wanted my forgiveness, and I told him that I agreed that you threw yourself at him."

"I threw myself at him?"

Penelope smiled like a Cheshire cat at Gabrielle's anger. "Whatever your little thing was is irrelevant to me. Max and I are going to be together and that's that."

"Oh. I guess that's why he was begging me for some this morning before he left?" Gabrielle told her with petty satisfaction. "You two losers have a wonderful life together."

Penelope held the phone away from her face as Gabrielle slammed the phone down. *"C'est la vie,"* she sighed as she ended the call.

She tried Maxwell's cell phone number again, this time leaving a message on his voice mail. Next she double-checked with the airlines that his plane had landed safely. When that was confirmed, she tried the gallery and was relieved to find that he had been there and gone.

"He'll be here soon," she promised herself. "And this time I won't take no for an answer."

Gabrielle was so mad and so hurt that Maxwell would divulge what had happened between them to Penelope that she swore she would strangle him until his very head popped off his neck. Any doubts she might have had at the validity of Penelope's statements never arose. How else could Penelope have known about it?

That slick wanna-be Picasso, that played-out son-of-a— The phone ringing cut off the rest of her thoughts. Thinking it was Maxwell returning her dozen angry voice mails left on his cell, she snatched up the phone. "Hello?" she snapped, her eyes blazing for battle.

"Gabrielle? Dang, who got you so pissed?"

At the sound of her sister's voice, Gabrielle sank to the sofa of her living room and let her head fall into her hands. "Penelope claims Maxwell told her that we slept together because I threw myself at him," she said, her voice weary and filled with pain.

"That's messed up. Are you sure?"

Gabrielle didn't realize she had begun crying until she tasted the salt of her tears. "How else could she know that we slept together if he didn't tell her?"

"Didn't you say she's always hanging around the house, and didn't you also tell me that you and Maxwell argued because he felt guilty over taking your virginity? Was she there that day?"

"Yes, but—"

"Yes but nothing, Gabrielle. This oh-so-wonderful Maxwell that you've been bragging on for years doesn't seem like the type of person to put his business or yours in the street."

Gabrielle wished she had April's way of always seeing the glass half full.

"I'm telling you I know the tricks that are played and the tricks that play them."

"Maybe he does want her. I don't know."

"Listen, if she does know that Maxwell slept with you just under a week ago, why in the world does *she* want him? And if she does know and is that desperate that she doesn't care, what type of woman is she? And what man is going to school his new woman on someone he just slept with? That's something you hide, not something you provide."

Gabrielle's head felt like it was spinning as April continued her tirade.

"All I'm saying is something about the whole thing don't make sense, and before you start to swinging on Maxwell, I'd slow my roll."

"If he did tell her or he didn't, I don't care because that's not even the worst of it. I mean, I am in love with this man, and no matter how much I hang around here, he's never going to love me the same way. I feel pathetic."

"Oh, Gabrielle," April sighed in sympathy. "So Hector pretending to be Miguel didn't work, huh?"

Gabrielle laughed bitterly. "Oh, it worked enough for Maxwell to want to sleep with me again. I was going for the whole picture and I messed up. Maxwell and I can never go back to the way we were. Now I don't even have him as a friend anymore. I should have just left well enough alone."

"So what are you gonna do, kid?"

Gabrielle shrugged as her eyes looked off into the distance. "A part of me wants to pack my things and run before he gets home. Ape, I never felt so lost and so out of control of my life," she told her in a whisper as she sniffed back the tears. "Loving somebody who doesn't love you the same way sucks, big time."

"I wish you were here so I could give you a big bear hug and feed you Oriental Oodles of Noodles."

Gabrielle actually smiled. "Don't talk too soon. I might be there sooner than you think."

"*Mi casa es su casa,* little sister."

Maxwell walked into his suite and immediately froze in the doorway at what he saw. Candles were everywhere, there was a trail of rose petals leading to the bedroom, and the faint sound of Barry White was a soft serenade. For a second, he thought that Gabrielle had flown out and planned this surprise for him, but common sense prevailed. There was no way Gabrielle would go to all that effort after the angry words they shared the previous day. No, this was Penelope's little scene for seduction, and Maxwell wasn't even in the mood.

Quietly he backed out of the suite, his garment bag still hanging from his finger behind his back, and closed the door. He picked up his packages from the hall floor and quickly walked to the elevator, smiling at a couple who stepped out of it and looked at him oddly. He hit the lobby button frantically, praying for God to be with him as he fled. He said a thank-you to the Great One above as the door finally closed and the elevator went down.

When it came to a stop on the lobby floor, Maxwell thought he would get another room in the very same hotel. But thinking of Penelope's persistence, he instead walked straight out the front door and signaled the doorman that he needed a taxi.

One pulled up seconds later, and Maxwell climbed into the back, leaning forward to instruct the elderly driver. "Take me to the Wyndham at Emerald Plaza."

"Yes, sir," the man replied, pulling his taxi into the traffic. "Nice hotel. Isn't it like a couple hundred bucks a night?"

"Trust me, with my life, I need and deserve it."

Chapter Twelve

Maxwell checked into a room at the Wyndham, had dinner at the hotel's restaurant, and enjoyed a hot bath before calling Penelope to let her know that he wouldn't be staying at the suite. He was embarrassed for her and had delayed the inevitable as long as he could.

"Max, I had a surprise for you," she whined after he gave her the news.

Yeah, so I saw. "Oh, I'm sorry, I didn't know. I just decided to stay with a friend."

"A female friend?" she asked.

Maxwell's eyes went to the ceiling as he swirled his snifter of brandy and relaxed in the lounge chair. "Does it matter, Penelope?" he asked pointedly.

"I just thought we could enjoy this beautiful suite . . . *together*," she said sultrily. "I was going to show just what you've been missing. And trust me, a good time was to be had by all."

"But we've already discussed this, Penelope, and I thought we decided that it was best that we keep our relationship platonic," he stressed, not wanting to hurt her feelings but wanting his intent to be clear.

"No, I think *you* decided that, and I don't know

why you're fighting what's between us," she insisted in soft tones that he could tell were forced. "Are you scared of all this woman? Please don't be, Max."

Maxwell knew that whatever she felt was between them was all in her head. He felt the annoying heat of her pursuit and definitely wanted out of the kitchen, by any means necessary. By rule, he didn't like to lie, but how could he say: "Penelope, I don't want you, so get the hell over it"? That would be too harsh, and he was never one for confrontation.

"Hold on one sec, Penelope," he said, setting his snifter on the table beside the chair and placing his hand over the mouthpiece just enough. "I'll be right there," he yelled across the empty room. "Listen, Penelope, I have to go. We're going out for drinks." He winced as the lies continued to roll off his tongue with the ease of water.

"Oh, where are you going? I could stand a night out on the town, and I could meet you there."

Maxwell swallowed his irritation. "Actually, it's a strip bar, but if you're into that kind of thing . . . Hey, to each his own."

"No thanks, I'll pass," she snapped.

"I gotta go," he told her again. "See you tomorrow at the reception."

"But Max, what about—"

He disconnected the line before she could offer herself up again. The woman was relentless in her pursuit, and she was beginning to annoy the devil out of him. She was an excellent consultant—very skilled and knowledgeable with great contacts on both coasts. If she could just get it through her thick skull that he was never going to sleep with her, they would continue to enjoy a profitable working relationship.

Sighing, Maxwell picked up his drink and looked down into swirling depths of the amber liquid. His gut clenched because the color was the exact hue of Gabby's beautiful eyes. Eyes that he would give anything to see smile at him again.

One night of incredible passion had destroyed a friendship. He was the older more mature one. He should have been in better control of his desires. He had taken Gabrielle's innocence, which he ironically considered himself to be protecting from men just like himself. "I let a sexy dress and a new hairdo steer me from what's right," Maxwell murmured into his glass before sipping deeply of it.

But if the truth was to be told, he knew that his attraction to Gabrielle had begun long before her makeover. How could he not admit it after his erotic dream of Gabrielle astride him in his bed? That was the closest he had been to an actual wet dream since he was twelve. He desired her, but he had never planned on acting out on that desire.

Gabrielle's makeover, though, had given her a new confidence, and her flirtations had driven him so mad that all he could think of was having her, right then, and to hell with the repercussions of their actions. And the night had been incredible. Gabrielle's passion and ardor had equaled his own. Her flirtatious and sexy style had drawn him until he was captivated by her. And her sex had him so sprung that he wanted no one else but her.

Right then his want of her rose in his loins, and he wondered how he could continue to work with her and damn near live with her when he couldn't keep his hands off of her. Where would their friendship and working relationship go from now on?

He was determined not to have sex again with Gabrielle. He couldn't because he knew that she deserved and probably wanted far more than he had to offer. He was not the marrying type. He liked his life the way it was—his home, his rules, his hours, *his* way.

Maxwell used his free hand to rub the stress from his eyes as he grimaced. He missed her terribly, and he hated the way they had argued the day before. He had to mend things or at least try. Lifting his hips up a little off the chair, he pulled his cell phone from his belt clasp and flipped it open. He frowned when he saw that it was turned off. He must have forgotten to turn it on when he departed the airport.

He pressed the power button and soon saw that he had a dozen voice mail messages. He hit the buttons to retrieve them, placing the cell on speakerphone as he did.

Maxwell deleted Penelope's voice mail without a second thought. His brothers had called to tell him they would make it to the reunion in May. He nodded at that bit of info. *I'll call them when I get back home,* he thought, hitting the button for the next message.

His face went from nonchalance to confusion as Gabrielle's angry voice echoed into the quiet of the room. One message later, she called him everything but a child of God and ranted about Penelope's telling her that he'd told Penelope about the night they made love.

Shaking his head for clarity, Maxwell hit the button to replay Gabrielle's first message.

Maxwell Bennett, you got some nerve telling Penelope that you slept with me because I threw myself at you. You better be glad you're not here, because I would plant my foot so deep in your behind that you'd think we were Siamese twins. . . .

Maxwell winced as she let loose a string of expletives that would put a sailor to shame. He flipped the phone closed and set it down next to his drink.

He had to take a moment to think it through. Penelope obviously told Gabrielle that he'd told her about what happened with Gabrielle. Penelope also told Gabby that he told her that Gabrielle threw himself at him. A bunch of he say, she say—something he abhorred.

Maxwell reached for the cell phone again and dialed first his house and then Gabrielle's, not getting an answer at either.

He would get things straight with Gabrielle and try like hell to mend their friendship. He also planned to deal with Penelope because he'd had his fill of her. One thing about Maxwell, his patience with people was much more tolerant than most, but whenever he'd finally had enough, it was definitely enough.

That night Gabrielle made the hardest decision of her young life. She was moving to Georgia. She had made up her mind. Although it was the most difficult thing she ever could do, she knew it was for the best. Their intimacy had made it impossible for her to love Maxwell and not be loved back by him.

She knew that she couldn't continue on the way that they were. Six years of friendship and a great working relationship gone in one night.

Gabrielle folded her new clothes and placed them in the open suitcase on her bed. Her old clothes had already been boxed and sent to Goodwill that morning. A moving company would arrive tomorrow to place her large pieces of furniture in storage. Those items that came with the cottage, she had covered with drop clothes to protect them from dust.

"Gabrielle, what's wrong with your phone? What on earth are you doing, Gabrielle Dutton?"

Gabrielle looked up to see Addie standing in the doorway of the bedroom. "I unplugged it and I'm moving back to Georgia with my sister." She answered both questions with a soft smile that didn't quite reach her eyes.

Addie's face moved from confusion to disbelief and back to confusion as she began to wring her hands together and walked into the bedroom. "Without telling me or Maxwell?"

Gabrielle dropped the T-shirts she'd been holding onto the bed and stepped over the boxes in the middle of the floor to pull Addie's short frame into a warm embrace. "I'm going to miss you, Addie," she whispered while tears gathered in her eyes.

Addie hugged Gabrielle's slender frame back fiercely as she too let her tears fall. "What's going on, Gabrielle?" she asked as they pulled apart.

Gabrielle shrugged. "Just time to move on, Addie. I can't work as Maxwell's assistant forever."

Addie didn't believe her and it showed.

"Haven't you always told me to get a life of my

own? Well, now I am," Gabrielle tried to explain as she turned to finish packing.

"I'm sorry that things didn't work out between you and Maxwell," Addie told her softly, with eyes that were far too wise.

Gabrielle diverted her face. "What do you mean?"

"I overheard your argument on the stairwell before Maxwell left for California, Gabrielle," Addie admitted quietly.

Gabrielle feigned nonchalance. "It's no big deal, Addie."

"Then why are you leaving if it's no big deal?"

"It's all a mistake that I'm trying to correct."

Addie stepped over the boxes to stand beside Gabrielle. She glanced sideways at her as she helped her fold the pile of clothes jumbled in the center of the bed. "Running away never solved anything," Addie said.

"What should I do, huh, Addie? Stay here and watch him party away his life and chase women?" Gabrielle asked with impatience, dropping the shirt she was folding and letting her head fall into her hands.

"I knew it. I saw it all these years, and I thought maybe I was just imagining it."

"Saw what?"

"You're in love with him aren't you?" Addie asked her, pulling Gabrielle's hands away from her face.

Gabrielle looked into Addie's concerned eyes and was unable to deny the truth. "So much that it hurts," she admitted in hushed tones.

"Ooh, poor baby," Addie sighed, moving the suitcase back so that they could sit on the bed.

Gabrielle leaned sideways and let her head fall into Addie's lap as her tears flowed like waterfalls.

Maxwell was not enjoying the reception for the opening of his exhibit. He had been unable to reach Gabrielle to set things straight, and he knew the evening would end horribly because of the conversation he planned to have with Penelope. Pulling the strings on his art career was one thing; dabbling in his personal life was entirely another. *Speak of the devil,* he thought as he sipped deeply of his champagne, watching Penelope advance toward him over the rim of the flute. He had been short with her, rude even, but the woman just couldn't take a hint.

"Another successful outing, Max. Aren't you pleased?" she asked excitedly and clutched his forearm with both her hands.

Maxwell's eyes pierced into her as he purposefully removed her hands.

Penelope's eyes widened at his blatant denial of her touch. "Is something wrong, Max?" she whispered, her eyes shifting around the room to see if anyone had noticed his bold and direct act.

"I'll talk to you later," he replied in a cold voice, directing his gaze away from Penelope.

Her spine stiffened. "If there's something you want to tell me, you can tell me now."

At her persistence, Maxwell again felt like fleas were nipping at his neck. He glanced down at his watch and then at the slowly thinning crowd in the gallery. It was near the end of the reception. *Now's as good a time as any.*

"You're fired," he said flatly.

Penelope did an actual double take. "I'm what?"

"Fired. Discharged. Released of your services. Don't need you no more. Bye-bye," he told her, leaning his head down so that she could see he meant business by his tumultuous, angry eyes.

"What is going on, Max?" she hissed, grabbing his arm to pull him behind her outside the gallery.

"Listen, I hired you to help direct my art career, not to get your behind up in my personal business. I told you before to not even go there when it came to Gabby."

Penelope felt alarmed by his behavior. Never had she seen such anger in the man. "I haven't a clue what you're talking about," she said with a weak smile as a couple walked past them on the sidewalk.

"You told Gabrielle that I discussed something personal about her with you, and that's a lie," he told her, his voice clipped as his jaw clenched and unclenched.

"I did no such—"

"Don't lie, Penelope," he roared.

Her eyes fluttered as she leaned away from him.

"Now it's up to you whether you stay for the remainder of the reception or not, but your services are most definitely no longer needed in *any* capacity," he told her, rudely raking his eyes over her body before he turned and walked back into the gallery.

Penelope looked over her shoulder and saw that several of the gallery's patrons were glancing out the window at her and whispering. She notched her head up high, placed her beaded clutch under one arm, and hailed a cab. She was glad when one rolled to a stop in front of her and she was able to climb in and speed away from the openly gawking eyes.

Gabrielle walked slowly through the cottage, which now looked like a ghostly version of its former self. She had six years of memories that she would carry with her always. She had to fight back sorrowful tears as she let her hand trail across the back of the couch where she and Maxwell had enjoyed some exciting moments.

She picked up her purse and walked to the front door. When she awoke in the morning she would be in a new environment, starting a new life in a new place. The hardest fact to face was that she would never see Maxwell again.

The cab waiting outside for her on the lawn blew its horn. She breathed deeply, and her chest heaved with emotions as she opened the door and hit the switch to turn off the lights. She allowed herself one more glance before shutting the door. She climbed into the back of the cab and closed her eyes against a wave of pain so intense that it felt like a heart attack. Through her tears she looked back at her little house and then at Maxwell's large manor until the taxi pulled through the open gates and sped away up the street.

Maxwell lay nude in the middle of the bed with his eyes to the hotel's ceiling. His thoughts were filled with Gabrielle. No matter how many times he tried, she refused to answer his calls to her cottage or to her cell phone.

An idea hit him suddenly, and he rolled over to reach for his cell phone on the bedside table. Quickly, in the darkness, he dialed Addie's home number.

"This had better be either real bad or real good and nothing in between," Addie snapped after several rings.

Maxwell swung his legs over the edge of the bed to sit up on the side. "Addie, this is Max."

"Boy, do you have any idea what time it is here?"

He glanced at the clock and grimaced when 12:00 A.M. flashed in crimson red; that made it 3 A.M. back home. "No," he lied, trying to hold off some of Addie's inevitable wrath. "Addie, where's Gabby? I've been calling her but she hasn't—"

"Gabrielle's gone to live with her sister. Didn't she call and tell you?"

Maxwell's gut clenched and he felt an anxiety attack nearing. He flopped back on the bed as his free hand came up to massage his eyes.

"Maxwell?"

He began to shake his leg in his usual nervous habit as he tried to think, to comprehend, to understand the blow he'd just received. *Gabby was gone . . . for good?*

"When did she say she was coming back?" he asked.

"She ain't coming back, baby," Addie told him with sadness.

"What did she say, Addie?" he asked, removing his hand to look up at the ceiling.

"That's not for me to say. Call Gabrielle, and you two work this out, Maxwell."

"She won't answer her cell phone."

"Well, she said she left you a note in your loft," Addie added reluctantly, not quite sure that Maxwell deserved Gabby. As much as she loved him, the truth was the truth and that was all there was to it.

"Maxwell, a girl—no, a woman like Gabrielle isn't to be taken lightly. You either go all out or not at all. You understand me," she told him. "If you ain't serious, then leave her be and stick to a barracuda like Penelope."

Maxwell felt guilt claim him as he released a heavy breath. "I fired Penelope tonight. I think she's part of the reason that Gabby left."

Addie snorted into the phone. "So you finally bought a clue, huh? Well, good riddance to her little sneaky butt."

Maxwell wasn't in the mood to hear Addie sing like the Munchkins from *The Wizard of Oz* that the wicked witch was finally dead. "Addie, I'll be home in the morning."

"What time?"

"About, um, oh Lord, about, um ten I think," he said struggling for clarity.

"I'll make you that oatmeal like your momma used to," Addie told him warmly.

"Thanks Addie," he said, knowing she meant well.

"Maxwell?" she called out before he could hang up. "I love you like my own son, but remember what I told you. All the way, or nothing at all."

Maxwell didn't even bother to answer as he disconnected the line.

He tried Gabrielle's cell phone again and felt crushed when it went to voice mail. Not sure he'd be able to maintain his composure, he left no message. He flung the phone across the room, ignoring it when it bounced against the wall. As he continued to lie on the bed, sleep eluded him, and a loss like nothing he had ever known consumed him.

Gabrielle sat on the window seat of her bedroom at her sister's apartment. Her knees were bent, and she wrapped her arms around her legs, leaning against the cool glass of the window. It was nearly two o'clock in the morning, and she couldn't sleep. Her dreams were just as filled with Maxwell as her waking thoughts. Any attempts April had made at cheering her up had failed miserably until she had begged her to just give her some time to get right. Nothing but time would heal her heart.

As incredible as the sex had been, Gabrielle would trade it in a millisecond to have her life back the way it had been before. *Damn, I miss him so much,* she thought as she rocked her body back and forth on the window seat. Before she new it, the rocking gave way to crying, and soon her body was racked with sobs that caused her chest to heave.

April walked in, sleep heavy in her eyes as she crossed the room. The reflection in the mirror showed one sister wordlessly comforting the other as she wept.

Maxwell entered the loft and walked slowly over to Gabrielle's desk. *It's not Gabby's anymore,* he reminded himself as he slumped down into the chair. His eyes focused on the small vanilla envelope propped against the phone. His name was in Gabrielle's neat handwriting across the front.

Maxwell didn't know how long he sat there and stared at that envelope. It could have been minutes, maybe even hours. Part of him wanted to know what she'd written, and another part of him was afraid that reading the letter would end all ties to Gabrielle.

"You know an elevator around here wouldn't be a bad thing, you know what I'm saying?" Addie's voice boomed when she walked into the loft, breathing heavily from the exertion of the stairs.

Maxwell's eyes remained fixed on the envelope. "Gabby suggested the same thing all the time," he answered, his voice as lifeless as his soul felt.

Addie watched him closely. There was no mistaking that Gabrielle's departure had affected him deeply. "You know, Maxwell, she did what she thought she had to do," Addie began, going to stand by the desk. Her eyes took in the unopened letter with a subtle nod of understanding.

Maxwell shrugged, forcing himself to sit up straighter in his chair. "She was free to quit. Two weeks' notice would have been polite."

Addie bit back a smile. "Two weeks' notice, huh?" she asked.

Maxwell cleared his throat and looked up at the woman, whose face was entirely too knowing. "What?" he asked softly as she continued to stare at him with hawkeyed precision.

"After what happened between you two, maybe it's for the best that you two part ways," Addie said, moving around the room to inspect things.

Maxwell looked up at her in surprise. "Who—"

"If you don't want your business told, you shouldn't tell it," Addie answered before he could even ask. "You especially shouldn't argue about it in a stairwell that carries voices so well."

Their argument the morning before he left for San Diego.

"Do you love her, Maxwell?" Addie asked him, cutting her eyes over to him as she frowned at the dust accumulated on the windowsill.

"I really don't want to talk about this, Addie," he told her abruptly.

"Well, don't get snippy with me, Maxwell Bennett," Addie snapped in return, her eyes flashing.

Maxwell leaned back in the chair, folding his arms over his eyes. "Addie, I didn't mean to snap. I just need some time to think."

"You know, if you're not going to let your little cleaning crew clean in your precious loft, you really need to acquaint yourself with a dust rag," she told him saucily before heading back to the door.

"Gabby and I would have never worked out, Addie," he said suddenly, compelled to explain himself to her.

Addie paused in the doorway before turning to face him. She started to say something but changed her mind and just left the room without another word.

Maxwell stood suddenly, sending the chair flying back against the wall with force. He circled the desk, his hand massaging his chin as he stared at the envelope. Curiosity won. Reaching out quickly, he tore open the envelope and unfolded the letter before he could change his mind.

Maxwell,

I am officially offering my resignation from my position as your personal assistant effective immediately.

Gabrielle

P.S. Under the circumstances I hope you understand why I handled this the way that I did and I hope you don't hold this against me. I did not know that the one night of passion would completely destroy our friendship and any chance of a working relationship. I would gladly trade it all back for things to be the way they were before. Maxwell, there are no words to express how much I will miss you as a boss and as a friend. For my own sanity I must wish you the best and say good-bye.

Maxwell read the letter again and again until her words were etched into his memory. Her scent hung faintly to the paper and he inhaled of it deeply, wishing it was her skin.

He walked the length of the loft and stood before the covered painting on the easel. Slowly, he removed the cloth, and he wished it was Gabrielle's clothes that he was removing to gaze at her naked form. His head hung low as he pulled a chair in front of the picture and slumped down into it.

"I'll miss you too, Gabrielle," he said softly as he allowed himself to get lost in the amber eyes of his painting.

Chapter Thirteen

One Month Later

Part of Gabrielle had secretly hoped that Maxwell would fly to Georgia, proclaim his love, and whisk her back to Virginia for the whole happily ever-after. After two weeks the dream started to fade; on the thirty-day anniversary of her resignation, she let it disappear completely with a *poof*. She knew that if she was at all serious about staying in Georgia, she had to eventually find a job and get on with her life. Her substantial savings would not last forever, and hopefully, neither would her love for Maxwell.

But first she was treating herself to a sixteen-day Caribbean cruise that was scheduled to leave the next morning. She was all packed and ready to climb into her one-way rental car headed to Florida, where she was to board the cruise ship. She looked at the trip as the kickoff to her fabulous new life. Okay, maybe it wasn't so fabulous, but it was at least new.

"Rise and shine, baby sister. Rise and shine."

Gabrielle turned her head on the pillow to look at April as she strolled into the room with way too much energy for seven A.M. "Morning," she replied, her voice still heavy with sleep as she reached for her glasses and pulled them on.

April frowned at the very sight of them, pointing as if they were a venomous snake. "I thought we trashed those things."

Gabrielle sat up in bed. "I took them back out of the trash and cleaned them."

"But why?" April whined.

"Because I refuse to wear contacts just so that I can read in bed, and I still need to see until I put the contacts in, Ole Big Sister Gorgeous One," Gabrielle teased, ducking as April reached for one of her pillows and tossed it at her.

"I'm on my way to work, but first I wanted to come in and have us say a little prayer together like when we were kids," April told her seriously, holding her hand out to Gabrielle.

She reluctantly took her it. "You woke me up to—"

"Shoosh," April cut her off, closing her eyes fiercely. "Oh Heavenly Father, I come to you today for someone in need. Someone who needs Your assistance, Heavenly Father."

Gabrielle looked at her sister like she was crazy.

"I pray to You, Heavenly Father, because I believe *only* You can help this lost soul. Sweet Jesus . . . please help Gabrielle get a life—"

Gabrielle snatched her hand away and frowned, sucking air between her teeth in agitation as April began to laugh hysterically. "I have a life, thank you very much."

"Sitting on the couch all day and watching raunchy talk shows or those home makeover shows is *not* a life," April told her, turning to leave the room.

Gabrielle childishly stuck out her tongue at her sister's retreating back. "Come tomorrow I won't be sitting on anybody's couch 'cause I'll be chilling on a cruise ship."

April paused in the doorway to turn and look at Gabrielle with serious eyes. "I hope this trip helps you get over your funk about—"

Gabrielle cut her eyes at her sister, reminding her of their vow to not mention *his* name.

"Anyway, I wish I could go, but some people got a job to do."

Gabrielle had enough savings to pay for her sister to go with her, but April couldn't take that much time off from work.

"Don't wait up for me this evening."

"Who's the next victim?" Gabrielle asked snidely.

"That brother Tyrone who just started at my job. Girl, he looks like Vin Diesel and I'm for sure going to see he can show me some of the Triple X, if you know what I mean," April told her, jiggling her buttocks in her silk skirt before she squatted to the ground and got back up with a laugh. "Bye, girl."

"Bye, Ape."

Gabrielle rolled onto her side and feel back asleep for a few more precious hours before she finally rose, flinging the covers back and rolling out of bed. She took a shower, put in her contacts, and pulled on a pair of April's sweat shorts with a tank top before heading to the kitchen to fix her usual brunch of bran flakes. She was just headed to the couch for a full day of serious television watching when the doorbell rang.

Gabrielle chewed on a huge spoonful of cereal while she headed to the front door and stood on her toes to peer out of the peephole. "Who is it?" she yelled, her mouth still full.

"Fed Ex. I have a delivery for a Gabrielle Dutton."

She dropped back down on the soles of her feet, holding the cereal bowl with one hand and opening the door with the other. She nearly choked on her food when she looked up into the face of one handsome man. *Well, I'll be damned.*

"Gabrielle Dutton?" he asked, smiling a little at her reaction to him and exposing a deep and delicious dimple in his right cheek.

Gabrielle laughed nervously as she forced herself to look away from him. "I'm Gabrielle. Um, sorry. Could you set that there?" she asked him, stepping back from the doorway to point to a spot against the wall.

"Sure, if you'll just sign right here," he instructed, handing her the clipboard.

Gabrielle took it in her free hand as she watched his tall, muscular frame stoop to place the large box on the floor. When he turned to face her, she looked down at the bowl in her other hand. "Could you, ah, hold this for a sec?" she asked him.

He smiled again as he accepted the bowl.

Gabrielle returned his smile before she lowered her head to sign the spot marked with an X. She looked up at him again as they swapped the bowl for the clipboard. "Thank you."

He nodded and stepped out the door. "You're welcome, Gabrielle."

"Bye," she said softly, closing the door slowly so that she could watch him walk away.

Gabrielle knew that the box was a care package from Addie. She had spoken to her last week, and obviously Addie was living up to her promise to send a box of home-baked goodies. She had just started to open it when the doorbell rang again.

She walked back to the front door and was surprised to see the oh-so-sexy delivery guy standing on the other side. "Do I have another package?" she asked, surprised to find that she was flirting. Funny how there was a time when she would never have had the confidence to even meet his eyes, far less throw him a little coquettish rhythm.

He returned her smile. "Actually, I hope you don't think this is too creepy, but I wondered if I could have your phone number to call you sometime?"

Gabrielle was surprised. This whole male and female mating/dating thing was so new to her. *What should I do?*

"I guess I should have asked if you're married or something?" he asked, shoving his hand into the back pockets of his uniform pants.

Maxwell does the same thing all the time, Gabrielle thought suddenly. *Stop it,* her voice screamed inside her. *You have got to get over Maxwell Bennett, Gabrielle. With a quickness.*

"Yeah," she answered him on impulse, surprising herself.

He tilted his head to the side. "Yeah, you have someone, or yeah, I can have your number?"

Gabrielle reached for his clipboard, removed the pen, and wrote down her name and number for him. "Does that answer your question?" she asked.

What am I doing? I'm leaving for a sixteen-day cruise in the morning!

He looked down at it and then back at her. "Cool. I'm Brandon by the way."

"Nice to meet you, Brandon."

He pointed over his shoulder. "I gotta get back to work, but I'll call you."

"Cool," Gabrielle replied. *What the heck? I can remember boys like him never paying me any mind in school. Now check me out!*

Unashamed, she watched Brandon jog down the stairs and smiled at him when he paused to glance back at her.

Her stomach felt aflutter as she closed the door and walked back to the living room. "Just wait until Ape hears about this," she said aloud to herself as she plopped onto the sofa and picked up the remote to turn the television to her secret passion—*Surprise by Design* on the Discovery Channel.

She finished her cereal during a commercial for winter get-away cruises. "Now that's what I'm talking about," Gabrielle sighed around her last mouthful as she clearly envisioned herself cruising to the Caribbean the next day. Of course, she had put a nice dent in her savings, which wasn't exactly practical with her current unemployment status. But she felt she needed it and she deserved it, and she was going.

Finished with her brunch, Gabrielle set the bowl on the coffee table and then reached for her care package. She pulled the tape off of the box and smiled as the scent of brownies and chocolate-chip cookies filled the air. An envelope sat atop the Ziploc goodies. Gabrielle smiled at Addie's unruly hand-writing as she removed the note.

Hello Gabrielle,

I made the brownies and the cookies with extra walnuts, just the way you like them. Hope these make you smile. The house sure isn't the same without you. Have you started job hunting yet or are you still on "vacation"? That's okay if you are. You deserve it.

Remember Sister Edwards from my church . . .

The rest of the letter was filled with gossip on all of Addie's church members. Gabrielle hated to admit that she was disappointed because Addie, just as she'd done the last time they spoke, neglected to mention Maxwell at all.

She wanted to call to check up on him, but she knew that for her own well-being it was best to leave Maxwell alone and move on in life with the Brandons and whoever elses in the world.

Addie was worried about Maxwell, but she didn't let on that fact to Gabrielle. He had become as testy as an injured bear and twice as mean as a rattlesnake. He barely left the house anymore, preferring to stay locked in the loft or his bedroom. He barely ate the meals she prepared, and when he did make an appearance downstairs, he looked as if he hadn't bothered to groom himself in days.

Concerned that the dinner she'd left for him in the microwave still sat untouched when she came in the next morning, Addie immediately set about making him a steaming pot of his mother's oatmeal. As soon as it was ready, she prepared a tray with a big bowl of it with cinnamon toast on the side and a glass of fresh orange juice. Although she disliked climbing those stairs, she would willingly hike to the top of Mount Kilimanjaro to get some food into Maxwell.

"One way or the other this food is going inside him," she said aloud with meaning as she marched out of the kitchen and up the steps.

Thirty days had passed since Gabby left. Thirty nights that Maxwell fell in bed and dreamed about her. Thirty mornings that he woke up praying that he would stop missing her.

Maxwell was sure that Gabby had to have put root on him or something. How else could he explain his distraction? Here he was bordering on becoming obsessed with a young virgin.

He went to the gym and saw her face smiling back at him from the punching bag.

He tired to work, and she was there in the paints he tried to mix.

He watched television, and her face replaced that of every women who crossed the screen.

His appetite was gone.

His desire to paint was waning.

He hadn't been with a woman since his night with Gabrielle.

What next?

It was easy to admit that he missed Gabby, his feisty assistant with the big heart and even bigger glasses, but fessing up to being whipped by Gabrielle was not at all setting well with him. Unfortunately, the two were one and the same person. Yes, the sex had been great but surely he, a man who'd had his share of women—and a share of some other men—had not been thrown off course by a woman.

Maxwell had just flung his pillow across the bedroom in frustration when he heard the knock at his door. He decided to ignore it.

It has to be root.

How did she do it? Was it something she put in his food? Or some concoction in his drink? Or something in her sex that held him beguiled? Is that why she had so willingly played the seductress that night, to feed him her wicked spells from some hoodoo woman? In this day and age, anything was possible, and what other excuse could there be for his behavior?

He frowned in annoyance as his door swung open.

"You better cover up what you don't want seen 'cause I'm coming in, Maxwell," Addie called into the room from the hall.

Maxwell flung the bed covers over his nakedness and saw Addie with her eyes tightly closed, holding a tray. "I'm decent and not hungry," he told her.

Addie opened first one eye and then the other, as if she was worried that what he considered decent wasn't the same as her idea of it. "Well, tough tit 'cause you're going to eat, Maxwell," she ordered, marching the tray over to sit beside him on the bed.

Maxwell looked at Addie and was pierced by her boy-you-know-I'm-not-playing-with-you stare. "My favorite oatmeal, huh?" he asked reluctantly, pulling himself to a sitting position in the bed and setting the tray on his lap.

Addie's eyes were concerned. "You know, this is the first time in weeks I got a close look at you. You're losing weight."

Maxwell knew she was right. He was slipping. He glanced at her as he took a big spoonful of his oatmeal. "Addie, you're from the south and old—"

"Hey, watch it now," she frowned.

"I meant older than me," he told her with a smile.

"And?"

"How do you know if someone has root on you?" he asked, his voice quiet because he was embarrassed to ask.

Addie did a double take. Her face changed to astonishment. "Who you think put something on you, boy?"

Maxwell dropped his spoon into the oatmeal as he scratched his growing beard. "Gabby," he answered with the utmost seriousness as he met Addie's stare.

"And what makes you think that?" she asked, talking slowly so that he wouldn't see that she was dying to laugh at him. *Talkin' 'bout Gabrielle got root on him. Jesus, help him.*

"My appetite is gone. I dream about her all the time. I feel depressed. I don't want other women. Me! Addie, *I* don't want any other women. The girl took my nature."

Addie burst out laughing, unable to hold it in any longer.

Maxwell regretted his revelations as soon as he saw the first tear of laughter fall from Addie's eyes. "I'm glad I provided you some humor this morning," he drawled disparagingly.

Addie wiped her eyes and bit her bottom lip to stop the laughter as she looked at him. "I'm sorry, baby, but you know good and well that Gabrielle don't have no root on you."

"Never mind. I don't want to talk about it anymore," he told her, closing her out and forcing himself to finish his breakfast.

"I don't know why I didn't see it sooner. These old eyes ain't as wise as they used to be," Addie said, looking at him with an enlightened face.

"Thanks for breakfast, Addie," he told her, handing her the tray and then flopping down flat on the bed to yank the covers over his head.

"You're in love with Gabrielle, Maxwell Bennett," Addie said as she reached for the covers and pulled them away from his face. "That ain't root. That's love. Plain and simple."

Maxwell looked up at Addie. "I am not in love with Gabby. I love her, sure, she's cool, but I ain't in love with her. She needs a husband who does the nine to five and wants three kids and a dog. She and I are good friends but not relationship material."

Addie rose from the bed with the tray in her hands. "Who you trying to convince? Me or you?"

He immediately shut his mouth.

Addie walked to the door. "I thought you were a little too wild for Gabrielle. Still do. Sometimes, though, your heart chooses who you love and not your head. I still say all or nothing when it comes to Gabrielle, Maxwell."

"Nothing," he called back to her, disgruntled.

"Ever think you're so busy fightin' your feelings that you haven't taken time to take a good look at 'em?"

Maxwell pulled a pillow down over his head.

"All or nothing," she called over her shoulder before leaving the room.

As soon as the door closed behind Addie, Maxwell hopped out of bed and headed for his adjoining bathroom. He'd shave, have a shower, and then he was going to find something to do besides sulk around the house. Root or not, he was not going to let a woman—any woman—be his downfall.

Maxwell stood at the sink, deciding to shave his head clean with his clippers as he waited for the water to get hot in his running shower. "I love Gabby," he spouted at the absurd idea to his reflection. "Addie must have lost her mind."

That ain't root. That's love. Plain and simple.

"See, that's the problem with women: they confuse sex with love," he continued, pulling down his upper earlobe to shave the hair from above his ear.

That ain't root. That's love. Plain and simple.

"Who's in love with Gabby? I sure ain't," he bragged with false bravado. He smiled and winked at his reflection. "Now there's the old Maxwell. Whassup, dog?"

That ain't root. That's love. Plain and simple.

Maxwell stepped into the shower and closed his eyes at the first feel of the steaming water pulsating against his skin as he rinsed the loose hairs from his head and shoulders.

"Miss me, Maxwell?"

His head shot up and his eyes widened at the vision of Gabrielle, naked and lathered with soap, standing before him in the shower. He backed up quickly and bumped his back and buttocks smack against the unrelenting wall of the shower. She advanced on him with that same flirtatious look that had drawn him in the first time.

"You know you love me, Maxwell," she said softly as she reached below his waist and began with a wicked smile to massage his hardness.

Maxwell felt his loins inflame as his maleness lengthened and swelled with life.

"Don't you love me?" she asked him softly before pressing her soapy breasts into his chest and sucking his earlobe.

Maxwell shook his head for clarity and blinked rapidly. Sure enough, he was in his shower alone, dreaming of her, seeing her, wanting her again and again. *See what I'm talking 'bout? Root. Nothing but root.*

He rushed through the rest of his shower, annoyed that his erection would not ease as it poked like a pointed pistol through the towel wrapped around his waist.

If he was honest with himself, the reason that he had been so overly protective of Gabrielle was that he wanted her for himself, not because of some outdated idea of chivalry. "Still, that ain't love," he spoke aloud to himself as he dressed in his usual painting garb of jeans and a tank top. "That's sex."

That ain't root. That's love. Plain and simple.

Anxious to clear his head, Maxwell left his room and jogged upstairs to the loft. As soon as he entered it his eyes darted to the nearly life-size painting of Gabrielle that now took prominence on the far wall. With long strides, he crossed the floor, reached up, and took it down. He turned the painting backward against the wall.

Today was *the* last day he would sit around with

his head up his butt worrying about Gabrielle. "I need to hire a new assistant and a new consultant. Both male," he stressed as he moved across the room to sit at the desk.

No one can replace Gabby.

His eyes fell on Gabrielle's letter sitting atop the trash in the wastepaper basket. *For my own sanity, I must wish you the best and say good-bye.*

"Funny, Gabby, you left, and I'm the one going insane," he admitted aloud as he raised his hands to massage the weariness from his eyes.

That ain't root. That's love. Plain and simple.

Images of Gabrielle floated through his memory like a slide show:

Gabby smiling at one of his jokes.

Gabby throwing back her head to laugh openly.

Gabby huddled in the corner of a chair, biting her fingernail as she read.

Gabby looking up at him as she straightened his tie.

Gabby snoring in her sleep.

Gabby the night of his dinner party.

Gabby's face alive and open with desire as he stroked deep inside her.

Gabby . . . Gabby . . . Gabby.

Maxwell reached down into the wastepaper basket and removed the crumpled note. He rose from the chair and walked across the loft as he smoothed it flat.

He turned the picture around so that he was able to look into her face.

For my own sanity, I must wish you the best and say good-bye.

There, in her eyes, he finally saw what had captivated him so much about the woman. What about her appealed to him. There was no denying his memory of the emotions brimming in her luminous eyes. He saw the truth of her feelings and was unable to deny his own. Six years of memories and one fabulous night of passion.

That ain't root. That's love. Plain and simple.

"Damn," he swore.

He left the loft and raced downstairs to the kitchen.

Addie heard his steps before he came to a sudden halt in the doorway.

"What's her sister's address?" he asked, breathing hard.

She studied him with piercing eyes. "So I was right."

Maxwell stood with arms akimbo and gave her a meaningful stare.

"Why don't you just call? Gabrielle has her cell phone."

Maxwell shook his head and prayed for patience. "I'm going to go get her."

"How do you know she'll come back with you?"

"Addie, please."

"All or nothing, Maxwell Bennett?"

He locked his eyes with hers. "All," he said with meaning, letting his feelings burst like fireworks inside his chest.

Gabrielle was enjoying a few of Addie's homemade cookies with milk and watching *Trading Spaces* when the telephone rang. Wiping her hands on her sweat shorts to free them of crumbs, she leaned across the back of the couch to pick up the cordless phone.

"Hello."

"Can I speak to Gabrielle?"

"Speaking."

"Hey, what's up? This is Brandon."

Surprised that he was phoning so soon, she glanced at the clock. It read 4:30 P.M. "Hey, Brandon. You don't mess around do you?" she joked as she used the remote to put the television on mute.

Gabrielle was already regretting giving him the number. She wasn't in the market for another male mess in her life. She had yet to recover from her one-night stand with Maxwell.

"I just got off work. I'm on my cell phone."

"How long have you worked for Fed Ex?" she asked for the sake of conversation.

"Um, let's see, ever since I graduated from high school. About three years ago."

Gabrielle frowned and held the phone away from her face for a second before she put it back to her ear. "That makes you twenty or so, right?"

"Yeah."

Oh, hell, no!

Loud music started to thump in the background. "What is that?" she asked, talking louder so that he could hear her.

"Oh, my boy T-Murder is giving me a ride home. That's his system. It's off the chain right?"

"Off the what?" Gabrielle asked, confused.

"Off the chain. That means it is real nice."

She heard his friend laughing in the background. "I say like Smokey, nigga. Puff, puff, give."

Gabrielle's frown deepened as she listened to Brandon speak to his friend.

"I guess you don't smoke, huh?" he asked, sounding like he was holding his breath and trying to talk at the same time.

"No, I hate the smell of cigarettes."

"Cigarettes," he balked. "I meant weed."

"You mean marijuana?" Gabrielle shrieked, her mouth forming an "O."

"No, dandelions," he joked. "That's cool if you don't. To each his own."

Gabrielle had had quite enough. "Um, Brandon, can I call you back? I gotta go pick my sister up from work and I'm running late," she lied easily.

"Why don't you and your sister stop by my mom's?" he asked, sounding eager.

"Your mom's?" she asked, even though she feared she knew the answer.

"Well, it's my house too."

Oh, double hell, no! "I wish we could, but we're going shopping tonight. I'm leaving for a cruise in the morning," she told him, praying he didn't get angry since he knew where she lived and had a friend who actually answered to the name T-Murder. *I got the worst luck with men.*

"Oh for real, for how long?"

"Sixteen days and then . . . and then . . . I'm . . . I'm moving back to Virginia."

"Damn, that's messed up," he said, sounding disappointed. "I thought we could hook up."

"Yeah, me too, but I was just visiting my sister *and* her husband. I should've told you that."

"Hey, I know your sister April, and she ain't married."

Oh, the devil's in control now. "She just got married, that's why I'm in town. Look, I gotta go, but it was good talking with you," she rushed to say before hanging up the phone.

"The boy's still got his mother's breast milk around his mouth," Gabrielle said aloud to herself. "I have got to remember to tell Addie not to send me anything by Fed Ex again."

Chapter Fourteen

Maxwell got hardly any decent sleep last night. This afternoon he would be flying to Georgia to find Gabrielle. He couldn't deny it or fight it any longer. He placed his hands behind his head in the bed. "I love her. I love Gabby," he said aloud to himself, reveling in the way his chest felt light at the very thought of it.

Since he was able to finally embrace that fact, a lot of things over the years finally made sense to him: His insane jealousy whenever he thought a man was sniffing around Gabrielle. His desire to always have her in his presence. His protectiveness of her. His inability to focus and paint when she went to visit her sister. She was his muse, his balance, the calm to his hectic life, his one true love.

This feeling of being in love was so new and fresh to him. This was absolutely the first time he could honestly say that his heart belonged to a woman who was not his mother, one of his sisters, or the irreplaceable Addie.

Maxwell didn't want to live without Gabrielle in his life. He couldn't. He'd tried and failed. He wanted to make love to her every night. Sleep with her in his arms. Awaken to her smile. And spend the days growing to love her even more.

Does she love me? Of that he was just about seventy-five percent sure. She had given him her virginity, and sex was obviously not something she took lightly, regardless of what she'd said. Still, he wasn't one-hundred percent confident since she'd refused to give him the time of day, but he was more than willing to run behind her and throw his heart out there on the line. He could only pray she felt the same. His love for her demanded nothing less.

Brrrnnnggg.

He rolled over in bed to grab his cordless phone. "Hello."

"What's the deal, little brother?"

"Oh, it's you," Maxwell said, flopping back down on the bed at the sound of his sister Darlene's voice.

"Glad to hear your voice, too," she told him with mock sarcasm. "Who were you hoping it was, one of your newest flavors of the week?"

"Real funny," he drawled, letting his forearm rest atop his forehead.

"You need to settle down before you get too old and just fall down."

Maxwell frowned.

"You are the only one of us not married yet. What are you waiting for?"

"I'm not ready to get married. When and *if* I'm ready, I will," Maxwell insisted.

"Little brother, there is nothing wrong with loving somebody, *one* somebody, for the rest of your life," Darlene said softly, her concern for him obvious.

"Who says I'm not in love?" he asked, as he used

the remote to turn on the plasma television installed in the wall across from his bed.

"Yeah, right."

"I'll have you know that today I am going to do one of the most romantic things in my life," he boasted.

"Do tell," Darlene said, intrigued.

"I'm flying to Georgia to surprise Gabby and . . . tell her that I love her," he finished with a smile.

"Why is Gabby in Georgia?"

"She moved there after she resigned."

"Gabby doesn't work for you anymore? What happened?"

Maxwell thought about all of the intricate details. "Long story. Anyway, I *said* I'm in love with Gabby."

"So when did she quit?"

"Could you focus on the romance?" Maxwell asked, exasperated. "I *said* I . . . am in love with . . . Gabby!"

"Oh, right, okay, I'm sorry. That is sweet and romantic. And I'm happy for you, baby brother. Gabby seems like a nice girl. So when's the wedding?"

Maxwell grimaced. "I said I'm in love, not insane," he drawled as he flipped through the digital cable channels. "I'm not ready to jump into marriage."

"Let me get this straight," Darlene stated slowly. "So you're going to Georgia to proclaim your love and ask this wonderful woman to return to Virginia with you to be your employee during the day and your love slave at night. Yeah, that's *very* romantic."

Her sarcasm was not lost on him. "Who says you have to marry every person you fall in love with?"

"Are you for real?"

"All I'm saying is that this is all new to me, and

why should I rush into a legally binding contract called marriage?"

"Don't you remember that song from when we were kids? Max and Gabby sitting in the tree, K-I-S-S-I-N-G. First comes love . . . then comes *marriage*—"

"Then comes a divorce rate of over fifty percent," Maxwell interrupted dryly.

"Little brother, you might want to rethink running to Georgia with an offer of *dating*."

"No, not just dating. A completely monogamous relationship between two people who are in love and want to enjoy each other's company," Maxwell insisted.

"Ooh, yes, I wish I was Gabby. To hell with a wonderful marriage and commitment. Let's just shack."

Maxwell did assume that Gabrielle would merely move into the house with him and that they would begin their move from friendship to relationship. What was wrong with that?

"Enjoy your cruise, Ms. Dutton."

Gabrielle smiled at the steward as she boarded the cruise ship. "Thank you, I will," she told him softly, pulling her carry-on bag behind her as she followed his directions to reach her stateroom.

She squealed in delight at the first sight of it. There was a private balcony with comfy lounge chairs that she immediately crossed the room to enjoy. As she leaned against the rail, she inhaled deeply of the scent of the ocean and felt excited about the adventure she was about to embark upon. This trip was the start to her new life.

Gabrielle took her time unpacking, hanging each

item in the closet as she hummed a tune. When she came to the lovely, and dry-cleaned, white dress she'd worn *that* night, she couldn't help but think of Maxwell.

All the memories of the night came flooding back to her in a rush. His initial reaction to her. She had seen it in his face: the surprise and then the desire. It had made her bold, coy even. She knew that he wanted her just as much as she wanted him. Him making sure that she sat next to him at dinner. His eyes locking with hers as they talked and flirted like she had always dreamed. Even her embarrassing scene, crashing into one of the servers.

I was lucky the dry cleaner got the wine out, she thought with a laugh as she turned to hang the garment in the closet.

She had been so bold that night, first telling him to kiss her and then actually planting her lips on his first. And then the night of passion had begun.

Come for me, girl. Come for me.

Gabrielle actually felt herself shiver as she remembered his hotly spoken words to her as she did just as he bade. That night had been better than all her erotic dreams of Maxwell over the years combined. He had lived up to her fantasies. Lived up to them and surpassed them.

But for her it was about more than sex. She wanted more than his male anatomy, as beautiful and satisfying as it was. It was his heart she wanted. She needed it.

Shaking off any tears before they welled up in her eyes, Gabrielle decided to finish unpacking later and reached in her overnight case for her string bikini. Quickly she changed, still not believing she had let April talk her into purchasing the skimpy thing. She surveyed herself in the mirror lining the wall over her bed and actually giggled.

There was a time when she wouldn't have dared wear something as revealing as this. Her last bathing suit had been a tank top and a pair of trunks that no longer fit Max.

The suit was a pale peach and the perfect complement to her bronzed caramel complexion. The top cupped her plum-sized breasts perfectly, and the bikini was cut so low on the hips that Gabrielle was glad for her Brazilian bikini wax. She slipped on clear high-heeled sandals that April had let her borrow and grabbed a sheer wrap, just in case some old geezers were looking for a free peep show.

Using her map of the boat, she made her way to the Lido deck and settled into a lounge chair with a contented sigh. The sun blazed against her skin and the gentle breeze from the ocean tickled it as well. *All's well that ends well.*

Gabrielle was reaching into her oversized beach bag for her book and shades when she looked up and saw a couple, so obviously in love, stroll past her on the deck. The brother's head was just as shiny as Maxwell's own dome.

She ached for him, wishing their "thing" had worked out so that they could cruise to all the wonderful destinations on the itinerary together. Exploring Aruba. Sightseeing in Acapulco. Shopping in Puerto Vallarta. Diving off the cliffs of Cabo San Lucas. All with Maxwell.

"Get it together, Gabrielle," she told herself, literally trying to shake off her sadness as tears threatened to fill her eyes. "I am not lonely, just alone. And there's a difference."

She cleared her throat, slipped on her shades, and forced herself to enjoy the sun and get lost within the pages of her latest Jordan Banks mystery novel.

Maxwell was frustrated. Everything seemed to be stepping into his path to Gabrielle. Not wanting to leave any of his cars at the airport, he called for a cab to drop him off. On the way there, the cabbie was rear-ended by another car at a light. To be honest the car had barely bumped the bumper, but the cabbie refused to move his taxi until the police arrived. Needless to say, once Maxwell relayed his opinion of the events to the police officer and hailed another cab, he had missed his flight.

He was able to get on the next flight, nearly three hours later. Not wanting to risk going home and returning in time to make it, Maxwell hung around the bustling airport instead. He had never drunk so much cappuccino and filled out so many crossword puzzles in his life. Nor had he ever realized that thirty minutes of listening to one baby's whiny cry was akin to fingernails being dragged across a chalkboard. He had been more than happy to see that family board their plane.

Finally, when he was able to board and claim his seat in first class, he was mortified when the man in the seat next to him proceeded to go straight to sleep and snore like a bear in hibernation. It truly took the cake when the man's head rolled over to lightly land on Maxwell's shoulder. All he could do was pretend to stretch and send the man's head

rolling back the other way, where he then proceeded to drool.

There was a delay in the departure, and so his
one-and-a-half-hour flight stretched into three
hours of pure torture.

The plane finally landed safely, and Maxwell
grabbed his carry-on bag and flew off the plane as
soon as he was able, only to discover that the garment bag he'd checked was now M.I.A. He could
only laugh as he filled out the appropriate forms with
airport personnel. "What next?" he asked himself.

Being splashed with dirty curb water by a cab
pulling away from the terminal, that was what.

So it was with wet pants and an almost mental
breakdown that Maxwell stepped out of the cab in
front of Gabrielle's sister's apartment in Savannah,
Georgia. He glanced at his watch only to see that it
had stopped.

Maxwell's eyes shifted up to the sky, and he
frowned at the dark clouds forming. He could
smell imminent rain in the air.

"With my luck today, no one's home," he muttered darkly as he climbed the stairs searching for
April's apartment number.

Considering that he hadn't bothered to book a
hotel in his eagerness to get to Gabrielle, her not
being home as rain threatened to pour definitely
not a good thing. "Uh, it's 2G. This is 1G and here
we go . . . 2G," he said as he stopped in front of the
door.

He knocked three times.

"Who is it?" a female voice asked.

"It's Maxwell Bennett."

He saw the peephole at the top of the door darken, so he smiled and waved.

"You're Gabrielle's boss. Uh, ex-boss," the voice said.

"Yes, is Gabby home?" he asked.

The next apartment's door opened and a tall, fair-skinned brother walked out, dressed to the nines in a three-piece suit that Maxwell immediately recognized as a Sean John. "What's up, man," he greeted, as the man's eyes fell to his wet pants.

"What's up?" he was greeted in return.

"Hey, Clayton," the female voice cooed from behind the door.

"Hello, Ape," Clayton said over his shoulder without breaking a stride.

Maxwell's head swiveled to look oddly at the man. *That's the Clayton that Gabby told me about?*

"Um, Maxwell, Gabrielle's not here," April told him through the door. The eye was still pressed to the peephole.

"Listen, would you mind opening the door? I feel a little silly talking to a peephole."

Seconds later the peephole lightened and the door opened slowly.

Maxwell looked down at a shorter and curvier version of Gabrielle. "Hello—April, right?"

"Hello," she told him coolly.

Maxwell felt chilled to his toes. "Can you tell me when Gabrielle will be home?"

"In two weeks," she answered with a frosty demeanor.

So Gabby's filled her in, huh? If the sister's this angry I could only imagine how pissed Gabby is. "Two weeks?" he asked in confusion.

"What happened to your pants? Couldn't hold your bladder?" she teased with an arched brow as she leaned against the door.

"Listen, April. I've had one hell of a day to get here to find your sister. I mean you cannot imagine the things I have gone through and ignored so that I would complete my task of coming here. I don't mean to be rude, but my patience has been worn just a tad bit thin today. So I must ask you to please at least extend me the courtesy for my oh-so-long travels and answer my question, which I will restate. *Where* is Gabby?" Maxwell inhaled a deep breath as he peered down at April with pensive eyes.

"She left for a sixteen-day cruise this morning," April answered finally.

"Damn," he swore, his streak of bad luck continuing.

"What exactly do you want with my sister, Mr. Bennett?" April asked as she folded her arms over her chest and looked up at him with eyes that were so much like Gabrielle's.

"I need to talk to her."

"A whole month and you finally got *something* to say to her, huh? Took you a whole month to get your line together?"

"Is Gabby as mad at me as you appear to be?" he drawled.

"Madder."

"Damn," he swore again, not sure what his chances with Gabby were now.

"What do you have to tell her so bad that you came all the way to Georgia?"

Maxwell looked directly in April's eyes with the utmost seriousness. "That I love her."

* * *

"Gabrielle. Gabrielle. Wake up, baby. I've come for you."

Gabrielle blinked rapidly as she awakened from her nap. Her vision focused and she started in surprise to see Maxwell kneeling beside her bed. "Maxwell?" she asked softly in disbelief, propping herself up on her elbows.

He climbed onto the bed beside her and immediately took her slender frame into his arms with a fierceness.

Surprise and pleasure filled her as she hugged him back. "Oh, Maxwell, I knew you would come for me."

He reached for her chin with his hand and tilted her face up to his. "How could I let you out of my life?"

His lips touched hers for a precious peck before deepening to plunge his tongue into her mouth to tango slowly with her own. Gabrielle's body instantly reacted to him and she felt herself purr in the back of her throat as she let her hands slip beneath his shirt to massage his nipples at leisure.

Maxwell moved his hand from her hip to caress her breasts with a warmth that caused her body to shiver. She whimpered as his fingers teased, rolled, and tugged at her nipples as he sucked deeply at her tongue as if he drew life from it.

"Ms. Dutton? Ms. Dutton. Are you all right?"

Gabrielle opened one eye and peered straight up into the face of one of the cruise bartenders. She smiled weakly at him as she realized that she had fallen asleep on a poolside lounge. She looked to her left, and an elderly woman with liver spots and over-sized shades smiled at her.

Her brain was a little fuzzy from being jarred out of her sleep, but she recalled having a rather erotic dream about Maxwell where she was moaning and . . . *Oh Lord, they heard me carrying on with Maxwell in my dreams. How embarrassing.*

She looked up a the bartender again and then back over at the older woman whose smile broadened until Gabrielle could almost count every one on her false teeth. "I'm fine, thank you," she told the bartender, sitting up straighter on the lounge chair.

"Can I get you something to drink?" he asked with a polite smile.

"I'll have another virgin margarita," she answered, picking up her book from where it had slipped onto the floor.

"And you, ma'am?" he asked the older woman.

She snorted. "Give me *whatever* she's drinking," she teased, jerking her thumb over at Gabrielle.

Again, Gabrielle felt her face warm in embarrassment.

Maxwell and April were at an impasse.

April refused to contact Gabrielle or to even tell Maxwell which cruise she was on. Maxwell refused to leave, determined to gain this woman's trust and in the process have his shot at winning Gabrielle back. The only reason April didn't throw him out was that it was raining cats, dogs, and every other animal outside.

"Listen, April," Maxwell began, moving to sit on

the edge of the chair as he met her gaze. "I can't wait two weeks for Gabby to return."

"So I should just call her back from her trip?" April asked in astonishment. "She's in the Caribbean! Seeing exotic places, eating fantastic food, and hopefully meeting all the buff, bronzed, and beautiful Caribbean brothers she can."

Maxwell's gut clenched at the very thought.

"My sister has put her life on hold for you ever since she met you. For once in her life she's doing something just for her, and you want to take that from her," April told him. "If your love is so great it should last longer than sixteen little days, Maxwell."

"Tell me where she is and I'll go to her."

"No."

"Damn it, April, why are you being so stubborn?

"Because I held my sister while she cried over you, that's why," April told him angrily, as she pointed her finger at him accusingly.

Max felt remorse over Gabrielle's tears.

"If I had known that giving her the makeover would lead to her hurting so much, I would have left her just how she was. In the end, all she wound up with was a sad heart and a wet behind."

"That's a little ridiculous," Maxwell drawled.

"That's life; deal with it."

The doorbell rang and April rose. "Let me see who this is."

Maxwell had said all the right words, made all the right motions, but the woman was even more stubborn than Gabrielle. She was not going to budge. It was looking like he was going to have to head home and wait until she returned from her cruise.

"Who is this?" a beefy male voice asked with plenty of attitude.

Maxwell stood and turned, his eyes level with a man's chest. Slowly he raised his head to look the man in the face, until he felt the back of his head was going to touch his back. "Maxwell Bennett," he said cordially, holding out his hand. When the man looked down at it like it was a vile thing, Maxwell stiffened his back. "Nice meeting you," he muttered dryly.

"Tyrone, this is my sister's friend, Maxwell. They broke up, and he didn't know she went on the cruise when he came here from Virginia to make up with her."

"Oh . . . okay," the large man replied.

"You mind if I use your phone? I want to make airline reservations," Maxwell interrupted.

"Sure, use the one in Gabrielle's room," April told him, pointing to a closed door down the hall. "Heading home, huh?"

Maxwell nodded as he turned to leave them alone and stride to Gabrielle's bedroom.

As soon as he stepped into the room, he was surrounded by the scent of Gabrielle. He inhaled deeply of it as he looked around the room. Her scented candles were everywhere, and there were books stacked on her nightstand nearly as tall as the lamp. Sitting in front of the books was a tiny crystal picture frame atop a notepad.

Maxwell walked over to the bed and sat down on the side. He picked up the frame and immediately noticed Gabrielle's neat script on the notepad. There in black and white were her travel plans. She was cruising on the Carnival *Paradise* departing from

Miami, Florida. He felt like he'd won the lottery and had to keep himself from giving out a hoot of joy.

He looked down at the photo in his hand and saw that it was a picture of himself. "Don't worry," he said aloud, not even bothering with the house phone as he reached for his cell. "I'm on my way, baby."

Maxwell scrolled through his phone book and hit the button to automatically dial his own travel agent back in Virginia.

"Elaine? Hi, this is Maxwell Bennett. I need a favor."

Thirty minutes later she had reserved a flight out of Savannah International Airport to Atlanta, where he had a room reserved at the Sheraton. The next afternoon, he had a flight out of Atlanta to Aruba—the first port of call for Gabrielle's cruise ship.

Closing his cell phone, Maxwell sat the frame back by the bed and stood. Using a curved finger, he pulled back the sheer curtain and was glad to see the sun now blazing in the sky. The rain had ceased.

Maxwell took in the light and airy decor of the small bedroom. "Nice room, Gabby, but I know something much better," he said aloud, confident that her belongings would soon be back in Virginia.

He picked up the apartment's phone and called the number he'd seen on the side of the cab that he caught from the airport. "Fifteen minutes," he said aloud to himself.

"Yes, Tyrone. You better work it, boy," April's voice echoed through the wall.

Maxwell frowned.

The pictures on the wall began to rattle and flap where they hung as something solid loudly banged against the wall.

Maxwell's face changed from confusion to shock.

April let out a high-pitched moan, and the banging increased in speed and vigor.

Maxwell headed out of the bedroom, not wanting to be a player in something that could've been one of those cheap porno videos. "April, I'm going," he called out, already walking to the front door. "Don't break the headboard," he hollered with a smile before he closed the front door behind himself, thinking, *they could've waited until I left.*

The phone rang for what seemed like forever. Finally giving up on trying to reach her sister, Gabrielle hung up the phone. *At nearly seven dollars a minute, maybe it's good she didn't answer,* Gabrielle thought with a laugh as she picked up her Bath & Body Works lotion and began rubbing some of it onto her hands.

She reflected on the days ahead as she turned off the light and snuggled down under the covers. The day after tomorrow the ship would anchor in Aruba, and Gabrielle already had her day planned. She was going to fill it and her mind with any and everything so that thoughts of Maxwell had nowhere to reside.

If only I could be so strong in my dreams.

April awakened from one of the deepest sleeps of her life. She lifted her head from the pillow and looked at Tyrone sleeping heavily on his back. The man put it down in the bed like he was a recently released prisoner. Once they were done, all she could do was fall asleep and hope to recoup.

She winced as she rose from the disarrayed bed

and pulled on her robe. The sun was gone, and there was an evening chill. Nearly seven hours after Tyrone first carried her over the threshold, April left her bedroom.

Of course Maxwell was gone, but she looked in on Gabrielle's room anyway. She spotted a notepad lying in the middle of her bed spotlighted by a ray from the full moon and walked into the room to pick it up. With it in her hand, she reached down to bathe the room with light from the lamp on the nightstand.

"No wonder he hightailed it out of here," she said aloud as her eyes skimmed over Gabrielle's traveling plans. "So he's on his way," she said, wondering how to deal with the new bit of information.

Okay, she believed he loved Gabrielle. And she *knew* that Gabrielle loved the handsome bastard.

"Let him find Gabrielle, and she'll make her own decision. She's grown," April said, throwing the pad back onto the bed.

"April, where you at, baby?"

She smiled, thinking the echo of a man's voice sounded good in her apartment. "I'm coming baby," she called back, closing Gabrielle's bedroom door behind her.

"Not yet, but you will be," he told her as she walked into the bedroom.

Tyrone sat in the middle of the bed, holding his fully erect maleness in his hand with a wicked smile.

April smiled seductively, licking her lips eagerly as she untied her robe and let it slip from her body. *Lord, give me strength.*

Chapter Fifteen

Aruba was even more beautiful than Gabrielle had imagined. The waters were turquoise, the sand she spotted in the distance was almost as white as rock salt, and the air was invigorating. She walked off the balcony back into her suite to grab her sun hat and purse from the foot of the bed before strolling out of the cabin. She felt as if her sandaled feet never touched the deck as she joined the line of people leaving the ship to enjoy hours of fun in beautiful Aruba.

"Enjoy Aruba, ma'am."

Gabrielle turned her head and smiled at the deck steward, who then tipped his hat to her. "Thank you. I will," she answered, her voice excited.

The port bustled with activity, and Gabrielle was ready to get into the mix. She was all about sightseeing, shopping, and exploring today. She'd hunt for some shot glasses for Addie, buy April something wicked, and then focus on herself. She refused to be sad. She refused to miss or even think of Maxwell Bennett.

"Gabby."

Her steps leading her deeper toward the market faltered at what she thought was Maxwell's voice.

"Get real, Gabrielle," she muttered. "Aruba is a Maxwell-free zone."

"Gabby."

A warm hand grasped her waist, and Gabrielle's heart pounded wildly as she whirled around and found herself face-to-face with Maxwell.

He smiled at her and used one strong arm to pull her body close to his. "God, I missed you Gabby," he murmured, his hand racing up her nape to pull her head toward his. "I missed the hell out of you."

Gabrielle's body shivered from head to toe, and she hated the tears that threatened to fall. "What in the world are you doing here, Maxwell?" she asked, with pleasure and surprise.

"I love you, Gabby," he whispered fiercely against her mouth just before his lips captured hers.

Gabrielle jerked her head and body back until she felt she could almost bend over backward to touch her head to the floor. She let her hands rise to his shoulders as she gaped at him. "You . . . you . . . what? What did you just say?" she asked him in a soft voice as she pummeled his shoulders with her fists, her face disbelieving.

Maxwell laughed and let his hands clasp against her lower back, drawing her back to him. "I said I love you, Gabby. I love you. I came all the way to Aruba like a nut just to tell you that I love you."

Gabrielle's knees felt weak and shaky, and she was glad that Maxwell supported her with his strength or she would have fallen to the street like a mound of Jell-O. "You . . . you love me?"

Maxwell nodded as his eyes scanned over her beautiful face.

But something had been nagging and eating

away at her and she *had* to know the truth. "The night after we made love you didn't stay home, Addie said, and then you showed up the next morning with Penelope. Were you with her that night?"

Maxwell looked confused. "Gabby, I said I love you."

Gabrielle waved her hand dismissively. "Yeah, I got that. Now answer me."

"I was up in my loft all night, painting. Penelope came over that morning, and we were downstairs going over contracts."

Relief flooded her on *that* point, but she wasn't done yet.

"And," he began, when he saw the fire still in her eyes, wanting to cut her off before she even began to chew him out. "I fired her for lying and telling you that I told her about the night we shared together. She must have overheard us talking, but I swear to you I didn't tell Penelope about any of it. She was a little more determined than I thought to snag me. I wasn't interested then and I'm not interested now."

"No more Penelope?" she asked excitedly.

Maxwell smiled broadly. "No more Penelope," he promised.

Gabrielle's breathing was heavy and her chest heaved as she looked up into his face and locked her eyes with his. She saw the love there in the cocoa depths. She'd waited and dreamed six long years about this very moment, but Maxwell's surprising her in Aruba surpassed all of her wild imaginings. "Six long years, dammit. What took you so long?" she teased with a smile, sniffing back tears and playfully swatting at his head. "By the way . . . I am loving the bald head."

"Come here, girl," he said low in his throat, finally capturing her mouth in a kiss.

His tongue traced her bottom lip and then her top before he teased her own tongue into a slow, heated drag. They clasped each other tightly, not caring that they were in the middle of a crowd as they savored a kiss that was filled with all of the love they had for one another.

"I still cannot believe you're here," Gabrielle told Maxwell, as they walked into his hotel suite together, laden with bags from a day filled with shopping and sightseeing. "I can't believe we're together and that we're in love and . . . and I'm turning my back on a fifteen-hundred-dollar cruise."

She felt overwhelmed by everything and it showed on her face when she slumped onto the plush sofa. Maxwell dropped down beside her and then pulled her into his lap to cradle her. "I'll take you on an even bigger and better cruise," he promised, nuzzling his face against the softness of her neck as she wrapped her arms around his strong neck.

Gabrielle closed her eyes and let her head fall back to revel in the light kisses he placed from her chin to her shoulder. "That feels divine," she purred like a kitten being stroked.

Maxwell laughed lightly. "Does it?"

"Um-hum," she sighed, nodding softly.

"I know something that feels even better," Maxwell told her, slipping his hands up her leg and under the hem of her dress. His journey continued until his fingers lay beneath the lacy trim of her panties.

Gabrielle gasped at the first feel of his fingers playing in her moist flesh. "I thought we were going to talk?" she asked even as she opened her legs a little wider on his lap.

"Okay. It's up to you," he told her, slipping first one and then another finger up inside her core to massage the walls deeply. "Talk now or talk later?"

Gabrielle's hips arched to meet his fingers, and she quivered in his arms. "Later," she whispered, tilting her head up to lock her lips heatedly with his own.

Nothing but the sound of Maxwell undoing the zipper of her strapless cotton dress echoed in the room. Gabrielle stepped off his lap and let the dress billow to a white puddle around her feet. Dressed in nothing but her high-heeled sandals and a sheer black thong, she backed into the bedroom, curling her finger for him to follow her.

Maxwell stood, reaching in his wallet to pull out a condom. He threw the billfold onto the couch and placed the protection between his teeth as he rushed out of his clothes, leaving them in a heap before the sofa. Nude and erect he followed behind her. *Well, I'll be damned,* he thought at the first sight of Gabrielle naked and on her knees in the middle of the bed.

She looked behind her and then wiggled her booty. "Come and get it, daddy," she said playfully with a lick of her lips.

Maxwell dropped the condom from his mouth into his hand, tearing the foil and strapping on their protection as he strode over to her. He climbed onto the bed behind her, his erection leading the way. He reached out and lightly rubbed her core, wincing at the wetness he discovered. "What you doing so wet, huh?" he asked throatily.

Gabrielle just moaned at the feel of his magic fingers.

With one hand massaging her buttocks and lower back, Maxwell used his other hand to guide his sheathed thickness inside of her core slowly. They both gasped hotly. Pausing with just the throbbing tip planted within her walls, Maxwell's body tensed as he struggled for control. "Damn, it's so tight, Gabby," he told her through clenched teeth.

Gabrielle bit her bottom lip and burrowed her head into the pillows.

As his climax eased away, Maxwell slid inch by delicious inch of hard length inside of Gabrielle until the majority of him was fitted with her walls like a sheath. She began to work her hips and Maxwell lightly touched her lower back. "Not yet, baby. Not yet. Please," he begged, feeling so very close to spilling his seed. He let his head fall back and his eyes shut.

Gabrielle quivered from just the feel of him stretching and pushing against her walls with strength and steely hardness. With his rod planted deeply within her, she rose off her elbows, sighing as his arms wrapped around her waist and pressed her back to his muscled chest. Her head fell back against his shoulder, and she let one arm rise to drape behind her on his other shoulder.

Finding the control he needed, Maxwell let his hands drop to Gabrielle's waist as he slowly circled his hips, sending his shaft inside her with mind-blowing tiny strokes. "Work back, baby. Nice and slow," he instructed in her ear before lightly biting the lobe.

Gabrielle began to circle her hips in perfect sync with his, her mouth gaping open when one of his hands lowered to tease the throbbing bud between her open legs. "Oh, Maxwell," she groaned as a fine sheen of sweat covered her body.

Maxwell eased his other hand from her waist to cup a breast, his fingers skillfully teasing her hard nipple. "You like that?" he asked.

Gabrielle nodded, glad that his body supported hers from behind as they made the most sensual slow love ever. "I love it," she told him in a rush and meaning it.

The feel of his hardness throbbing inside of her. The tiny hairs of his groin tickling her backside. The feel of his chest against her back. His hands lightly teasing both her bud and her nipple. All of it was pushing her very quickly to the first delicious wave of release, and she *wanted* to come. She felt it rising and welcomed and craved the feeling like it was a drug. "I'm gonna come, Maxwell," she told him in a raised voice as her body began to tingle and her hips jerked of their own accord.

"Come for me, baby. Come on," he demanded softly, increasing the temp of his strokes and reveling in the way her bud swelled and thickened under his fingers. "Come on."

Gabrielle howled out harshly with the first burst of white-hot spasms. She felt unable to take it all, and she tried to move from Maxwell but he tightened his grip on both her breast and her core, locking her into place. Gabrielle felt out of control of her body as she began to wildly jerk and thrash with her release. "I'm coming. Oh God, I'm coming," she cried loudly.

Maxwell felt his own climax building inside him, and he lowered them both to the bed. There he lay atop her back and grabbed her hips from the sides as he worked his hips at a fast pace that soon had him yelling out and quivering with his apex. "I love you, Gabby," he murmured against the side of her face.

"I love you too, Maxwell," she answered before falling into a deep sleep.

"This is our first date," Gabrielle told Maxwell as she sat across from him in a Caribbean restaurant.

"It is, and you never looked more beautiful," he told her, reaching under the tablecloth to massage her inner thigh.

She flushed under his praise as the candlelight flickered in the depths of his eyes. "Thank you," she told him softly, letting the love she felt for him glimmer in her own eyes. "Are you saying that because you picked out this lovely ensemble and purchased it for me?"

"What other choice did I have with all of your clothes still on board the ship?" he mused.

"You should have thought about that before you whisked me away," she countered with a smile, coquettishly flipping her hair away from her face. "The ship doesn't leave until ten, and it's just after five. We have time to pick up my things after a little nap."

"You really are beautiful, Gabby," Maxwell said with an intense look in his eyes.

"You just refuse to call me Gabrielle, don't you?"

Maxwell nodded.

They fell into a comfortable silence as they both looked about the elaborately colorful restaurant.

"I can't believe that we're doing this. This . . . us," Maxwell told her. "But it feels so right."

"We should have done it sooner."

"I agree."

Gabrielle picked up her flute of champagne and raised it in a toast to the man she loved with every inch of her heart. *Finally, he's mine.* "To us."

Maxwell raised his flute as well. "To love."

"God, we are *sooo* corny," Gabrielle said with a smile before she took a deep sip of her drink.

Maxwell laughed as well, the lines at his eyes deepening. "Yeah, that was a little corny."

Gabrielle looked down at her dinner of *shrimp in coco.* The shrimp cooked in a mixture of coconut milk and brandy and then topped with coconut flakes looked delicious. "Maxwell, this looks wonderful," she sighed. "But do you know what I wish I was doing right now?"

Maxwell met her look with a question in his eyes.

"Riding you," she told him huskily.

Maxwell held his hand up and signaled for their waiter. "Check please."

"When did you know you first loved me?" Gabrielle asked Maxwell a couple of hours later as they lay tangled among the sheets on the bed.

His hands massaged the length of her arm where it lay against his chest. "I think I've loved you since the first time I saw you at the Art Expo, but it was

Addie, believe it or not, who made me realize just what I was feeling for my little Gabby."

"Addie?" she asked in surprise, tilting her head up off his chest to look at him.

Maxwell smiled as he placed a kiss on her forehead. "I thought you had root on me, girl. I couldn't eat, sleep, think. I was pretty much jacked up around that house."

"Root?" Gabrielle shrieked, poking him in the ribs.

"Ow," he yelled, tightening his grip around her.

"I don't deal in root, thank you very much," she told him, laying her head back down on his chest. "I just got some good stuff."

Maxwell tickled her sides and Gabrielle burst into uncontrollable giggles.

"I dreamed about us making love before I even saw your makeover, you know," Maxwell said after they settled back into each other's arms.

Gabrielle frowned. "Yeah, right," she muttered against his chest in disbelief.

"I did," he insisted as he played in her riot of curly hair. "I loved you even then, and I just didn't want to face it. I hated to think of you on that date with the psychiatrist."

Gabrielle began to laugh.

"What's so funny?"

"The psychiatrist, or head doctor as Addie called him, actually turned out to be an employee for a lawn-care company named Hedge Doctors."

Maxwell laughed. "Good ole Addie."

"And he had the audacity to offer to clean my pipes."

"What?" he asked, serious now.

"That's nothing. When I was in Georgia I gave my

number to this Fed Ex guy who delivered my care package from Addie. Turns out he smokes weed, lives with his mama, and has a friend named T-Murder or something like that."

Maxwell's body went still.

Gabrielle looked up at him and was surprised to see that he was obviously angry. "What's wrong?" she asked, puzzled.

"So you were living it up in Georgia?" he asked her.

Gabrielle's face became enlightened as she shifted her body so that her face was closer to his. "You're *jealous*. Oh God, I love it, love it, love it," she told him, planting tiny kisses all over his face until the angry line dissipated.

"So were y'all dating or something?" he asked, sounding like a disgruntled child.

"God, no," Gabrielle exclaimed. "We talked just that once on the phone. It was no big deal, Maxwell."

"I hate to think of somebody all over you."

"Imagine how I felt, loving you and watching Penelope damn near throw her cha-cha at you like a ball every day," she told him.

"From now on it's just me and you," he told her, rolling them over in bed so that he lay atop her.

"Forever and ever," she said, burying her face into his neck. "You know Acapulco would be a great place for a honeymoon . . . or even a wedding."

Maxwell was placing a love bite on Gabrielle's delicate shoulder, but he froze at her words. His sister's words of doubt floated back to him with way too much clarity. *Little brother, you might want to re-think running to Georgia with an offer of dating.*

Gabrielle immediately noticed the change in him. "What's wrong, Maxwell? Why are you so tense?"

"No reason," he replied, forcing himself to relax as he continued to kiss her.

Gabrielle made a weird face. "Why did you get tense when I mentioned a honeymoon or a wedding?" she asked him, placing her palm against his forehead to dislodge his lips from her shoulder.

"I didn't."

"You did."

Maxwell rolled off of Gabrielle to lie on his back, letting his forearm rest atop his forehead as he released a heavy breath.

Gabrielle pulled the sheet up around her chest, sat up in bed, and looked down at him. "You thought I was trying to get you to propose, and you got tense. I mean you felt like dead weight lying on me for a second there."

His silence was damning, but he wouldn't lie to Gabrielle.

"So you love me, but you wouldn't marry me?" she asked in disbelief.

"Gabby, don't you think it's too soon to talk marriage? I love you. I mean I *really* love you—"

"But you want to put a deadline or an end date on this relationship before it even begins?"

"I didn't say that. Gabby, where are you going?" he asked as she flung back the covers and rose naked from the bed.

"What are we doing? What is all this, Maxwell? A game? What?" she asked, searching beneath the blankets on the floor for her underwear.

"So you're saying right now, this minute, if I asked you to marry me, you would?" he asked.

Gabrielle rose with her panties in her hand and

locked her eyes with his. "In a heartbeat," she told him softly with meaning.

Maxwell looked at her in amazement. "I'm not saying that I would never marry you. I'm just not ready to be married right now, but that doesn't mean that I don't love you."

A sole tear slid down Gabrielle's cheek as she looked at him with pained eyes. "So you're saying right now, this minute, if I asked you to marry me you wouldn't?" she asked him, flipping his own question on him.

Maxwell rose from the bed and came to pull her stiff body into his arms. "Gabby, I love you so much and I want to be with you. All I'm saying is let's take things slow and get to know each other as more than just friends."

"Okay . . . okay, I understand," she told him in a dry tone, her arms still at her side.

"Good," he said, kissing the top of her head.

She let him lead her back to the bed, but she climbed under the covers and rolled over onto her side away from him. She felt numb. When Maxwell rolled over behind her to wrap his arm around her waist, she let her eyes close and hoped for anything to take away her disappointment.

"Did you enjoy your day in Aruba, ma'am?"

Gabrielle handed the steward the card that the cruise line issued to her as proof that she was a passenger. "Yes, I really didn't want to leave," she said, her thoughts filled with Maxwell. She just thanked God that she hadn't canceled her trip prematurely.

He handed her back her card. "Enjoy the rest of your evening."

"Thanks," she told him softly as she boarded the ship.

In her cabin she immediately slumped against the door. Her eyes ached from crying, and her stomach was a pit of nerves. *Had she made the right choice? Did she do the right thing?*

Only time would tell.

Maxwell rolled over in his sleep and immediately reached for Gabrielle, but she wasn't there. Only a piece of paper lay in her place. He snatched up the note and then leaned across the bed to turn on the night lamp.

Maxwell:

I must admit that your words of love made me happier than anything else in this world. I have dreamed of being able to express my feelings for you for what seems like forever. Finally, I could hold you and tell you I love you without any shame, fear, or doubt, because I do love you, Maxwell. I have loved you from the first moment I saw you, and I am not ashamed to admit that I would love nothing more than to be Mrs. Maxwell Bennett.

It confuses and hurts me to know that you love me but not enough to make the ultimate commitment to me. I can't help but question the depth of your feelings. I don't think that you believe in our love like I do.

I'm not saying this is the end of us, just a little

break to give us both time to see what exactly it is we want from one another. Will it be your way or mine?

I'm going to finish my cruise. I hate that I snuck off, but I knew you would never let me go. Please give me this time to think because I feel like getting seriously involved with you is a risk I'd be taking with my heart. I don't want you to love me only until you feel it is time for you to move on. I love you much more than that.

I probably won't call you from the cruise. Do not meet me at the next port, Maxwell. Please be patient with me like I've been patient with you all these years. Remember that I love you, Maxwell. And please be good (smile). Lots of XOXOXOs to you, my love.

Your Gabby♥

Maxwell read her words three times before he finally set the letter down on the nightstand. He knew without a doubt that he had messed up . . . again. He climbed out of the bed that felt all too empty without her in it and reached into his open suitcase to pull out a pair of jeans. He slipped them on before moving to the hotel balcony to brace himself against the railing. His eyes were troubled as he looked at the calm harbor. The same water that helped carry Gabrielle away from him.

"Damn," he swore, knowing that he had put his foot in his mouth big time. There was a very good possibility that he would never have this incredible woman back in his life. But was marriage the only answer.

Will it be your way or mine?

Although he had every intention of having

Gabrielle in his life, marriage had not been a part of his plans. Now he might have no other choice. Is *this* what Addie meant by all or nothing? He had assumed that his words of love and fidelity to Gabrielle were enough.

Maxwell sat on the balcony long into the night, looking at the situation from every possible angle. He ran over the pros and the cons of marriage. Then he ran over the pros and cons of marriage to Gabrielle, which was an entirely different thing. The pros definitely outweighed the cons on that one.

Gabrielle was not just the woman he loved. She had been his friend and his confidante for six years. Although they had only been on their first date tonight, they had a history, a chemistry, a relationship that was based upon their friendship. They got along well. Some of the best moments of his life had been spent with Gabrielle at his side, supporting and cheering him on.

Maxwell looked out at the ocean blanketed by night. He liked his life the way that it was. Uncomplicated. With a wife came responsibilities, compromises . . . changes.

No more parties.

I did say I was tired of them anyway.

No more painting at odd hours of the night.

Gabby already knows that I do that.

No more other women.

Hell, I've lost my taste for anyone else ever since Gabby.

No more getting up and flying off at a second's notice to sightsee the world.

Gabby could fly away with me.

No more . . .

No more?

No more excuses.

For the life of him Maxwell couldn't find any other reason *not* to share his life with Gabrielle.

Will it be your way or mine?

Clearly, he could remember the time Gabrielle had told him of her dream wedding. The memory came back to him in a rush.

It would be a small wedding, probably in a garden, with lots and lots of lit candles. The people I'd invite are there to be happy for me because they love me and not to just gawk. I'd have lots of gardenias, including one in my hair. And everyone, even the guests and my future husband, would wear white. The reception would be kind of casual just as the sun sets, with a buffet of good old-fashioned southern food and lots of soul music. And our first dance would be to "Always and Forever."

Maxwell could see the vision so clearly: he was the groom standing at the end of the aisle waiting for Gabrielle, his soon-to-be bride, to come to him.

Will it be your way or mine?

"Yours it is, Gabby."

Chapter Sixteen

Ten Days Till I Do

"Maxwell, you know you're insane, right?"

Maxwell looked at Simone Love, the event planner, who sat, along with Addie, at the island in his kitchen. "Why?"

Love's mouth shaped like she was going to say something, but she stopped herself to frown and then held up a hand, which she then dropped. "You really want to plan a wedding in eleven days?"

"Ten," Maxwell corrected her.

They looked at each other across the island. Her face was amazed. His was blasé.

"And the bride?"

"Doesn't know," he answered her matter-of-factly.

"She . . . she . . . ah, she doesn't know. Okay then, um. Will she be in attendance?" Love asked lightly with a nervous smile.

Maxwell released a heavy breath, glanced over at Addie and then back at Love. "I sure hope so."

Love could only look at him oddly.

"I think it's romantic to surprise her with a wedding," Addie added, looking at Maxwell with pride. "Don't worry, *she'll* be there."

"And what of the marriage license?" Love asked, positive that Maxwell was out of his mind. "Even though Virginia does not have a waiting period, she *does* have to be in attendance to apply for the license with you before they will issue it."

"I have all that under control."

She arched a questioning brow. "Okay, well first thing is for you to show me where you want to hold the wedding, and then I'll try to take all of her ideas that you told me about and make them happen . . . in ten days," Love said with a professional smile. "Because of the short notice things are going to run a little higher."

"Sky's the limit," Maxwell told her with ease.

Addie beamed. "That's my boy. You better work it."

April's face changed from straight confusion to surprise and back to confusion as she listened to Maxwell lay out the details of his plans via the phone. "Let me get this straight, Maxwell," April spoke into the phone as she swatted Tyrone's hands away from her thighs.

"I'm listening."

"You are planning a wedding for you and my sister," she began, ticking off her fingers.

"Right, right."

April was intrigued and pulled the phone closer to her face. "You don't want me to say anything to her about it *and* you want to send me money to shop for her wedding dress and my maid-of-honor dress here in Georgia."

"Yeah."

"I will then take the dresses with me to Virginia. I

will then call and trick her into going to Virginia and not coming back here to Georgia after the cruise."

"That's it exactly."

April moved completely from Tyrone's wandering hands, needing a clear head. "You know I know that you met her in Aruba?"

"I kind of figured that."

"And you know that she called me all sad because you were dead set against marriage," she told him in an accusing voice.

"It's natural she would call her sister, yes."

"Well, since you know it all, I guess you already knew that I would help you, right?" she asked.

"I hope you would."

"Glad you got your act together. Wanting her to shack in this day and age, *please*," April said with attitude as Tyrone reached for her toes and began to suck them like grapes. "Listen, Max," she sighed, shivering as she licked her lips. "I'm gone to have to call you back. But don't worry, Clayton and I will get to dress shopping today. Uh, right after I handle some business of my own."

"Just let me know how much it is."

"Yeah, uh-hum, whatever," she told him, hitting the button to turn off the phone just before she let it unceremoniously drop to the carpet.

Tyrone knelt on the floor between her legs, using one of is beefy fingers to pull aside the edge of her panties. She began to purr before he even lowered his head and tongued her core like it was going out of style.

"You are so nasty," she said hotly. "And you can do this as much as you want to, baby . . . just as long as you don't ask *me* to return the favor."

* * *

Maxwell hung up the phone, frowning as he caught on quickly to just what business April had to handle. He picked up the pen from the desk and drew a line threw "wedding dress" on his list. He also crossed off "wedding planner" while he was at it. Next in line were the guests. Love had told him she needed a list by tomorrow. Then on top of that he had to contact everyone via phone because of the short notice.

He hated to admit it, but it sounded like more than what he wanted to bite off by himself. Smiling broadly, he picked up the phone and dialed his sister's house.

"Hello."

"Don't say I told you so," Maxwell said before he even offered a greeting.

"See there. I told you—"

Maxwell cleared his throat.

"No need to speak the obvious. So what happened in Aruba, baby brother?" Darlene asked.

"I realized that Gabby is the woman I want to marry," he told her in an ultra-serious voice.

"Congratulations. Congratulations," Darlene sighed with pleasure. "Where's the bride-to-be? Let me holler at her for a second."

"She's in Costa Rica."

"What in the devil's drawers is she doing in Costa Rica?" Darlene shrieked.

He took his time and explained exactly why Gabrielle continued on with her cruise and why he was back in Virginia planning a surprise wedding.

"So she doesn't even know?"

"Nope. I've hired an excellent wedding planner, her sister is shopping for the dress, and all I need is a beautifully talented slightly older sister to help me pull all this off in—" he looked down at his watch. "Nine days and four hours."

"I wouldn't miss this for all the ivory in Africa. Let's see, I have to use some of my sick leave, and my hubby can fly down later in the week with the kids. Is tomorrow good for you? I'll catch the first thing smoking."

"See, now that's why you're my favorite," he told her with a broad smile.

"Uh-huh, whatever," she told him lovingly.

"I want the whole gang there, and I'll fly in whoever I have to," Maxwell said, scratching "invite guests" off his list because he knew that as sure as he could spell his last name that Darlene would take care of it for him.

"I'll start calling all the family, and don't you worry, I will not let any of them beg you for money during the reception."

"You got my back, huh?"

"Now you know that's right."

Gabrielle wanted to call Maxwell but she refrained. This cruise was her time and being a little selfish was something she had not allowed herself to be in nearly six years. Besides, not only was she having a wonderful time, she was supposed to be thinking through exactly what she was going to do about Maxwell after she left the security of the cruise.

What to do?

Yes, she loved him completely, but was it wise to settle when the man clearly had told her that he did not want to be married?

Had she wanted him to propose to her in Aruba? Truthfully, yes, she had. It would have been the final piece to the puzzle that made the picture complete.

True, she didn't have much experience with men, but she had plenty of common sense to know that you could not change a man. She could hang around for years, letting Maxwell give her the best sex of her life drinking up all her milk for free, but in the end if he still abhorred the idea of marriage, he was not going to buy the cow.

Then on the flip side, did she want things between Maxwell and herself to end before they even began? How romantic was it for him to fly to Aruba just to proclaim his love? That was something from a romance book. Besides, he hadn't said he would *never* get married, right?

A maddening gamble.

Gabrielle flopped back onto her bed and let out a short, frustrated cry.

Four Days Till I Do

Maxwell's entire estate was alive with activity as preparations for the wedding continued at a fevered pace. Some of his family members had already begun to arrive, and Love's crew were all over the yard beginning their setup.

He couldn't find a single moment of peace anywhere in his whole house. "Gabby, only you are worth all of this," he muttered murderously while he quickly moved out of the path of two burly men carrying materials through the front door.

Somehow he had hoped he could just relay Gabrielle's dream wedding to Love and let her take over every other detail. He had been sadly mistaken. What did he want on the menu for the buffet-style reception? What flowers? Which cake sample did he like? What type of music for the reception? Any special traditions he wanted to honor during the ceremony? What favors did he want to use? Who was his best man? What type of tuxedo? Go get fitted for the tuxedo. Do this. Do that. Want this? Want that?

He felt like screaming . . . but he didn't. Even though Darlene had arrived as she promised, no one involved, except maybe April who wasn't scheduled to arrive until the day before the wedding, knew Gabrielle the way that he did. Not even Addie. No one else knew that she loved devil's food cake. No one knew that she was allergic to strawberries. No one else knew that champagne made her dizzy so she would need sparkling cider instead for the wedding toast. If he wanted this to remain *her* dream wedding and not someone's else's, he had to stay involved. No, this was his idea, and so he counted to ten before he answered every single question with patience that was quickly wearing thin.

He'd been so busy entertaining guests, helping to plan a wedding, pacifying Addie, who was upset about the people trudging in and out of *her* kitchen at their whims, that he barely had time to go to the bathroom.

Needing a break, Maxwell climbed the stairs to his

studio and locked the door behind himself. Visions of Gabrielle dressed in a skimpy bikini and smiling up at buff island men while sipping on fruity beverages irritated him until he felt like putting a fist through the wall.

The doorknob rattled as someone unsuccessfully tried to open it. "Open up, little brother, we know you're in there."

He smiled at the sound of Darlene's knowing voice.

"Yeah, we *know* you in there."

His smile dropped to a frown at the sound of April's voice. She was early.

"Max, open this door."

He rose and moved to the door, unlocking it. "Can't a man have a moment's peace in his own house?" he asked.

"No," the ladies said in unison, pushing the door open wide.

He noticed that they got quiet, and he turned to look at them.

"Ooh, you got a naked picture of Gabby. Y'all so freaky," April told him, walking closer to the easel at the other end of the loft.

"I thought you and Clayton weren't coming early because you couldn't get off work?" he asked her as he strode past both of them and quickly covered the painting with the cloth.

"Don't hate me because I can make things happen," she said saucily. "Clayton's gone off with Hector. Oh, I mean Miguel," April teased.

"What can I do for you, ladies?" he asked with an exhausted air.

"We were thinking that Gabrielle is going to need a hair stylist—" Darlene began.

"And a pedicure," April added as she wandered around the loft, observing Maxwell's paintings.

"Fine," Maxwell agreed, steering April by the shoulders away from the covered painting of Gabrielle. "Anything else?"

Darlene saw the signs of aggravation on her brother's face and wisely put off the rest of their questions until later. "No, that's it," she said, grabbing April by the wrist to lead her out of the room. "Oh, and be on the lookout. I heard Raymond talking about some new get-rich-quick scheme he wants you to invest in. I won't tell him you're hiding up here."

Maxwell smiled his thanks before he closed the door and locked it behind them.

In four days, Gabrielle and he would be married, and he couldn't wait to throw every single person, except for her, out of his house.

Correction. *Their* house.

He liked how that sounded.

Two Days Till I Do

"Gabrielle, Maxwell is in the hospital."

Gabrielle sank to the bed in her stateroom as she felt the energy drain from her body. "What happened? Is he all right?"

"I can't talk long, this call is already costing me a fortune, but you need to fly to Virginia tomorrow. Maxwell's sister is in town, and she's going to pick you up at the airport," April told her.

"I have to call somebody—"

"She's at the hospital, and Addie's home," April added quickly.

"Which hospital? Doesn't anyone have a cell phone?" Gabrielle asked, frustrated at how far she was from him when he needed her the most.

"Yeah, his sister has Maxwell's cell phone, and she said you could call her on that in the morning because she'll have it off while she spends the night at the hospital."

"Okay."

"I gave you all the info I have, Gabrielle. I don't think it's too serious, though, but you got to get to Virginia. If I get any other updates here, I'll call you."

"I'm leaving this ship now," Gabrielle insisted.

"Gabrielle, just slow down and think, okay? The cruise will be back in Miami in the morning, and you can catch the first plane headed to Virginia," April told her calmly.

"You're right, but how can I sleep knowing Maxwell is hurt?" she asked, wringing her hands nervously.

"I know, but everything will be all right, okay?"

"Okay," Gabrielle said softly before hanging up the phone.

April hung up the phone in Maxwell's loft. "She's worried out of her mind, Romeo," April told him, upset at the lie she had just told her sister.

Maxwell leaned back in his chair. "We had to get her to Virginia or all of this was for nothing," he explained to April, waving one hand toward all the pre-wedding activity outside.

"You could have just told her the truth," April insisted.

"Then that would have ruined the surprise,"

Maxwell flung back calmly. "I plan to marry your sister and work hard at making her happy for the rest of our lives. I think she'll forgive one white lie for the greater good of love and romance. Don't you?"

April rolled her eyes heavenward.

Nine Hours Till I Do

Gabrielle had nearly rubbed the skin on her hands raw with worry. She had tried calling Maxwell's cell, but just as April said, the voice mail answered. She had barely slept all night and looked and felt a mess when she caught a cab from the pier to the airport.

As soon as she purchased her ticket, Gabrielle canceled her car rental reservation and then reached into her purse for the cell phone she hadn't been able to use at sea. She quickly dialed Maxwell's cell phone and said a "Thank you, Jesus" when it actually began to ring.

Maxwell's cell phone began to ring on his hip. He snatched it up, looked at the Caller ID, and saw Gabrielle's cell phone number displayed. "Darlene," he hollered from the middle of the yard, where men were busy at work assembling the gazebo.

Darlene looked up from watching the florist placing the arrangements down the aisle and saw Maxwell heading toward her with the phone up in the air. She grabbed the whistle dangling from a chain around her neck and blew into it as she raced to grab the phone from her brother's hand.

All activity on the grounds ceased.

"Hello," she said trying not to sound out of breath. "Hi, Gabby."

"How's Maxwell? How is he doing? Can I talk to him?"

"Max is fine he . . . um, he just had an asthma attack," Darlene said, shooting a look of horror at Max. "But he's fine now. Where are you?"

"Asthma attack? Maxwell doesn't have asthma," Gabrielle said, confused.

Darlene frowned comically and then laughed nervously. "Yeah, I know he doesn't, so imagine how surprised I was too, girl."

"Can I talk to him?"

"Actually, I'm back at the house for a little bit. You know you can't have cell phones in the hospital."

"My plane lands at 12:30. What hospital is he in? I'll just a cab straight there."

Maxwell's eyes were intense on his sister as she fought to keep up the ruse.

"Actually, I'll come and get you, sweetie. Which plane?" She nodded as Gabrielle gave her the flight info. "Well, I'll see you at twelve-thirty then, okay. Bye-bye," Darlene said, talking over Gabrielle's questions about which hospital.

"How did it go?" Maxwell asked anxiously as she gave him back his phone.

"Good, she's on her way," Darlene told him, reaching up to tweak his nose. "Today's your wedding day. How you feeling?"

Maxwell looked around at his transformed garden and thought of the pleasure he hoped it would bring his bride. "A little scared that she won't say yes."

Darlene arched a brow. "You're kidding . . . right?"

Maxwell gave her a weak smile.

Five and One-half Hours Till I Do

"Darlene, I wonder if someone's getting married. There's a beautiful limo parked in front of the courthouse," Gabrielle told her as they drove up the street.

"Actually I have to stop there and pick up something really quick while I'm in town, if you don't mind."

"I *really* want to see Maxwell, Darlene," Gabrielle insisted, placing both her hands atop the other woman's on the gearshift of Maxwell's Land Rover.

"It won't take but a minute, I swear. You might as well come in, too," Darlene told her, pulling in with ease behind the limousine.

"Couldn't you just drop me at the hospital and then come back later?" Gabrielle asked, trying not to show her annoyance. *Her brother is hospitalized and she's worrying about picking up papers?*

"Come on, girl," Darlene instructed, hopping out of the SUV before Gabrielle could put up any further resistance.

Gabrielle left the vehicle and climbed the steps to the courthouse behind Darlene. "This woman is crazy," Gabrielle muttered to herself as she walked through the courthouse door.

"Gabby."

She froze at the very sound of Maxwell's voice and felt an intense feeling of déjà vu from when he had surprised her in Aruba. But Maxwell was in the hospital, right?

Gabrielle turned and looked up into Maxwell's handsome, smiling face. She squealed in delight before lunging herself into his open and waiting arms. She kissed his neck a dozen times as she wrapped her arms and legs around him.

"Welcome back, baby," he whispered into her ear as he spun her around.

Gabrielle opened her eyes and caught sight of Darlene and April stand off to the side. *April? Hold up. Wait a minute.* She pulled back out of his embrace. "What's going on? They said you were in the hospital and I flew straight here."

Gabrielle climbed down from Maxwell and landed on her feet to whirl and glare at her sister and Darlene. "That ticket cost me like six hundred dollars. And . . . and April, what are you doing here? And what on earth are we doing at the courthouse? Are you people crazy?"

Maxwell grabbed her left hand, and Gabrielle turned back to him just as he slid a gorgeous three-carat emerald-cut solitaire onto her ring finger. Her mouth dropped open as he dropped to one knee before her.

Gabrielle felt her whole body go weak with surprise and pleasure. She began to tremble uncontrollably, and her breaths came in heavy huffs. "Oh my God. Oh my God," she kept whispering like a chant.

"Gabby, when I first laid eyes on you that day at the Art Expo I knew that I wanted you in my life. Foolishly I thought as just my assistant and later as my friend. But now I know that I love you and I have loved you for years. And I also know that I refuse to live another second of my life without you in it. Happiness was right under my nose for the past six years, and I didn't even know it . . . until now."

Gabrielle did not try to fight the tears that streamed down her cheeks as she bit her bottom lip and looked into the mocha depths of his eyes.

"Gabrielle Dutton, will you marry me?" Maxwell asked with an intensity and even an uncertainty that made her heart surge with more devotion for him.

"In a heartbeat," she answered softly, smiling through the tears.

Maxwell stood and pulled her body close to his, raising his own shaky hands to embrace her beautiful face and kiss her with a tenderness that brought her tears back in full force. "I love you so much," he told her fiercely against her lips.

"And I love you."

Darlene cleared her throat, and Maxwell shifted his eyes to see her point to her watch.

"Right," Maxwell said, reaching for Gabrielle's hand to pull her behind him toward the elevator.

"Where are we going now?" Gabrielle asked as she followed him into the now open elevator.

"To get our marriage license," he replied as he pushed the second-floor button.

"Why the rush?" she asked, confused.

"We're getting married today."

"We're . . . we're what?" she asked slowly.

"Surprise!" Darlene and April yelled in excitement just before the elevator door shut them from Maxwell and Gabrielle's view.

Fifteen Minutes Till I Do

"Oh God, I still can't believe it," Gabrielle said in amazement. "Maxwell planned all of this?"

"He sure did, sweetheart," Darlene told her in the back of the white limousine that had sped the ladies from the courthouse to a suite at the Hilton, where Gabrielle had been pampered and primped in preparation for her wedding later that evening.

"I knew he was a great guy, but I never expected anything as sweet as this," Gabrielle gushed, trying hard not to cry and ruin her make-up.

"Oh, Gabrielle, wait until you see how beautiful everything is," April sighed, pulling out a white silk blindfold from her beaded purse. "But not until you get to the aisle. Sorry."

"Say what?" Gabrielle asked with a frown.

April moved carefully in the back to sit nearer her sister and loosely tie the blindfold over her eyes. She lightly kissed her cheek. "See you in a little bit when you're Mrs. Maxwell Bennett."

The Wedding

Gabrielle's first sight of the wedding grounds took her breath away as soon as Clayton Wilkes removed the blindfold. It was beautiful and it was perfect. It was the wedding she had always dreamed of. Hundreds of candles were lit in every available spot, including the sides of the aisle. The heavy scent of gardenia was in the air. Everyone in attendance emitted a brilliant glow in their white attire against the darkening sky while the sun set. As the pianist played

the final strains of "Ave Maria" and began a slow and
sultry jazz-inspired rendition of the wedding march,
Gabrielle locked eyes with the man of her dreams,
standing handsomely in his white tuxedo inside a
grand gazebo draped with a beautiful floral arrange-
ment. She placed her arm through Clayton's and
began to walk to her future husband filled with so
many emotions, never once letting her eyes leave his.

Maxwell's first sight of Gabrielle took his breath
away. His heart pounded wildly in his chest, and
he actually felt himself well up with tears that he
refused to let fall. The dress she wore was absolutely perfect for her. The strapless ivory sheath
was simple and elegant, conforming to the curves
of her slender frame before falling to a delicate
puddle around her feet. Her hair was swooped to
the side in the front and then twisted into a beautiful chignon with a gardenia over one ear. Even
though it was early evening, she still wore natural
and light make-up with just a little more drama
around the eyes and only diamond studs and a
bracelet for jewelry.

She looked gorgeous and radiant as she walked
to him, their eyes locked.

And he wanted nothing more than to have her
at his side so that he could take the ultimate vow
and make her his mate for the rest of their lives
and beyond.

Maxwell held Gabrielle's body close to his and
buried his face into her neck when she reached
him. She wrapped her arms around his neck securely and sighed in pleasure as she leaned back to
smile up at him with love. "I've waited six years for

this day," she whispered into his ear before lightly biting his lobe.

"Was it worth the wait?" he asked in return, lightly kissing her shoulder.

"This was beyond my wildest dream, and I love you for that, Maxwell Bennett."

Epilogue

One Year Later

"I cannot believe I'm letting you do this," Gabrielle said to Maxwell, her nude and obviously pregnant frame draped on her side across the bed.

Maxwell's face was pensive as he took a step back from the easel. "Why?" he asked, finally shifting his eyes from the painting to look over the canvas at his beautiful wife.

"I don't know. Maybe because I do not look like *that* anymore," she told him, pointing her finger up to *The Muse*, the large nude painting of her, which Max had hanging over the bed.

"Your body is perfect, Gabby," he said.

Gabrielle wasn't buying it. "You just like it 'cause I finally have a ghetto booty," she told him.

Maxwell smiled broadly and wiggled his brows.

Gabrielle growled, reaching for a throw pillow to fling at him.

Maxwell caught it easily. "Come on, baby. I'm almost done," he pleaded with her.

Gabrielle saw the end of the road of the four-week project. "And I finally get to see it?"

"Of course," he told her, his head bent as he began to mix paint.

She sighed and positioned her body. "Well, your son and I say hurry up, Picasso."

"Uh-huh," he said, his voice already distracted as he added shadow to the painting.

"You do know these nudes will have to come down, once little Armond is older," she told him, being sure to remain in her pose.

"If you mean *Junior*, we'll just keep our door locked," he replied. They hadn't quite agreed on the name.

"I'm so glad that Addie agreed to come and live with us," Gabrielle said, not moving her lips.

"Yeah, me too, baby."

Bored, Gabrielle shifted her eyes about the room.

"Gabby," Maxwell chastised.

"Sorry," she said, looking forward again.

They fell into a comfortable silence.

"I'm done," Maxwell said, ten minutes later, stepping back again from the easel.

Gabrielle rose from the bed and strode across the room to stand next to her husband. "Oh," she sighed, her breath completely taken at her first sight of the painting.

Maxwell wrapped his arm around her shoulders and pulled her body close to his. "You like it?" he asked as he stared down into her face.

"I . . . I love it," she whispered softly.

Maxwell's painting captured both Gabrielle's nude pregnant body draped across the bed and *The Muse*, hanging above the bed. In both, she thought she'd never looked more beautiful. "What's it called, *The Before and After*?" she teased lightly as she leaned into his warmth and strength, her hands splayed on her womb.

He covered her hands with his own. "It doesn't have a name. I think it pretty much speaks for itself."

Gabrielle smiled. "You do have a way of making me look fabulous."

Maxwell's eyes smoldered, feeling himself aroused by her even as she swelled with nearly eight months of pregnancy. Her slender face was now a bit more full and she glowed. Her breasts were nearly twice in size and the nipples were darker and larger. Her legs were thicker and more sturdy. Her stomach was perfectly round as she rubbed it in full protective mother mode. She was absolutely gorgeous.

"You never looked more beautiful, Gabby," he said to her with honest emotion that made his voice husky.

Gabrielle turned in his embrace and kissed his mouth. "And I have never loved you more, Maxwell."

Dear Reader,

I derive so much joy from completing a novel and breathing life into these fabulous characters that I hope you all enjoy. Writing is very important to me, but even more important is the satisfaction I receive when all of the readers contact me and let me know how much they have enjoyed peeking into the lives of my characters.

I hope you all have taken pleasure in the story of Gabrielle and Maxwell. I treasured creating them and getting to know them as I breathed life into them. Honestly, they are two of my favorites. I can see a little of myself in Gabrielle during my awkward teens. Unfortunately, it took her a little longer than me to find her confidence. And in Maxwell lives my love for the inner city in which I grew up and my hope to see it continue to flourish into the great landscape it deserves to be.

Currently, I am working on my next novel, *Let's Do It Again*, and hopefully, you'll enjoy my next creation as I welcome Serena and Malcolm into my world with open arms.

Love 2 Live & Live 2 Love,
And I'm out.

About the Author

After having ten romantic short stories published within eighteen months, Niobia Simone Bryant promised herself in 1999 that she would have a book published before she reached the age of thirty. She submitted *Admission of Love*, her first completed novel, to two publishing houses in early 1999, and later that year both houses offered her a two-book deal. Deciding to go with BET's Arabesque line, Niobia saw her dream accomplished with the nationwide release of *Admission of Love* in August 2000. *Three Times a Lady* (BET Books) followed in June 2001. Both works received critical acclaim with top reviews, awards, and nominations. *Three Times a Lady* became a national best-seller and a Doubleday/Black Expression Book Club Selection. Niobia's heavily anticipated third novel, *Heavenly Match*, was released in August 2004 and instantly became a national best-seller and received top reviews. She is currently working on *Let's Do It Again*, which is slated for a December 2005 release.

This savvy writer and hopeless romantic is a proud native of Newark, New Jersey, although she currently resides in South Carolina. She's a graduate of Seton Hall University with a Bachelor of Science in Nursing and a Bachelor of Arts in Social

& Behavioral Science with an accompanying Psychology minor. A true lover of reading, she enjoys many genres of fiction and hopes to one day write mainstream contemporary fiction. Until that time, she continues to write novels that are filled with the realism, humor, and raw sexuality that her legions of fans have come to cherish.

She can be reached by e-mail: niobia_bryant@yahoo.com or by joining her free online Yahoo group (Niobia_Bryant_News) via her Web site: www.geocities.com/niobia_bryant.